That Certain Spark

By Isobel Hart

ISBN 978-1-9999568-5-1

Dedication

For Nicola, R.I.P.

The original 'lasagne-in-the-eyebrow' lady

Chapter 1

"Claire, why is there a lawnmower in your front room?"

I pull my gaze away from the fence panel that's blown down in the back garden and turn to look at my friend.

She's leaning forward, hands clasped around her wineglass, eyes narrowed with one eyebrow arched.

I'm not ready for this conversation so I turn away again.

It's remarkable, I can see straight through into next-door's garden. Their small plot looks like something Alan Titchmarsh might have created, not like the dandelion field below that first inspired me this evening. My patch of what might optimistically be called grass is almost anything but. Not that it's all mine, exactly.

"Claire?" Nicole presses me, like an annoying wasp. "The lawnmower?"

I glance across at the new addition now decorating the corner of my living room and shrug. "I collected it today. The grass needs a good cut." She didn't see the palaver involved in getting it up here in the first place. Those things are heavy. I won't be moving it again any time soon.

Nicole's eyes widen with alarm. "You didn't go over there again, did you? In this weather?" She glances towards the window. Wind shivers the pane, as if to emphasise her point.

In fact, it had taken the perfect blend of righteous, burning anger, laced with deep-seated misery to drive me out of the house earlier. I've barely gotten myself dressed, let alone found the front door, for months. My email is bulging with essays on The Egyptian Influence on Interior Design to mark. I'll get to them at some point. Best thing about it is it's a job that doesn't require me to get out of my pyjamas.

But tonight, inspired by my absolute need to cut the grass, and despite rain heavy enough to wet me through to my bra by the time I ran from my front door to the car, I'd ventured out. I'd pressed that doorbell so many damn times even *she* couldn't ignore me.

Residual anger simmers as I turn back to Nicole. "Daddy left it to me. It's worth a lot of money. I wanted it back."

It is. It's a Honda. Daddy took grass cutting and turned it into an art form spending almost every weekend of my childhood, and all his retirement, cutting stripes into the grass at the cricket club. Until he passed away. The mower was an indulgence; top of the range. I suspect it has a better engine than my Mini.

"Did you see her? What did she say?"

Hatred, oily and bitter, burns in my chest at the memory of Bella's fake smile teasing the corners of newly plump lips. She'd propped herself against the doorframe, pretending she wasn't surprised to see me. It was the slight tic in her jaw that had given her away. "She looked good," I admit to Nicole. There was a time I'd have been impressed by that, but not now. This time, I'd looked directly into Bella's eyes, the windows to her soul, and seen the cold, calculating bitch she was staring straight back at me.

Of course, it's too late now. I never realised my life – *my* life – was the steak Bella planned to sink her teeth into all along. I thought she'd had my back. She did, but only because it made it easier for her to slide the knife between my ribs.

"She's had her fingernails sharpened into points," I say, remembering the flash of red as she'd tilted her head to tuck a wayward strand of hair back behind her ear.

Nicole grimaces. "All the better for digging into your husband."

Why wouldn't he choose her over me though?

I shudder at the memory of Bella's eyes sweeping over me, from my unwashed hair to the pair of battered Vans. In my wisdom, I'd also worn yoga pants, odd socks and a sodden, sloppy Fruit of the Loom sweatshirt that used to be Ben's. I'd stood there held under her gimlet gaze as rainwater formed small puddles around my feet.

"What did she say?" Nicole asks, with another anxious glance towards the lawnmower.

"She wanted to know how I was doing, and then added a '*really*' with one of those faux-sympathy head tilts she does."

Nicole grunts. "God, I hate it when she does that."

"I ignored her," I continue. "You'd have been proud of me."

"Did you see him?"

I shake my head. "He wasn't there. She had the cheek to ask if *she* could help me."

Nicole makes a very unladylike sound. "I hope you told her where to go!"

"I told her she'd done quite enough already."

Nicole nods approvingly. "So how did you get from that to..." She swivels to look at the lawnmower again.

How indeed? I press my forehead against the cool glass of the window.

"Claire, please tell me you didn't just take it?" My friend no longer sounds amused.

I shrug again. "What if I did? It's mine."

"Claire..."

I swing round to face her fully. "No, I can't let her get away with taking everything. It's *my* bloody lawnmower."

Nicole raises her hands placatingly. "Sweetie, you don't want the lawnmower; you want your husband back."

"I don't."

Liar.

Nicole quirks that eyebrow again.

I sniff. "He's a lying, cheating bastard. And she's even worse. It's not enough she's taken my husband, my house and my business. Now she wants my lawnmower too. And she's got a bump!" I wail the last words as I admit, finally, the agony of seeing it in the flesh. It makes everything so real, her words still stinging me as they were intended to. *Maybe you should stop bothering us and start taking better care of yourself. Ben needs to focus on his new family now.*

"It's true then? She's six months gone?"

I nod. "She looked *so* bloody pleased with herself." Ben and I had tried for ages and ages to get pregnant.

An echo of the searing chest pain I'd felt at the sight of her hand dropping to cradle the swell of her lower abdomen, has me reaching to steady myself on the window frame. I'd wanted to avoid looking at it but she'd given me no choice; my eyes had lowered involuntarily, the bump unmissable, emphasised by her form-fitting dove-grey jersey dress.

Somehow, I'd dragged my gaze away, back to her face, trying to hide my hurt. No doubt, I'd failed miserably. Then I'd drawn a deep breath and told her I wanted my lawnmower.

Your *lawnmower?* she'd said, eyes widening, even as her eyebrows remained resolutely still. *You want our lawnmower?*

My anger had ignited then, flaring like a match held against gas.

I take a deep breath, anger fanned afresh by the memory. "She spluttered something about me living in an apartment. Said

I didn't have a proper garden. And anyway it was November and blowing a bloody gale." She wasn't wrong, I just hadn't cared.

And now I'm crying again.

"Oh, honey." Nicole stands, wrapping her arms around me, then leads me over to the sofa where she pulls me into her shoulder. I sob until her pale pink cashmere is damp beneath my cheek. When I pull away a silvery trail of snot marks where I've been. I'm still hiccoughing little sobs as she hands me a tissue before reaching over to grab the bottle and refill my glass.

The front doorbell rings. "Let me get it," she suggests, standing again as I blow my nose into the tissue. She walks back into the lounge moments later. "Umm, Claire? It's the police."

"Claire Everett?" the uniformed man shadowing her says. "Are you Claire Everett?"

I swallow, mouth dry despite the wine, forcing me to take another quick sip. "Yes?" My voice is little more than a whisper.

His eyes flicker towards the lawnmower and my stomach lurches. "I believe there may have been an altercation earlier. . . with a Ms Preston?"

"It was hardly an altercation. I just went to collect something." My heart is galloping – ba-boom, ba-boom, ba-boom – shortening my breath, anxiety pinballing around my body.

"Did you force your way into the premises? Did you use threatening language?" the police officer questions me.

I think for a minute. Did I? It's hard to know for sure what I said out loud and what was just inside my head. "I might have called her a husband-stealing whore," I say after a moment.

"That may be what she was referring to." There is the suggestion of amusement in the crinkling at the corners of his eyes.

"But it's mine, or... it was." It's not. Not anymore. The house had been in Ben's name. Stupid me. I never imagined the love of my life – the man I met at age nineteen on my first day of university, fell in love with and then married – would run off. Not after fifteen years. Ben and Bella were co-directors of the interior design business Bella and I had set up and run together. I'd never been all that bothered about the business management side of things, happy to let him do all that for us when he had the time. He was an accountant, after all. I just wanted to design and take a salary that would cover the cost of my monthly Visa bill. Bella took my husband, my home, and together they'd stolen my business. Now I face lengthy settlement discussions I can ill afford and am marking essays for the local college's online interior design course.

"Ms Preston has filed a restraining order against you." The police officer looks uncomfortable, the tips of his ears now a raspberry pink colour.

Nicole splutters: "Hold on! How's that even possible? Don't you need some sort of criminal conviction before you can be issued with a restraining order?"

The policeman just looks at me. Waiting.

Nicole swings around. "What did you do?"

"It was ages ago, while I was still terribly upset." I push a shaking hand through my hair.

Nicole's hands are on her hips. She's still waiting.

"I poured paint over Bella's BMW."

"What! When?"

I wave my hand dismissively. "I told you, ages ago."

My friend frowns at me, fingertips drumming silently against cashmere.

"Really, it was right back at the start. All done and dusted. I agreed to pay for the respray and I've not done anything terrible since."

The policeman sighs, looking down at his paperwork. "You're not permitted to go to the property or within one hundred metres of Ms Preston… or Mr Everett."

Panic bubbles up inside me at the thought of not being allowed to see Ben. It threatens to engulf me. I splutter, "That's ridiculous, there are matters we still need to resolve." This is all Bella's doing. She was looking for another reason to prevent me being alone with Ben. He's been feeling sorry for me. I swear he still has feelings for me… This is all her. She's determined to take everything away from me.

I gasp, dizzy now, my breaths coming short and fast, lungs straining for oxygen. I can't seem to draw enough in. I'm suffocating, I realise, as darkness envelops me from every side…

"Put your head between your knees and breathe into this bag," a voice says from somewhere beside me. I'm slouched on one of my wooden kitchen chairs. Someone must have brought it into the lounge. I have no idea how I got here. "Breathe in and out, slowly and deeply." There's a brown paper bag pushed against my face. It smells of French fries and chicken nuggets and... something terrible. I gag. Someone must have fished the McDonald's bag out of the bin. The same one I shovelled cat poo out of the litter tray with earlier. I gag again and push it away from my face.

I blink up at Nicole. She's frowning down at me. "What happened?" I ask. The policeman is crouched at my side, poised to catch me.

"You fainted," Nicole says, worry furrowing her brow. "Officer Brown only just caught you in time. You could've really hurt yourself."

The policeman's caterpillar-thick eyebrows pull across his forehead to meet in the middle. "You need to take it easy for a moment or two, until you get your breath back." He stands, passing me a glass of water from the coffee table.

I take it, then change my mind and put it down again, grabbing for my glass of wine instead. I take a sip. "It was probably just another panic attack."

"Another? What do you mean, another panic attack? Why didn't you tell me?" Nicole frowns again, bringing me additional guilt about the wrinkles I'm causing her.

"You've got enough on your plate looking after your husband and kids." I pat her knee. "You don't need to worry about me. I had a little one a couple of days ago. I was in Sainsbury's, looking at the meals for one and feeling a bit emotional. Then, the next thing I knew, I was on the floor gazing up into a face young enough to be my son's – if I'd had a child in my teens. Not that I would have... had a child in my teens, I mean. At any age actually. I'm infertile, you see." My mouth is running away from me, as unrelenting as the rain pitter-pattering against the window.

Nicole's not giving up. "Should you be fainting from a panic attack? Do you need to see a doctor?"

I wave her concern away. "I did. I have a condition called syncope. It means I sometimes faint when I have a panic attack."

The policeman glances towards my glass of wine. "It might help to ease off on that a bit."

The doorbell rings again. "Oh, for God's sake. Who is it now?" I'm at my limit with guests.

"I'll get it." Nicole darts into the hallway for a second time whilst I nurse my wine glass defiantly.

"Darling!" My mother sweeps into the room with an audible crackle of polyester. "Nicole says you had a bit of a funny turn. Are you feeling any better now?" She presses the back of her hand against my forehead, startling me with a burst of static electricity. It cracks against my skin, making me jump.

"Fuck!"

"Now, dear, there's no need for bad language." She looks up and spots the lawnmower. "Goodness, what's your father's mower doing up here?"

I stare at a spot of dirt on my carpet.

"Claire?" She uses that inquisitorial tone of hers – a perfect blend of Mary Berry crossed with a drill sergeant – that has me spilling my guts in seconds.

"I went to collect it."

"You didn't go near *that woman*?" my mother says, looking aghast. She whispers, 'that woman' as if she were saying 'that child molester'. I love her a little bit more for it. "What on earth were you thinking?"

"Daddy left me the mower – I didn't want *her* to have that too."

"Rotten thing. Never did work very well. It was in pieces on the kitchen table more times than he used the bloody thing. Still, it's true, he did leave it to you," she confirms.

"See!" I say triumphantly, looking towards the police officer who appears to be inching closer to the hallway, presumably hoping for escape.

"That doesn't excuse forced entry and threatening behaviour," he says, attempting to look stern. It's a losing battle. "You need to pursue your rights through the courts, not take matters into your own hands. Not unless you want to end up down at the station with me."

My mother has finally taken note of the burly policeman in our midst. She's looking at him the same way she assesses the fillet steaks at Waitrose. She extends a well-manicured hand. "Hello, I'm Claire's mother, Daphne. It's lovely to meet you. Are you and Claire… you know." She winks at him.

"No, Mummy!" I say, jumping to my feet at the same moment as he exclaims, "No, we are not!"

I glare at him, because there's really no call for him to sound quite so appalled. My head swims and I put out a hand to steady myself. Maybe I really should ease up on the wine.

The officer straightens his patrol vest. "I'm here on official business, ma'am." He looks at me again, stern expression softening. "Perhaps you should take it easy for a bit after that panic attack."

"Panic attack!" Mummy's level of horror is more suited to a genital herpes diagnosis. The affection I was feeling for her moments ago withers away. She purses her lips as she surveys me. "I've told you before, you need to go on a Mindfulness course. It will help you to sort out these *feelings* of yours. Marjorie went on one and it was the making of her. She meditates twice a day now and does something called The White Crane Spreads its Legs every morning." Marjorie is my mother's seventy-eight-year-old best friend.

I ignore her. "Are you finished?" I say to Officer Brown. The poor man deserves to be let out.

"Do you understand what the restraining order means?" he asks me pointedly, zipping up his vest.

"Restraining order!" Mummy squeaks, eyebrows heading for her hairline.

"Yes," I say, ignoring her, my heart clenching painfully at the thought of not being allowed to see Ben. We spent fifteen years with each other. Barely a day apart. He's a hard habit to break, despite what he's done to me... to us.

"What you need is to find another man," my mother says, once I've shown Officer Brown out.

"I certainly don't need another man. I hate men."

"You should try Grindr. Marjorie used it, and now she's having sex three nights a week."

"I think you mean Tinder." I giggle as Nicole snorts into her glass. "Although who knows? Either way, I could do without this unwelcome insight into Marjorie's sex life, thank you very much. I don't need a man," I say again, with more conviction this time.

"Well, at least think about the Mindfulness. You need to put a stop to all these negative emotions before you end up with a criminal record." Mummy smoothes back a strand of her long mercury-grey hair. "It'll help you get some perspective on life."

I can feel Nicole itching to tell her I've already got a record. I glare at my friend who bites her lip. "I'll think about the Mindfulness," I tell my mother. "By the way, do you need a lawnmower?"

Chapter 2

I scan the group with interest, glad to be out of the relentless wind and rain. It's all thanks to a weather system that's parked itself over the country for the foreseeable. The room's warm, its many lamps giving the place a womb-like feel, pulling out rich burgundy tones in the carpet and flock wallpaper and pressing back the darkness outside.

A jug and glasses sit on a small table pressed up against one wall. I make a beeline, picking up the jug to pour myself a glass of water as I try to decide which of the remaining free seats in the small circle to choose. I hate these sorts of moments: not knowing anyone, the weight of curious eyes on me as I hover at the periphery, wishing, not for the first time, I'd arrived a little earlier so I could have been one of the ones sitting in the comfort of a chair watching the new arrivals. The judging, not the judged.

Mr Wilson, my next-door neighbour's ill-timed call, informing me my cat was up the tree – again – had put pay to that plan. It's not even wholly my tree. It belongs half to me and half to the man who owns the ground-floor apartment. I've barely seen him in the two weeks he's been in residence, but he's already taken to leaving the door at the back of the hall unlocked so I can retrieve her, given the frequency with which her tree-climbing turns into a rescue operation. This is an exercise that requires me to use a ladder to climb up onto the shed roof, then heave the ladder onto the roof with me and prop it against the trunk of the tree as close to the branch she is stuck upon as I can manoeuvre it. All whilst I'm making encouraging, non-threatening noises to entice her out the branches. I can make 'come down here, you spawn of the devil' sound like the sweetest of endearments as I wait until she deigns to tiptoe down the rungs towards me. Today this delightful episode was conducted in a storm-force wind and yet more torrential rain. Most of my friends have commented, 'if she can get up there, she can surely get herself down again'. The memory of four excruciating days spent catching glimpses of her in her tree prison plus receiving an anonymous threat to call in the RSPCA, thanks to the yowling that commenced after day two, tells me otherwise.

Sukie's Ben's cat. She never had any time for me when he and I were together, despite my having bought her as a baby substitute when I didn't immediately fall pregnant. She used to follow him around the house like a puppy, crawling onto his lap any time he sat still long enough. She loved him as much as I did.

When he gave her to me a few months after the split, I'd thought it was a sweet gesture. An acknowledgement of my lonely situation. Suffice it to say, Sukie wasn't any more impressed to have been relocated from a four-bedroom semi-detached house with a conservatory and south-facing garden, to a one-bedroom apartment with creeping damp and a cat litter tray, than I was. She employed a strategy of dirty protest – doing her business on the rim of the tray, just outside the tray, on the doormat immediately inside the front door, anywhere but inside the bloody litter tray – combined with escapology. Any open rear window enabled her to descend onto the flat roof of the extension to the flat below, onto the fence, a small hop, skip and a jump onto the shed and then straight up the tree. Every time she did her business I was forced to open the windows. It was a vicious cycle, made worse when I realised she'd only been dumped on me because of the risk of toxoplasmosis to Ben and Bella's unborn baby. We'd both been dumped by him, and neither of us was taking it well. I just haven't resorted to dirty protesting... yet. For now, I'm making do with comfort eating excessive amounts of junk food, and panic attacks.

Ice from the jug cascades into my glass, leaving little space for any water, and no ice for anyone else unless I fish it back out again. Given the scrutiny the clatter has drawn in the otherwise silent room, I choose to make do and turn to face my audience. I have a choice: either the chair between a large woman wearing a tie-dyed shirt and an elfin man wearing shorts despite the icy wind; or the seat flanked to one side by a middle-aged couple holding hands and to the other by a giant. His pumped forearms and thick-set neck are decorated in a colourful, yet intimidating, patchwork of body art. I hesitate.

A beautiful girl with long, dark hair reaching nearly to her waist, sweeps into the room, leaving a delicate floral scent drifting in her wake. "Sorry I'm late." She walks straight past me towards the chair between the hippy and the elf. "My singing lesson ran late," she explains to anyone who cares to listen, unwinding the scarf then unzipping her coat to reveal a lean figure encased in skinny jeans and a fitted jumper. She curls one leg beneath her and settles into the seat. I use the cover of her self-assured entry to take the remaining chair. The seat is hard. I wish I could curl my leg beneath me, but my thighs are too fat.

"You're not late," our instructor reassures her with a smile. He's distractingly handsome. "Welcome, everyone. I'm so happy to see you all here tonight. Welcome to our eight-week Introduction to Mindfulness course. My name is Alex, and I'll be guiding you over the coming sessions." His voice flows over us, like golden syrup across warm pancakes.

He launches into a description of what we might expect from the course as my gaze springs locust-like between the other participants; we're a perfect symmetry of tightly crossed arms and legs. "Okay," he says. "Before we make a proper start, I'd like us to take a moment to greet one another. Tell us your name, and then the rest of us will greet you back with a 'hello'. So, I'll start. I'm Alex."

"Hello, Alex," we all respond dutifully.

"Oh… um… Jennifer," the hippy lady says in a breathy, high voice. She sounds nervous. That makes me feel a little better.

"Hello, Jennifer," we chorus again, getting into the swing of things now. I'm glad I manage to stop myself from putting the 'um' in front of her name.

"Willow," the pretty girl introduces herself. She has a pretty name too. Go figure.

"Hello, Willow."

"Malcolm." This from the shorts-wearing elf.

"Hello, Malcolm."

The couple are Sarah and Gavin. I spend most of the time we're greeting them worrying I might forget my own name when my turn comes. "C… Claire," I manage, with only a slight stutter.

"Hello, Claire," bounces back to me, minus the stutter.

The giant is called David, which is ironic. The last three are also men; James, Mike, and Colin, they declare in turn. I pay little attention, too relieved to have passed the first hurdle of remembering my name without any major blunders or significant embarrassment.

"Good." Alex smiles, his face warm and welcoming. "Welcome again. I think most of you came to the taster session." He scans the group, his eyes coming to rest upon me. "Well, nearly everyone," he amends.

I'd only confirmed my place this morning. It had all been a bit last minute, a decision made after receiving a fortieth birthday party invite from a friend. It was addressed to me, plus one. I've never been to a party without Ben. Not since we met anyway.

And before that, any parties I was invited to involved jelly, ice-cream and Pass-The-Parcel.

I woke up on the kitchen floor after another panic attack.

So it's this or Valium. And Valium's probably worth keeping in my back pocket as a fall-back option.

Alex is still speaking. ". . . so, I thought we could spend a little time getting to know one another a bit better. I'd like you to split into groups of three and take a moment or two to share the reason you're here. What's brought you along to the course tonight? What are your expectations? What do you hope to get out of being here?" He pauses and looks around the group as we dither, uncertain how to form ourselves into sets of three. "Sarah and Gavin." He's looking at the couple next to me. "Maybe you should split up and go into different groups?"

I glance at Sarah. She appears more than a little panicked at the prospect of being separated from her husband/partner, if her wide eyes and frantic glances around the room are anything to go by. She nods with some relief when I catch her eye and we pull our chairs to one side of the room. Then I look at David, because everyone else is already forming into triads but he's still sitting motionless in their midst. He says nothing but grabs the edge of his chair and drags it towards us. We blink at one another with an awkwardness I recognise as that of introverts being forced to be sociable.

Sarah sighs, "So, shall I start?"

"Yes, please." I'm pathetically grateful to have someone else take the lead. "Why are you here?" I ask her.

"My husband says it's because I'm mental," she says. I expect her to smile or give some other sign that she's joking, albeit in a somewhat able-ist way. Instead, she returns my look with a poker-straight face.

I swallow. What the hell am I meant to say to that? "What makes him…" I pause to clear my throat, taking a sip from my glass of water only remembering it's full of ice when the cubes barrel into my nose. I put the glass down again. "What makes him say that?"

"I spend most of the day telling myself how crap I am. It makes me... depressed."

Doesn't everyone?

Maybe they don't.

"I can see how it might," I concede.

"My doctor didn't want to give me any more anti-depressants. She thought I might benefit from this course instead. I suspect I just need the drugs, but we'll see."

"And what do you hope to get out of it?" I ask.

"Well, I guess if I can find ways to stop feeling so bad, stop putting myself down, then it has to be worth it. But my expectations are very low. Gavin already thinks it's a complete waste of time and money."

Across the room, Gavin is hanging on Willow's every word. I turn back to Sarah. "I hope you find it helps."

She releases a breath fraught with hopelessness. "Yeah, me too."

"Is your husband – Gavin – here for the same reason?"

"He's here to support me."

"Well, that's nice," I say, with another look over at him. He's leaning back in his chair now. Malcolm's speaking. Malcolm's obviously less interesting than Willow if Gavin's body language is anything to go by. I'm certainly not getting a supportive husband vibe off him.

"What about you two?" Sarah says, dragging my attention back. "Why are you here?"

I look at David to see if he wants to go next, but he stares at me as if waiting for my answer. "Oh, well... okay...well... I've been having a bit of a tough time. At home," I clarify. Understatement of the bloody century. "My marriage ended just over eight months ago. Since then, it's been... a bit difficult." Ah, the joys of good old British understatement.

"I'm sorry to hear that," Sarah says. Her head is tilted to one side, the way people do when they're trying to be sympathetic. I've received a lot of it lately. I have a quick flashback to my last meeting with Bella.

I plough on. "The thing is, I've become a little anxious about... well... a lot of things." A flush of heat creeps upwards from my collarbones and rushes towards my face. "I was hoping... well, it was suggested to me, that this course might help me to manage..."

What will it manage, really?

My feelings about the divorce?

My ruined career?

My complete mess of a life?

"…some of my negative feelings. About myself."

Unwanted memories crowd into my mind, sending my heartrate off at a gallop: the moment I walked into the studio and found Ben and Bella having sex on my desk replays in glorious Technicolor. She knew I was coming back to the studio that afternoon. She'd even sent me a text to remind me of some invoices I needed to send. To make matters worse, she'd dressed up for the occasion, donning the new underwear she'd bought in La Perla after we'd gone shopping together to celebrate her landing a big new corporate client.

My first thought had been, *Oh, she's wearing that lovely suspender set. It looks so good on her.* My second thought was; *Oh, that's Ben. My Ben.* I don't remember much else, only odd details; like the hurt. As if someone had reached into my chest and ripped out my heart. Agony. The betrayal cut so deeply I thought I might never be able to draw a deep breath again. That was the day of my first panic attack. I woke from it to find Ben beside me on the floor, Bella behind him straightening her skirt.

"Are you okay?" David's first words bring me back from the brink. Sarah's eyebrows are drawn together, her hands extended, ready to catch me.

"Yes." I take a deep breath. "Yes," I say again with a little more determination. I have to be okay. "What about you?" I look at David. "Why are you here?"

"I need to control my anger." We wait for him to explain, but he doesn't.

A bell chimes across the room, its sweet notes lingering, signalling an end to our discussion time. We shuffle back into our original places.

"Okay," Alex says, ignoring the oppressive silence that now fills the room in place of the earlier chatter. "Let's settle ourselves for our first guided meditation. I want you to make yourselves comfortable on the chair, or you're welcome to grab a mat and lie down if you prefer. When you're ready, close your eyes."

I opt for lying down. I know my jeans will dig in and distract me otherwise; I've gained weight since Ben left.

Self-pitying tears seep from behind my closed eyelids as Alex tells us to relax. I sniffle, then try to hide it as a sneeze. I force myself to focus on what he's saying

"Think of your mind as being like the sky on a clear day. Let your thoughts pass by like clouds, noticing them with curiosity, without judgement.

"Ideas take flight, like birds. Just let them go." Alex's voice rises and falls, like the tide. Despite my racing thoughts, it's pleasant. Relaxing.

I take a deep, shuddering breath, then exhale.

I'm fine. I will be fine.

There can be a life for me without Ben.

That's if he doesn't come back. There's still a chance he might come back…

"Notice your body, how does it feel? Observe the contact with the chair or the floor, the touch of your hands where they rest upon your legs. Relax the muscles in your hands... your arms... your shoulders."

My shoulders are up around my ears. I attempt to relax them, the process more difficult than I'd anticipated. I force them down, finding the new position unnatural, almost painful, making it even harder to relax. I suppose I've been wearing them up around my ears for the last eight months.

"Focus on your breath; your gentle, tidal breathing. Notice how it moves the muscles in your stomach and chest. Release your breath." Hissing fills the room, the sound of eight simultaneously released breaths. "How does it feel in the moment between one breath ending and another beginning?"

I release my own breath in a long, steady stream, then panic. I can't breathe – I've forgotten how to breathe! I gasp, the sound fracturing the hypnotic silence around me. A droplet of saliva travels with my breath into my lungs and sends me into a coughing spasm.

"Notice the sounds around you, look at them, then let them go," Alex soldiers on, as I attempt to stifle the racket caused by my coughing fit, turning the choking coughs into muffled, heaving breaths.

I'm such an idiot. I've ruined it for everyone. I can't even meditate properly. The thoughts hammer into me. My body's now rigid as a plank again. If thoughts are like birds then mine are vultures, pecking away at the carrion of my mind. The clear tones of the bell marking the end of the session are a relief.

I blink my eyes open, too embarrassed to meet the non-judgementally judging looks from my companions.

"So," Alex says brightly, hands clasped in his lap. "How was that?" He looks around the group, waiting for one of us to speak.

"I think I fell asleep," Jennifer admits. She shifts in her seat as all eyes swing towards her. "I may have snored. I'm so sorry."

"No need to apologise," Alex says, sending her a reassuring smile. "It's always a risk when you're so relaxed. That's good. Well done." She blossoms under his praise, hands fluttering as she smooths out her tasselled skirt. "It's a fine line between relaxation and sleep. As you practise your meditation at home, you'll find what works for you. The trick is to relax but maintain awareness. You might find sitting up straight works better for you."

She nods, blinking at him with wide eyes and slightly parted lips. I don't blame her; Alex manages to combine emotional intelligence with the kind of rugged masculinity that would be welcome on the cover of any men's health magazine. It's a surprise the group consists of more men than women. Word obviously hasn't gotten out yet.

"Anyone else?" Alex scans the small circle. Seven pairs of eyes focus anywhere but on him as he leaves a long, weighty pause.

Unable to stand extended, awkward silences, my voice rushes in to fill it. "I'm sorry for coughing." All eyes swing towards me. Bloody nervous babbling.

"Not a problem." Alex smiles, and I think Sarah's ovary pops. "It happens. How did you find the meditation?"

"Umm, my mind wandered a bit. I had to keep reminding myself I was meant to be meditating." A bit! Try ninety percent of the time.

"And when you became aware your mind had wandered, what did you think? What did you feel?"

"That I was failing, that I wasn't doing it right. Disappointed." Why do I choose now to be so honest?

"Failing? Disappointed? With what? With whom?"

I stare at the swirly pattern on the carpet. "With myself." It comes out as not much more than a whisper.

"With yourself," he echoes, nodding as if I've said something profound. "With yourself." His eyes sweep around the room and then settle back upon me. "Claire… it is Claire, isn't it?"

I nod.

"Do you remember what we said at the beginning of the session?"

I stare at him, my mind desperately backtracking through everything he said earlier, trying to separate my thoughts from reality.

"About approaching the thoughts we have with curiosity, without..." He hesitates.

"Judgement," the hippy snorer, who is clearly now assuming the position of class know-it-all, supplies.

"Exactly, Jennifer."

She beams. Teacher's pet.

"We're all inclined to do it," Alex says, blessing me with one of his reassuring smiles. A dimple puckers one of his cheeks and Willow sighs. "What would happen if you just let those thoughts go? If you recognised how you were feeling in that moment, but then let it pass? We're going to focus on teaching ourselves how to be able to do that. Mindfulness is a way of being, a way of experiencing and improving the balance you have between the different parts of your life."

By now the rest of the group are hanging on to his every word. I'm lost. I tighten my arms around myself, wishing he'd focus on anyone else for a bit.

Alex rocks back in his seat, breaking the moment. "Okay," he says. "I want to do one last exercise. Close your eyes and place your palms open out in front of you. I'm going to put something into your hands."

"Will it be clean?" Willow asks, her voice high and anxious.

Clean? She's looking at him as if he suggested placing pre-chewed chewing gum in her palm.

"Yes. It's perfectly fine," he reassures her. "Close your eyes," he says a second time. I'm still staring at Willow. Seeing her in a new, slightly less perfect light.

I blink my eyes closed, listening hard for the movement that will signify this new exercise has begun. Impatient after nothing happens, I open them a sliver. Alex treads quietly around the room, placing a small object into each outstretched hand. As he passes me, a slight weight drops into my palm – a raisin. Without any thought, I pop it into my mouth.

"Keeping your eyes closed, as I place the object in your hand I want you to feel it, touch it, smell it. Use all your senses to explore it."

Horrified, my eyes spring open again. The rest of the group still have theirs closed and are fingering their raisins. Alex sees me and glances down at my now empty hand. Heat rushes into my cheeks. He grins, reaching into the bag and pulling out a second raisin. He drops it into my palm.

"Roll it between your fingers," he says, "what does it feel like?"

I blink my eyes closed once more, rolling the small soft object between my fingertips, before bringing it up to my nose and sniffing. The fruity aroma is stronger than I remember, but then I don't believe I've ever sniffed a raisin before.

"Bring it to your ear. Listen to it as you roll it between your fingers." Now, I want to laugh. This is ludicrous. How the hell he thinks this will help with my panic attacks or anxiety I have no idea, but I dutifully bring the raisin to my ear and roll it around, just like he asked. There's a slight squelching from within the fleshy fruit. A raisin makes a noise – who knew! After several minutes more the bell rings. I open my eyes and am greeted by big smiles as we all blink ourselves back into the room.

"That's Beginner's Mind," Alex explains. "You were open, looking at the raisin with fresh eyes, without preconceptions. It's a mindset we'll be trying to work on over the next few weeks." He rocks back in his chair. "Okay, so that's about all we have time for today."

It's home time already? How did that happen?

"This week I want you to practise the first meditation we did as many times as you're able. Just keep practising. We'll talk about how you've got on next week. Make a note of anything that comes up in your logbook. I also want you to choose a routine activity. It can be anything you do regularly, but try to do it mindfully. Make an effort to create that in-the-moment awareness we've begun to focus on this evening. Have a go at eating at least one meal mindfully. It doesn't mean you need to eat slowly, just be conscious of what you notice. Like you were with the raisin."

I snort, remembering the fate of my first raisin.

Alex grins at me. "Thank you, everyone, it's been a wonderful session. Let's take a moment just to say goodbye to one another."

We do another circuit of the group, taking time to say goodbye this time. Then there's the awkward moment of departure. I don't want to be the first to leave, but I can't think of any reason to hang around. I can think of nothing to say. About anything. I've been nowhere, done nothing. I'm about as interesting as wallpaper paste. No one will want to discuss Egyptian Design essays with me.

The thoughts pop any residual good feelings from the raisin session. I tighten my coat around me and hustle out of the room. Wind and rain buffet me as soon as I step outside, so I run all the way back to my car.

By the time I start the engine I'm feeling no better than when I arrived.

Chapter 3

"Darling, what are you doing?"

I turn to look down at my mother. I'm standing on the shed roof, the bottom rung of the ladder propped against my hip to hold it steady against the trunk of the tree. I can barely hear her over the noise of a passing airplane. "What does it look like I'm doing?" I yell. "I'm getting the fucking cat down."

"Language, darling. Oh, did you get another one?"

"Another one? What the hell are you talking about? Have you finally become demented?"

"Another cat." She points up at the window of my apartment. Sukie is visible on the windowsill, watching me. I gape at her for a moment, then look back up at the unmoving lump I have been prodding with the ladder assuming it was her. Now that I look at it more closely, it does appear slightly green-ish. And perhaps a bit shiny. More like... like a Marks & Spencer's plastic bag.

"For fuck's sake," I curse under my breath. I've been trying to talk a plastic bag out of the tree for the last half hour. After a couple of failed attempts, I hook the bag with the tip of the ladder and yank it out from the branches.

"That will have been Storm Doris," my mother says, taking hold of the bottom of the ladder as I slide it down towards her.

I grab the bag off the top before the wind can catch it again, and stuff it into my jacket pocket, then begin the climb down off the shed. "Bloody stupid name for a storm."

"You seem a little out of sorts darling, anything the matter?"

"Apart from wasting my life getting a plastic bag out of the tree?"

"The whales will thank you. Plastic bags are killing them, you know."

"Not up my tree they're not. Why are you here, Mummy?"

We walk through the back door and back into the hall. "Morning." My new neighbour greets us with a smile. There's the suggestion of broad shoulders under the jacket he's wearing today. His blonde hair is as neatly cropped as ever.

I nod back, wondering if he's been watching me retrieve the plastic bag too.

"He seems nice," my mother says, eyes swivelling to study his back view.

"He said 'good morning'. How can you possibly know if he's nice or not? He could be another Fred West, for all you know." Unfortunately, my aggravated mood causes me to speak more loudly than I mean to. My neighbour's shoulders tense.

I hustle my mother up the stairs, into my flat, and close the door behind us. "Why are you here?" I ask again. "It's Saturday – we never see one another on a Saturday. Sundays are our day."

"Ben called me."

"Ah." I grab the kettle and fill it, just to have something to do. Anything to avoid showing my mother the tears that have pooled at the mere mention of his name. "What did he want?"

"He was worried about you, sweetheart. Seemed to think you might need some TLC today."

I blow my nose loudly on the piece of kitchen towel my mother hands me. I know exactly what he's referring to. Yesterday evening, as I was gazing down at my beans on toast and trying to eat them mindfully, the doorbell rang. A special delivery: the divorce papers. I'd known they were coming, but despite that it still hurt like hell. The sight of our names on the top of the legal separation document hit me like a blade to my heart, causing me to hunch over with pain as I gasped for air. I'd eventually come back to my senses to find an empty plate and a heap of Cadbury chocolate wrappers. I'd spent the rest of the evening wallowing in a pit of self-loathing and, I imagine, on the verge of a diabetic coma. I'd not fared much better today, my thoughts cycling in a never-ending spiral;

He doesn't want me anymore.

Why would he? Bella's much more beautiful than me.

Cue binge-eating session to make myself feel better. Then:

Oh God, why did I eat that? I'm gross.

No wonder he doesn't want me anymore.

The thoughts go around and around and around.

"Any biscuits?" Mummy asks, hunting through the cupboards. "You haven't got much food in, darling. I thought you went to Sainsburys yesterday."

"I did. I've eaten it all."

"Since yesterday?"

I jut my chin out, just a little. "Yes," I say, inviting her to make something of it. I'm so ready for a fight.

"Oh, darling." She swishes over to me, her slim frame draped in her usual twinset and tweed, wrapping her thin arms around me.

Damn her for cutting straight through all my defences. Now I'm a blubbering wreck. I tell her as much, garbling the words out between mucus-laden sobs.

"My darling," she says again, stroking my hair like she did when I was eight.

"I still love him. I don't know how to make it stop."

"I know you do. He's an idiot, but he won't learn that for a while yet. You can't worry about him. You need to focus on yourself. On your life." She presses a tissue to my nose and holds it there until I blow. "It's time to move out from under the shadow of yourself as part of a couple and rediscover what it means to be Claire. I know it's hard – I felt the same when I lost Daddy. But you have a bright, beautiful future waiting for you when you do, my darling."

I sniff, and blink up at her with bleary, teary eyes. "That was remarkably sensible, coming from you."

"I have my moments."

"Not often."

"There's my girl," she says with a smile. "Now, wipe those eyes and let's write a shopping list."

"As long as it has ice cream and chocolate on it."

I always think of Sundays as couples' days. I used to like them. Ben and I would wake late, then, after he'd popped to the shop to collect the Sunday papers, we'd laze around, maybe make love, eat a late brunch. Sometimes take a long walk via a decent pub in the afternoon, then see Mummy for Sunday roast in the evening. Sure, it had all become a little predictable, but it was comfortable, easy, familiar.

Now, I find myself wide awake at…I squint at my bedside table clock. Six. I groan, and flop back against the pillows. Having demolished a pint of ice cream before nine last night, I took myself off to bed for fear I would finish off the second weeks' worth of shopping in as many days. The result is a reintroduction to parts of Sunday I haven't seen in fifteen years. I force my eyes closed again, hoping I can compel myself back to sleep.

It's futile.

Instead, I reach for my phone and scroll down until I find the body-scan guided meditation. It's sent me off to sleep every other time I've tried it this week. Hopefully this time it will do the trick too.

Alex's warm tones are immediately relaxing. "*Let your hands lie alongside your body and keep your feet uncrossed so they fall away from each other.*" My feet flop apart in a most undignified fashion. So far so good. "*And notice the sense of the body as a whole, lying here.*" The only sense I have is of my body's resemblance to a slab of lard. "*We're trying to create awareness of what's already here. We're not expecting anything special to happen.*" I release some of the tension I didn't even know I was holding inside as I exhale all the breath out of my lungs, then suck in a fresh lungful.

"*Relax the fingers in your right hand.*" Mine are gripping the duvet as if someone might rip it off me at any moment. I uncurl each finger in turn until they're lying flat on the cover. "*Feel the contact with whatever is supporting you. Notice the sensation. Feel where it's strongest.*"

Each instruction unfurls a new piece of my body. I become leaden, my arms sinking down into the mattress, legs like dead weights. Yet my body's humming. I've never really noticed it before. I must be less tired than when I usually try this, because I've never made it further than my left arm without falling asleep. I congratulate myself on a job well done. At least I'll have something to share with the group next week.

"*Now, bring your attention to your breath. Focus on your abdomen, noticing the stretching of the abdomen wall on the in breath, and the falling away on the out breath.*" I hiss a long outward breath, preparing to inhale again when a warm, furry mass smashes into my face. I scream as claws lacerate my skin, my arms flailing.

I sit up in time to see Sukie rush from the bedroom.

I'm oddly sorry to see her go. This is the first time she's made any effort at contact since she was forced to live with me. I just wish she hadn't chosen the middle of my meditation to jump from the top of my wardrobe onto my face. I've frightened her now.

Hammering on my front door startles me a second time. "Claire?" The voice is unfamiliar. *Bang, bang.* "Claire, are you okay?"

I shuffle into my slippers and trudge to the door, sliding back the deadbolt. Peering out into the hallway I find my new neighbour, wearing only his pyjama bottoms. The guy is cut. Huh, I didn't know he knew my name.

"Is everything okay? I heard you scream." He pauses as we stare at one another. "Dear God! Whatever happened to your face?"

I lean sideways to catch my reflection in the hallway mirror. Vivid red scratches line both of my cheeks. Blood is welling out of the cuts and now dripping off my chin. I consider myself for a moment, then look straight back at my neighbour as I tell him; "My cat jumped onto my face from on top of the wardrobe whilst I was meditating."

He blinks at me for a second, then the corners of his mouth twitch. His shoulders start to shake and his body shudders as he struggles to compose himself. He fails and finishes up bent double, wiping his eyes.

As I wait for him to get control of himself again, I find myself oddly bewitched by the effect his laughter has on his abdominal muscles. Ben has turned a little fleshy over the years. This fellow's abs are out and proud and dancing along to his surprisingly pleasant laughter. Then I recall what he's laughing at. "Was there anything else?" I ask with as much dignity as I can muster when he appears to be in a position to hear me again.

"No." He looks at my face and starts laughing again.

"Okay, well, good – have a nice day," I say, closing the door.

I walk into the bathroom and dig out the TCP, then spend several uncomfortable minutes dabbing at the scratches with disinfectant-laden cotton wool. I'm quite the vision. I look like a character from one of the *Scream* movies. One of the characters that dies.

Sukie is cleaning her paws when I walk into the kitchen. Sitting in the middle of my table, paw curled to her mouth with her claws outstretched, she is pulling at each one in turn. Probably removing the pieces of my flesh she extracted. She ignores me as I walk past and flick on the kettle. "I'm sorry I screamed," I tell her, wondering why I feel the need to apologise to a cat. "Just, next time, give me some warning you're coming," I say, reaching a hand towards her. She pauses her cleaning, blinks at my hand, then jumps off the table, running across the lounge, up the curtain and out the top window. She runs along the fence and straight up the tree. It seems we're back to where we started.

Chapter 4

"Well, it's great to hear how well you were getting on with the meditation practice."

I love the way Alex manages to find something positive in my recounting of the cat-on-face debacle. The rest of the group are staring at me, several with mouths agape. Colin snorts but at least tries to pretend it's a cough.

"Aloe might help, or tea tree oil if they're deep," Jennifer says, peering closely at my face.

"Okay, how about we split into groups and talk a little more about how we're all getting along?" Alex suggests, bringing a halt to my facial scrutiny. Sarah immediately scoots towards me; surprisingly so does David. I'm assuming it makes them feel better to be with someone whose life is just a little more fucked-up than their own.

They both look at me. "Someone else start," I insist. It feels like they're waiting for my second instalment. "How did you get on?" I ask David.

He rocks back in his chair, making it creak with the effort of holding him. "I practised every day," he says.

"Gosh, well done." I admire his commitment having only achieved three successful meditations. And *successful* is a term I'm using very loosely. "How did it feel?"

He tilts his head, thinking. "I find it easier to do it in here. I relax into the meditation more."

"Oh, really? I find it more distracting here, the apartment's quiet – well, apart from my cat. What do you think makes the difference?"

He's silent for a moment. "I don't worry so much that someone's going to attack me."

That was not what I expected him to say. I struggle to form a response; aware of my mouth opening and then closing at least once without making any sound.

Sarah comes to my rescue. "Is that likely then?" She's looking at him with new interest.

David stares back at her. It's clear he's never really considered this before, and he seems surprised we're surprised.

"It doesn't sound terribly relaxing," is all I can think to add.

He pauses to think about it. "No, I guess not," he says slowly. "It's just how I feel when I'm at home." He shifts a little in his seat.

"How did you get on with the mindful activities?" I divert attention towards Sarah, aware we're ill-equipped to deal with the 'ah-ha' moment David's having.

"I was okay with the mindful eating. Gavin said it made a change to see me chewing for once." I smile, but can't help thinking it's not the most loving observation I've ever heard. "Then I chose brushing my teeth. God knows, it meant I did a much better job. I was aware some of the time my mind wandered, but when it happened it became easier to notice and focus back on the task. I've found that happening a few times this week."

"Wow, great, good for you," I enthuse, thinking back to my own mindless eating. "I'm still trying to crack that one."

"Okay," Alex says, once we are back in the big group. "I'm going to take you through a couple of exercises. What I want you to do is think about the situation I describe. After I do, take a moment to consider your immediate thoughts and feelings. What are you telling yourself? What are you thinking or feeling?" He looks around the room. We're all leaning forwards a little. There's a sense of anticipation. "Okay?"

As a group, we nod.

"Okay. Close your eyes and centre yourself. I want you to imagine you're walking through the park. It's a lovely sunny day. Someone you know is playing Frisbee with a friend. They look up and you wave at the person you know, but they don't respond." He pauses, allowing his words to percolate.

I'm there; The sun's shining, warming my shoulders, the very slight breeze lifting the edges of my skirt. I pass a man – he looks a lot like my dad – riding a lawnmower, the rich, green scent of freshly cut grass pungent. In my imagination, my rather handsome downstairs neighbour's playing a game with someone I don't know. A girl. She's far more attractive than me. I raise my hand at him in an awkward, half wave, certain he sees me. He looks away. Toe-curling embarrassment sends heat rushing to my cheeks. My heart races and my breaths shorten.

"Okay." Alex's voice startles me, drawing me back into the room. "How are we all doing?"

I blink, then take a couple of deep breaths. My palms are sweating.

He smiles. "How did you feel?"

I can't yet bring myself to speak. The emotions are still too real. I'm a little afraid I might cry.

What the fuck is wrong with me?

Willow surprises me by speaking first. "Rejected. I know they looked away on purpose. They pretended they didn't see me, but I know they did."

Alex pierces her with his gaze. "How did you know?"

She runs a hand through her hair, pushing it from one shoulder to the other and then back again. I'm beginning to recognise it as one of her nervous tics. "I just know. She didn't want to admit knowing me in front of the other person."

"Why?" Alex presses.

"Because then I would embarrass her in front of her friend."

Alex nods. "Thank you, Willow. Anyone else? Anyone feel something different?"

"I was embarrassed. I wanted to make a joke of it – laugh it off – but really, it was to cover my embarrassment. It felt humiliating." Colin shifts in his seat, two bright spots of colour on his cheeks.

"I was angry," David chips in. "I wanted to cross the park and thump him. Tell him not to fucking ignore me… Sorry." I assume he's apologising about the bad language rather than the ABH.

Words are tumbling out of my mouth before I have a chance to check myself. "I felt ashamed. It made me very anxious," I admit.

"Ashamed… anxious… angry… embarrassed…rejected. Do you hear those words? All different. What do you think about that?"

"It's amazing how different they are," Sarah says. "They can't all be right. I felt like Claire did, as if they ignored me on purpose." We share a smile, a connection.

"Yeah, well, they probably *were* ignoring you." Gavin snorts at his own lame joke. No one joins in with him. Sarah tries to smile, but the pinched look around her eyes tells me she's hurt.

Alex nods at her, bestowing one of his healing smiles. "You're right, Sarah. Our interpretations are all different. Interpretations of the same situation. And as you say, they can't all be right. It's the interpretation and meaning *you* place upon an event that causes the accompanying emotion. They're assumptions, they don't acknowledge the actuality of the situation. It could, for instance, be that the person left their glasses at home and didn't see you."

I'm struck by this. The differences in how we process the same scenario. The physical response triggered by little more than thoughts. How much of how I feel is based upon my own assumptions of what was meant by an action? How much is fact?

I'm still dwelling on that thought when I walk back into the apartment, and step straight onto a deposit Sukie has left for me on the doormat.

I get to work scrubbing the mat, while Sukie watches me from the windowsill. I employ my new skills and contemplate whether this is really a punishment, directed at me; whether my assumption – that she hates living with me, so she craps anywhere but the tray to express her unhappiness and punish me – is a truth, or another narrative that serves to make me feel even more rubbish about myself than I already do. I don't know it to be the truth. If Alex were here, he would tell me it's only a thought, and to let it go.

I release my tension, taking a deep breath, which I quickly release again because the place still stinks, then look at Sukie. She's watching me from the windowsill, waiting for me to open it, so she can race back up the tree. Or maybe she only wants to get away from the smell. I can't blame her for that. "Want to go out?" I say. She blinks at me. "Need some air?" I unlatch the sash window, and jiggle the pane until it lifts high enough she can pass through. She doesn't run straight out. "Everything okay?" I ask, tentatively reaching a hand towards her. She allows me to stroke her. Once. Arching her back into my hand, before stepping out on the ledge and jumping down onto the flat roof.

A day later, Mr Barnes, the glazier, makes the sort of whistling sound between his teeth that suggests this is going to cost me. "Won't be easy," he says.

I supress my annoyance, force a smile and say, "I'm sure not. But can it be done?"

"It'll have to be specially made."

I take a deep breath, telling myself to be calm. "I understand. I know it will be difficult…and expensive," I say, before he can remind me. "But I'd still very much like it done. Can you do it?"

"Yeah, I can do it."

"Wonderful. When?"

"Well, I can take the measurements today, I'll get the boys to knock one up for you in say…" He looks towards the ceiling for inspiration, "…a week?"

"Marvellous." I step back as he whips out a tape measure then proceeds to write down the dimensions of my window in a small notebook, having conjured a pencil from behind his ear.

I'm having a cat-flap fitted into the pane. This will allow Sukie to leave the flat whenever the mood takes her.

"All done," he says, smiling at me as he tucks the notebook back into his top pocket. "Nice little place you've got yourself here."

I look around the flat, my gaze snagging on the patch of grey mould growing in the corner where the wallpaper is peeling away, wondering what he means.

"You on your own?"

I take a step back as the alarms in my head start to ring.

Is this still normal banter? Or is he making a pass at me?

Ben used to deal with anything to do with home maintenance. I have no idea what's acceptable. Should I be friendly, or will that send the wrong message?

I swear, the man's staring at me now, in much the same way I look at chocolate fudge cake.

Movement in the garden catches my eye. "No. My brother's here too." My voice is little more than a squeak. "Downstairs." I nod out the window - towards my neighbour. He's bending down and stroking Sukie, who's loving every moment of it. She pushes herself against his leg whenever he stops until he reaches down to stroke her again. What a tart. Although... he's easy on the eyes, those jeans and that shirt look amazing on him, I can't really blame her. I mean, I might rub my face against his leg given half a chance.

My neighbour looks up, and our eyes meet.

"Not married though?" Mr Barnes asks, pulling my attention back into the room.

I blink at him. "Um, yes actually. But separated." No, no, no. Why did I tell him that!

He pushes the pencil back behind his ear, then turns towards me, feet planted slightly apart. "Well, if you're up for it, I am."

Up for it? What the hell does that mean? "Um, well that's very kind." I move towards the front door. "I'm not really *up for it* right now. It's a little soon." I sound like a character from a Jane Austen novel.

"We don't have to date; we could just ..." He waggles his eyebrows at me suggestively. Not really a Jane Austen novel then.

"Oh," I release a ridiculously high-pitched giggle. "Well, that's frightfully nice of you, but…" Dear God, I sound like my mother now. When did that happen? I open the front door, "…so you'll call next week to arrange to fit it? The window, I mean?"

He's still not moving. "Yeah, I'll call next week. Are you going to give me your mobile number?"

Not a chance. "The landline's fine. You can leave me a message on there." I want him to leave.

"Everything okay up there?" my neighbour's voice calls up from the bottom of the stairs.

"Richard!" I say, conjuring a name out of thin air, because I don't yet know what his first name is. "Dinner will be ready in about half an hour."

"Sorry?" His head pops around the bannister, looking confused.

"Dinner," I say again, brightly. "It won't be long." I turn back to the glazier, who is still rooted to the spot. "Thank you again, Mr Barnes, for coming at such short notice. I'll look forward to your call." I stick out my hand, which finally galvanises the man into action. He grips the offered hand tightly, his damp, cool palm unpleasant to touch. He's still holding it when my neighbour reaches the top of the stairs.

"Everything okay?" he says, eyes dropping towards the overly long handshake.

"Mr Barnes was just leaving," I say in a forced-bright voice.

"Your sister said she's making you a meal. You're a lucky man, Richard."

"My sister?" He looks at me and must see some facial leakage of my desperation. "Aren't I," he murmurs. He looks back at the man still gripping my hand. "I'll show you out," he says.

"Thank you," I say, when he taps on my door again five minutes later. "He seemed to like it here a little too much."

“No problem, glad you’re okay.” He turns to leave, then hesitates and turns back to me. “Your brother?” He raises an eyebrow.

My cheeks heat. “It was all I could think of. I… I’m sorry, I didn’t know your name.”

“I’m Jack.”

“Well, hello Jack, I’m Claire… as you already know,” I say, putting out my hand for the second time. How *did* he know? “Thank you again for helping me out.”

He takes my hand, his touch warm and pleasingly dry. “My pleasure. Any time you need a brother… or something... I’m your man.”

I come over all of a fluster as my mind toys with the ‘or something’ possibilities.

There’s a thud behind me as Sukie arrives back in the room. A second thump as she jumps off the table, followed by a brush of soft fur as she rushes past me and rubs herself against Jack’s legs again. I watch her, feeling the sting of betrayal. Tears prickle my eyes.

Stupid. Now I’m crying over a cat. “Yes, well, thanks again,” I say, hooking Sukie with my foot as I close the door.

“You’re a tart,” I scold her as I fill a pan with water and set it down upon the hob. She blinks up at me. “I thought we agreed that people with penises are not to be trusted. Haven’t you learned anything from Ben?” Haven’t I?

She blinks again, watching me as I wait for the pan to boil. When it's ready, I drop some frozen coley fillet into the pan and prod it with a fork. I stay there watching it until it's cooked through and falling apart into little flakes of fish, then spoon some into one of Sukie's dishes. I'm not above buying her love if I have to.

I stare down at the blank page in my notebook. My task for the class this week, on top of the meditation practice, is to make a note of any pleasant events that have happened to me. So far, I've drawn a blank.

"There must be something," Nicole says, sitting back in her armchair, glass of wine in hand as she watches me. "There must have been at least one time this week someone did something unexpectedly nice for you, or you were pleased with something you'd done? What about work – something with one of your students?"

"Nope," I say, eyes fixed on the page as I will some words to materialise.

"What about the ex-client you said called you?"

I grunt. "She didn't know I'd left the partnership."

Nicole's eyes roll. "But she still wanted you, didn't she? Even after you told her you weren't with them anymore."

"Yes, but I explained to her, I'm not doing design work. Not anymore." No, I'm spending my days marking the assignments of nameless, faceless students. A job I can safely do from under my duvet.

She makes an exasperated noise. "But you could. She said she wanted you to do up her house. There's nothing stopping you from taking on the work. You could set yourself up as an independent. You don't need to work with Bella to be a successful interior designer. She wasn't an active client; she won't breach any of the separation terms. Plus, in any case, you didn't approach her, she came to you." She sips her wine, looking at me over the edge of her glass. "I love you, Claire, but you can't spend the rest of your life festering inside this flat. You need to get out. Live your life again."

I cross my arms. "I'm not festering."

She raises a single eyebrow. "You're still wearing your pyjamas at seven thirty in the evening."

I cross my legs now too. "They're called loungewear."

"Not if you wear them to bed. Have you even had a shower today?"

"I've been busy. Anyway, it's been a very dry year. I'm helping to save water."

She grimaces. "That's just nasty, Claire. You need to wash, and you need to sort out a job. Your savings won't last forever. You don't know what sort of settlement you're going to get at the end of all this – as little as possible if Bella has anything to do with it – you can't afford to sit around and wait."

"I'm working."

Nicole snorts.

"I know you're right… I just-"

Nicole huffs a breath, making her fringe flutter in the process. "It's been nearly nine months. That's long enough."

"I'm no good at anything. Well, not on my own, anyway." I give voice to my fears. The ones that eat away at me in my darkest moments. That, without Ben, I'm about as much use as a chocolate fireguard.

Nicole sits forward. "Bollocks. What evidence do you have for that conclusion?"

"Evidence?"

"This 'I'm so crap' version of yourself you come out with all the time. Your husband was unfaithful to you. That says more about his character than yours. Otherwise, until that point, you were – are – a talented designer who delivered more clients to the business than anyone else. One who was featured in House & Garden. Why *wouldn't* someone want to work with you? All Bella's able to design is expensive Ikea rip-offs. All chrome and glass and sharp edges."

"Corporate clients like chrome and glass."

She makes an exasperated growling sound. "Because most of them are soulless like her. You design from the heart. You make people homes that reflect who they are." She makes a fist and presses it to her chest. "In here." She looks around at my apartment. "Well, I maybe wouldn't use this as an example of what you can do… but why don't you set up a new company? Put it out there to some of the contractors you worked with that you're available again. Focus on houses, not corporate – that will keep Bella off your back – and see where it goes. It's got to be better than marking essays and eating your own body weight in chocolate every day."

I look down at the half-eaten box of Milk Tray on the coffee table.

Nicole sits back in the chair, slightly out of breath, blinking at me. I think she may have surprised herself with that outburst. To be fair, she's had my back throughout this whole episode. For the last eight months she's said nothing, allowing me to vent, violently agreeing with everything I said. This is the first time she's suggested anything other than a future of pyjamas and wine.

"Sukie let me stroke her yesterday."

"Sorry?"

"Yesterday, Sukie let me stroke her. Twice. She never lets me stroke her. That was good."

Nicole sighs. "Write it down then."

I scribe the words carefully into the page in my workbook. "I know you're right," I say when I finish, keeping my eyes on the book. "I know I have to get on with my life. I'm pathetic still to be letting it affect me so much. Trying to convince myself Ben'll see the light and come back to me." My eyes blur with tears.

Nicole moves closer and takes hold of my hand. "You're not pathetic, sweetheart. You've been grieving for the life you thought you were going to live. But now it's time to look around you and consider the life you do have. The life you could have if you let yourself. You're still young and talented. Your future is bright with possibility."

"Mummy said the same thing, the other day."

"Well, that was unusually good advice from her."

"I know. She just has these moments of clarity every now and again."

"To be fair, she went through something just as bad when she lost your dad. You don't see her wallowing about in her pyjamas all day."

I shake my head slowly.

Nicole jabs at the book still resting in my lap. "So, will you think about taking on some clients? I know at least one person looking for an interior designer."

"I'll think about it."

"And will you write it in that damn book?"

"I'll write it in my book."

"Well, go on then." She folds her arms across her chest, watching until I've written the words down.

Chapter 5

Willow's in the middle of relating all the good things that have happened to her this week. "My mother told me she'd never seen my house so tidy. Goodness knows how, but I managed to get the mark out of the carpet that she'd brought in with her the other day. She never takes her shoes off, it drives me mad. Just the thought of all the dirt she's walked through outside being trodden into my beautiful cream wool carpet." She shudders. "It's filthy. Anyway, I got the stain out – it took about half a pot of Vanish, and some heavy-duty elbow grease – but it was worth it-"

"That's wonderful, Willow." Alex holds a hand up, halting her litany of cleaning successes. "Anything else make you feel good about yourself? Any other pleasant events-" she draws a deep breath "-other than cleaning?"

She releases it again. "Umm." She frowns, thinking for a moment. "Well, I got selected to sing a soprano solo in Rock Choir." The group exclaims with delight on her behalf. Partly because it's an awesome achievement, and partly because it's not cleaning related. Willow looks taken aback at the group's general level of enthusiasm. "Oh, it's not a big deal. It's only because the woman who normally does it has a nodule on her vocal cord."

Alex holds up his hand again. "Hold it there for a moment," he says. He looks around at us. "Do you all hear what she did there?"

I see exactly what she did. It's exactly what I would have done: the default to self-deprecation.

"Did you see how she immediately tried to diminish what was good, and find reasons why the accomplishment meant less than it did?" The group murmurs in agreement. "Willow, tell me, are there other people who sing soprano, like you?"

She nods slowly. "Yes."

"So, there are other people who could have been chosen when the first lady damaged her throat?"

"I suppose so, yes."

"But they chose you. Out of all those other people, they chose you to sing the solo. Which is awesome! Enjoy that moment. You should feel proud of yourself."

Flustered, Willow begins flicking her hair from side to side. "I'll probably cock it up."

Alex shakes his head. "You don't know that. You're catastrophising. Your mind won't let you enjoy a moment of peace. The only thing we know as a fact right now, is that of all the people they could have chosen to sing the solo, they chose you. Your mind immediately wants to focus on what's not right, what might go wrong. Don't let it. Be in the moment. Enjoy now."

Enjoy now. It sounds so easy. It's so much easier to assume the worst. Willow's reaction is just like my own.

Most of us struggle to find anything positive to tell the group about until Alex teases it out of us. The session turns into a celebration. My potential new client is joined by David securing a meeting with an account he wants, Colin getting a date, and Sarah's big project at work being nominated for a prize. We're all uncomfortable under the spotlight of praise from our companions, but it does feel good to bask momentarily in our success. "We need to practise being with ourselves, experiencing the sensation in our bodies in each moment," Alex explains, wrapping up the session. "Recognise the good moments when they come. Now, this week is harder – or maybe some of you will find it easier – I want you to keep a calendar of unpleasant events. What was the experience? I want you to describe the unpleasant feelings you have while the event is happening. Be specific: how does your body feel? Then I want you to describe the other feelings and thoughts that go with it."

There's only a single page. Will there be enough space to capture everything likely to happen to me in the space of a week? I stop myself. I'm doing it again. I stand and pull on my coat, reaching for the zip.

"Claire." Sarah stops me with a hand on my arm.

I turn to look at her, ignoring Gavin who's frowning at me over her shoulder.

"I wondered if you might like us to meditate together one night this week. I find it helps me to be able to talk about it afterwards, and Gavin's not really all that keen."

A warm flush of pleasure leaves me smiling. "That would be wonderful," I say. "I have to get some marking done Monday, Tuesday, but I could do Wednesday? You're welcome to come to mine, if you like? I'll make sure there's no chance of the cat jumping on your head." I touch the fading scars on my face self-consciously.

Sarah smiles. We're grinning at each other like kids now. "That would be perfect." We exchange details, then I hang back a moment to thank Alex, before heading out.

Sarah and Gavin are a little ahead of me, her hand clutched within his. He bends towards her and I think he's going to kiss her cheek. Instead he whispers something into her ear. In the short time it takes them to reach their car her posture deflates, shoulders rounding, until, as she opens the passenger door, she appears almost curled into herself. "See you Wednesday," I call, walking past them. I don't get an answer.

I look down at my workbook. I've already filled half the page. I've only done one day so far, but it's been a humdinger.

Day One

What was the experience: Call from my solicitor.

Unpleasant feelings: Anxiety, tightness in my chest, tingly body, breathing fast. Panic attack – woke up on the floor.

Mood: Worried, scared, feeling of hopelessness, despair

To say my solicitor had been annoyed with me would be an understatement akin to suggesting Usain Bolt is quite nippy. Apparently, being cautioned for breaching my restraining order isn't helpful for my settlement case. They're likely to paint me in a less than positive light now, citing Ben's infidelity is understandable given my aggressive, unreasonable behaviour. He suggested it might make the judge less well disposed to look favourably on my situation. I allowed him to rage at me over the phone, then, as soon as he disconnected the call, I had my first full-blown panic attack since I started the Mindfulness course. Waking up on my lounge floor had been a blow to my confidence. I thought I'd been making progress. As if.

I look down at the second entry.

Day One

What was the experience: Text from Ben.

Unpleasant feelings: Weepiness, pain in chest, breathing fast.

Mood: Despair, broken heart

I pick up my phone and re-read his text for the thirtieth time.

'How could you, Claire? Hitting a pregnant woman! Can't you at least consider our baby and what all this stress might do to it? I'm so disappointed in you. Please don't contact us again. Our solicitor will be in touch.'

Oh, Bella's good. She's played me like a fiddle, stitched me up like a kipper, well and truly stuck the knife in and twisted.

And it all started out so innocently. . .

Still on a high after the group, I'd decided to get some advice on starting my own design company. Half an hour later, following a call to my new accountant, I'd set the wheels in motion to form my own small interior design business.

Twenty minutes after that, I'd booked my first client in. The same lady who'd contacted me to begin with. She'd been delighted to hear I'd reconsidered.

Feeling rather pleased with myself, that was the point I'd realised some of my older folders and notebooks were still at the studio. Full of swatches and colour books, they were where I'd dumped all my ideas in the early days. Most were just doodles and random colour boards, pages from magazines and notes about lighting, but every now and again inspiration struck. I was sure I remembered a design that fit perfectly with what my new client had said she wanted.

I knew I still held a key to the studio.

I'd looked at my watch. Bella never got into work before twelve. I'd figured I could pop in and pick it up. I'd be in and out again and she'd be none the wiser.

I didn't think. I'd grabbed my bag, picked up my phone and keys, and run out the house ignoring Jack's shouted greeting as I'd bundled past him. It had taken me less than ten minutes to reach the studio.

Letting myself in through the front door, I'd taken the stairs two at a time before pushing into the main studio space.

What I hadn't counted on were the memories. They'd hit me like a punch to the gut.

I'd fully intended to run in and straight out again once I'd found the folders. Instead, I'd found myself in the middle of the room, staring around at what had once been a focus of my life. For more than ten years.

Photos lined the walls, frames holding pictures from my magazine features. I'd lost myself, staring at the smiling faces, trying to remember what it had felt like to be that happy. I'd tracked through the beams of light that filtered in from the high windows, over to my desk, watching the dust motes dance. I'd always loved the light in the studio on a sunny day.

Remnants of my last project lay untouched, exactly where I'd left them. So many months later, no one had even bothered to clear my desk. I'd fingered the fabrics, wondering who had finished the work for my client.

Then, unable to stop myself, I'd walked over to Bella's desk. Mood boards for her latest design lay scattered across the desk; Chrome and glass. Same old same old. Next to a framed photo of her and Ben. Laughing together. She had a hand pressed proprietorially against his chest.

At that point, I'd seen enough. I'd walked back to my desk and pulled open the drawer where I'd known my folders and notebooks lay. They were still there – exactly where I'd left them. I'd grabbed them, tucking them under my arm.

That was when I'd heard the key in the door below.

Panic hit. I'd taken a second to look around for somewhere I might be able to hide. Then stopped, wondering what the hell was I doing. Determined I wasn't going to cower from the bitch again, I'd pulled back my shoulders and straightened up just as Bella appeared at the top of the stairs.

Her hand had dropped protectively over her bump, as she'd stopped and stared. "What the fuck are you doing here?"

"I wanted to pick up a couple of my things. I'm not staying. I don't want any bother." I'd found it was true.

She'd ignored me. "What have you got there?" Her eyes had narrowed, laser focused on the folders under my arm.

"Nothing of yours. Only my folders."

She'd crossed her arms over her chest, more confident now. "That's where you're wrong. Those are company assets. They belong to me."

"Oh, give it a rest, Bella. You'd never use any of this stuff. It's not your style."

She'd reached as if to snatch the folders from me. "That's where you're wrong. Since you let the business down, I've stepped in to support a number of your clients. I've found I'm a natural at the cluttered look. Those books belong to the business."

I'd clutched them tighter to my chest. "Any designs I created for clients while at the company belong to you. These scribbles are mine. Most of this stuff was done before we even started the company. You don't even like what I do."

She'd rolled her eyes. "That's irrelevant. I'm doing a design for the Plumbers. I need some of that shit to help with my mood board." She'd nodded towards a board I hadn't noticed leaning against the wall.

I'd wandered closer. "God, that's horrible." The words had slipped out without any filtering. It was true though. Her attempt at what she'd referred to as 'cluttered-shit' was more shit than anything else.

She'd turned on me then. "You're so fucking rude. It looks exactly like all the crap you do." I'd touched a nerve; she'd never been able to combine colours and fabrics the way I could. It had always pissed her off that, as a result, it was my designs featured in the articles on the walls, not hers.

"Well, good luck with it," I'd said, striding towards the door, hoping for a clean exit. I should have known better.

"Give me those fucking books."

I'd turned back, frustrated. "Bella, you've taken my business, my home and my husband. Don't you think I should at least be allowed to keep my designs?"

"No. You don't deserve them. Stop acting like such a victim. It's pathetic. You're pathetic. Really, you only have yourself to blame. If you'd appreciated Ben a bit more, he'd never have even looked at me. Then you walked away from this business." She gestured around at the studio. "You walk away from everything the minute it gets a bit difficult. You've always been a spoiled brat. Expecting everything to land straight into your lap. Well sorry. It's time you learned life's a bitch."

"And you'd know all about bitches," I'd shot back.

She'd lashed out then, cracking me across the cheek with the flat of her palm.

I hadn't thought. My hand had swung round on instinct and slapped her right back. It had resounded with a satisfying crack. Only, where my engagement ring had turned around on my finger and was now facing out from my palm, it had caught the soft flesh on her cheek.

She'd shrieked, raising her fingers to touch her face. They'd come away bloody.

"You cow. You attacked me! I'm calling the police."

Adrenaline had punched through me. Fight or flight. Fight. "You slapped me first!"

"You shouldn't be anywhere near me to begin with."

She'd had me there. I'd grabbed my folders, tucked them under my arm and run.

"I suppose you'd better come in," I say a few hours later, pressing the button to open the front door to Officer Brown.

"Hello, Ms Everett." He plods up the stairs towards me. "Been visiting old friends again?"

I hold my door a little wider for him to step inside, then lead the way into my kitchen. "I don't suppose you'll believe this, but she slapped me first."

He'd tilted his head, looking weary. "You weren't meant to be within slapping distance in the first place."

I'd sighed. "I know." Lifting the kettle, I'd looked at him. "Did you want tea?"

He'd nodded. "For what it's worth, I do believe you. I can see a mark on your cheek."

"Oh." I'd flicked the switch on the kettle, pausing to examine the palm-shaped mark on my cheek in its curved reflection. It looked red and sore. "Am I in a lot of trouble?"

He'd sighed. "A fair bit. She's threatening assault charges in addition to a complaint about your breaking the conditions of the restraining order. I think, now I've seen you, I can probably get her to back off on the assault. But there are some files she mentioned – property of the business allegedly. Apparently you stole them?"

I'd huffed, gabbing a couple of mugs out of the cupboard. "I didn't steal them. They were mine to begin with. I was just trying to start again. Setting up my own business. She doesn't even know how to use them; it's just enough for her to stop me using them." I'd poured the boiling water over the teabag, stirred it for a moment then fished it out again before holding up a carton of semi-skimmed milk.

He'd nodded. "With one sugar, please. Can you prove they were yours?"

The items in question were still on the kitchen table. I'd picked one up and turned it towards him so he could see my name in ancient ink swirling letters all over the front.

He'd sighed. "Look, for whatever reason this lady has got it in for you-"

I'd huffed, placing the mug down on the table in front of him. "I don't know why; she's already taken everything that mattered."

He'd picked up the mug, blowing gently as he'd cupped it in both hands. "Regardless, you're making this very easy for her. Stay away. Speak to her through your lawyer. At the moment she's making you look like the bad guy in all this."

"You don't think I am though?"

He'd offered me a smile. "I don't want to speak out of turn…"

"But…"

"No, Ms Everett. I've met ladies like her many times before. I don't think you're the bad person here. Stop running her race. She'll win if you do. I don't mean Mr Everett or all that stuff – I mean yourself. You'll lose yourself if you descend to fighting her on her terms. You're better than that."

I'd let him out a little later, after he'd finished his tea, his words still circling around in my brain. Oddly comforting in their own way.

Then Ben's text had arrived.

Chapter 6

Sarah looks at me open-mouthed as I relate the latest chapter of the telenovela commonly known as my life. "Did they arrest you?"

"No. She backed off the assault charge after the policeman mentioned the bruising on my cheek."

"What about the folders?"

I sigh. "They're with my solicitor now. It's all still a bit up in the air."

"God, Claire. I don't know how you do it."

Neither do I. I think about the wastepaper bin full of family sized bags of Minstrels and Maltesers. My self-loathing levels at DEFCON One. Forget mindful eating, mine was mindless all the way.

I wave a hand, literally trying to push the thoughts away. "Enough about me. What's going on with you?"

She shifts, her turn now to look uncomfortable. "Oh, you know. Gavin isn't really a fan of the course."

Well that was hardly news. The man made his disdain for everything mindful very apparent. "Yeah, I kind of got that vibe from him. But you're finding it helpful, right?"

She smiles, the tension in her face lifting a little. "Oh yeah. Really helpful. It's made me stop and question all the shit I tell myself most of the time… about how crap I am. It's helping me a lot with my depression. I'm managing without the pills for the first time in a long time. I wish I'd found it years ago. Of course, Gavin's convinced they're brainwashing us. Do you think they are? He claims it's all hippy trippy clap trap."

I want to tell her what an arse her husband is. Instead, I choose a more diplomatic approach. "I don't think they're brainwashing us. They never tell us what to think. All they do is help us examine our thoughts and recognise the ones that aren't constructive. I don't know about you, but I've found it incredibly helpful. I mean, I've had a bad week, but even so, I've still been meditating. I've handed in my notice to a job I hated and started my own business – it's helped me believe in myself enough that I've felt able to start my own business – and while the shit with my ex and his lady has been somewhat less than ideal, it hasn't made me less determined. If anything, I'm determined to prove her wrong. I'd say that's progress."

Given only a few short weeks ago I'd been living in my pyjamas and having panic attacks most days, I figure I'm doing okay, despite the occasional slip. "I mean, I've got a way to go. I'm still ridiculously punishing on myself most of the time, but at least I know when I'm doing it now. I see the thoughts for what they are. Hopefully Alex will show us some magic trick to help us turn them off, or down, or something."

Sarah leans back against the chair looking thoughtful. "I know what you mean. Gavin wants me to stop the group, but

I've refused. We had a massive row about it." She rummages in her bag and pulls out a tissue, dabbing at the corner of her eye.

"If it's helping you..." I don't know what else to say. I don't really want to get caught in the middle of her relationship drama. It wouldn't be the first time I've made the mistake of slagging someone's arsehole of an ex off, only to have them reunite the next week. It makes for awkward dinner parties. On the plus side, now that I'm single again, I don't get invites to dinner parties anymore. "Anyway, at least we both have plenty to put in our books."

I'm humming to myself when I let Mummy into the apartment. She's been checking up on me almost daily since my latest brush with the law. I think she's worried I'm going to have a panic attack when I'm here alone, and no one will know or come to help me. "What have you been doing, darling?" she asks, following me into the lounge.

"Tidying up the flat a bit," I say. "Well, taking the lawnmower downstairs anyway. Jack's letting me keep it in his shed." I return to hoover to finish sucking up the old grass cuttings it left behind.

"That's kind of him. You didn't think the *lawnmower in lounge* look was something that would catch on, then?"

"No, sadly not. Daddy would have disagreed though, wouldn't he?" I grin. "Cutting the grass always reminds me of him. Just having his mower here... it's been nice."

Mummy grins at me. "You're as mad as he was." She kisses me, then pats my cheek as if I were five, not thirty-five. Static cracks against my skin. "I do so miss him terribly. Fancy a cup of tea?"

"Please," I say, rubbing my cheek. She grins at me again, disappearing into the kitchen.

I've finished hoovering and I'm sitting in the armchair when she re-emerges with two cups, steam billowing from the top. "So, I bought myself a new mobile telephone device," she says, taking care to put my tea down on a coaster. Goodness only knows why she bothers; the table is a piece of second-hand mass manufactured pine. Every time I look at it, I hate it a little more. Last time I checked there was an ancient lump of chewing gum welded to the underneath. When I left Ben's I really didn't bother to take anything. I didn't want the reminders. Every piece of furniture I own has been bought since. I think I was punishing myself in some way when I chose this table. It really is time I did something about the state of the flat.

"It's just called a mobile, Mum."

She rummages in her bag, whipping out the latest iPhone. "Goodness," I say. "That must be costing you a fortune." The salesman obviously saw her coming.

"Yes, well I have unlimited textuals."

"Texts."

"Yes, and what did he say, thirty giga-somethings of data."

"Goodness, I'll cancel my TV package. We'll watch it on your phone."

She peers at the device in her hand. "I'm not sure the screen is big enough."

I push a hand through my hair. "Don't worry, I'm just being silly. What did you buy a phone for?"

She gives me one of those *don't be so silly* looks. "Well, so you can call me if you need me, of course. In case you have one of your panics."

Emotion catches me by surprise.

"I didn't mean to make you cry, darling."

I didn't know I was. "It's good crying, not bad crying," I manage, swiping away a tear. I take the phone from her and enter in my number to her contacts. When I check, I'm the only one. My mum bought herself a gazillion pound phone that she'll be paying through the nose for monthly, just so she could make sure I was okay. It's humbling. She's in her mid-seventies. I'm meant to be looking out for her; instead she's still checking I'm okay. "I'm getting better."

"I know you are, darling. I can see it."

I feel the need to reassure her some more. "The to-do with Bella last week was just a little set-back."

"Those designs are yours, my darling. She's just jealous of you. She saw your life and your talent, and instead of making a life for herself just as lovely, she wanted to take yours. That's because she's not a very nice person. I was telling William all about it last week."

"William? Who's William?"

She waves a hand dismissively. "Oh, a friend of mine, from bridge club. He's hopeless at bridge, but he's quite good company."

I squint at her. "Are you having a dalliance?"

"Goodness, no." Mummy laughs, waving her hand again as if my question were an annoying fly buzzing around her head. She stands and wanders over to the window. I can't tell, because she's not looking at me, whether she's fibbing or not.

"I wouldn't mind," I say quickly, just in case she thinks she needs my permission. "I don't think Daddy would mind either. Not after all this time." It's nearly ten years. We've both taken a while to recover from it.

She turns to look at me. "Oh, I know that. He wouldn't mind a bit. But there was really only Daddy. For me, anyway." And now I'm crying again. "Anyway, who wants to get saddled with an old man? Really, what's the point? They're mostly awfully selfish, just want a woman to look after them – cook and clean and all that. Take care of them. You don't even get the bedroom perks because of their prostate problems, and they're back and forwards to the lavatory all night… It's like having a baby again. Well, unless you're as lucky as Marjorie. She's the exception, not the rule. Who'd want that? I'm quite happy on my own, thank you very much. No, I was talking to William about your business. He owns a company. Mentioned they'd used your old design firm…."

What the hell? What's she talking about?

"… so I told him what a two-faced b-i-t-c-h," she whispers the letters, "your old partner turned out to be. Suffice it to say, he's not planning to use them again."

Alarm bells, loud and jarring like my old school's fire alarm, sound in my head. "Mummy, what company does William own?"

"Oh, they're a funny lot. I didn't really understand it, to be honest. They sell clouds, or something. As if! Who sells the weather, for goodness' sake? Anyway, he's the one who suggested this phone would be perfect for me."

Oily nausea swills in my belly. Mummy's friend William sounds like he may well be William Flack of Nebula. They're a massive cloud storage provider, one of the biggest. They have offices all over the world, and just before all hell broke loose in my life, they'd become our biggest client to date. Or Bella's biggest client. Hence the reason for the La Perla knickers. We'd been commissioned to draw up a design for their flagship UK offices. The plan was that if they liked what we came up with they would roll the designs out, or a version of them, worldwide.

Bella had let other clients go to get this project right. As far as I knew, although given we didn't talk much any more things might have changed, the designs had been submitted. She had been waiting for the finances to be approved, and a decision to be made on the other sites. It sounded like Mummy might very well have torpedoed the whole project. Dear God!

"Oh look, darling, that nice man from downstairs has bought himself a puppy. They're out in the garden. Let's go down and see them." She's already halfway out the front door before I'm even out of my chair.

I sigh and follow her down, still preoccupied with what she has just told me.

"Oh, how absolutely gorgeous!" Mummy crouches down, exclaiming over the ball of fluff in front of her. I have to admit, it is rather divine. One black ear, one white. Jack is grinning like a proud parent. "Look of the size of his feet," Mummy says. "He's going to be enormous. Isn't he one of those Durex puppies?"

Jack's face turns bright red, as he attempts to stifle his laugh.

"Dulux, Mummy," I hiss. I'm convinced she makes these slips of the tongue on purpose purely to mortify me.

Chapter 7

I stir my vodka, because I hate it when the lime cordial sinks to the bottom, then take a long drink. It's been another rough day. The walking meditation didn't work for me at class tonight – my mind caught up with too much self-destructive chatter. I'm going to have to find time to practise that one again.

"So, did your ex bugger off with a younger woman then?" Willow asks, pulling my attention from my own thoughts. She rummages in her oversized bag and pulls out a packet of antiseptic wipes. Extracting one, she proceeds to wipe the top of her fruity cider bottle. She looks at me expectantly, replacing the packet in her bag before picking up the bottle to take a sip.

It takes me a second to recall the question. Bella – was she younger or older than me? *Urgh.* I don't think Willow meant the question to be unkind because she seems genuinely curious. So do the others, judging by the way they're all leaning in to hear my answer. A few of us de-camped to the pub after our class this evening. It's turned into a kind of 'getting to know you better' session. With alcohol.

"No, she's older than me. Five years older." That's always been a bit of a kicker. I mean, at least when a man dumps you for someone younger and prettier than yourself, you kind of know where the shallow bastard is coming from. Still, I couldn't compete. Not when she has the added benefit of her fecundity. Ben really wanted a child. We both did.

"Bummer," Willow says.

Yeah, that about sums it up. I hum in agreement.

Sarah grabs my hand under the table and squeezes it. She's a nice person. Gavin didn't come tonight and I'm not sure if it's a coincidence, but Sarah's seemed chattier... less weighed down... happier. The continual put-downs he directs her way can't be good for the soul. She winces a little, settling back into her chair.

"I think I need help," Willow announces, in much the same way she might tell us she needs to stop at Tesco Express on the way home to buy some milk.

She's successfully diverted all the attention away from me. I'm grateful.

"I think I need help for my OCD. I've always denied it, until now. But this course... Talking about all the stuff we let go on in our heads. Well, I think mine is more than just the normal crap we mess ourselves up with. It's fucking up my life; I'm paranoid of dirt, public places like this." She looks around, then shudders. "I can barely stand having to sit on these chairs. God knows how many other people have sat on it. That's why I curl my leg up underneath me, so the smallest possible surface area I can rest upon and still be considered sitting is in contact with the chair." She sighs. "Even touching other people... Well, you can imagine it makes having any kind of proper relationship hard."

I look at her. Really look at her, beyond the great hair and straight white teeth. To the hands, twisting in her lap, teeth worrying at the edge of her lip. She's waiting for our judgement. It's amazing how much I envied this girl and her good looks that first evening she breezed into the room. I imagined she had it all. Shows what I know. The only ordinary people are people you don't know very well. It's not my saying, but it fits.

Sarah speaks first. "That's a huge step you've taken: acknowledging the problem. You should be really proud of yourself. What are you planning to do?"

"I'm going to ask for a referral. My mum's been wanting me to get help for ages. I think I'm ready now."

I want to hug her, but I know it would be just about the worst thing I could put her through, so I tell her what I'm thinking instead.

She grins. "Thank you for not hugging me. That's so thoughtful of you."

I return the smile.

A buzzing noise distracts us, breaking the moment.

Willow looks down at the dark wood table, its surface marked by years of coaster-less drinking. "Who's that?" she says. My phone is shuddering its way across the tabletop, still on vibrate after I silenced it before the session earlier.

It seems I have a facetime call. "My mother." I sigh. "Or, at least, her nostrils." We have a perfect view up her nose. I swipe to answer, ignoring the snorts of laughter from the people around me. "Hello Mummy."

"Darling, isn't this marvellous. I can see you now when we have our little chats. It's better than our textual intercourse, don't you think?" She giggles, knowing perfectly well she's using the wrong words.

"You can just say texts. And I think the word you're looking for is discourse." I'm really wasting my time. And still staring up my mother's nostrils. "Can you move the phone a little further away from your face?

"Oh, sorry darling. Yes, yes, of course. Is that better?" Her living room wall comes into view, and the entirety of her face. Her bright blue eyes sparkle with joy. I find myself smiling because she's smiling. It's infectious. She has a gift for bringing joy with her. I'm appreciating it a little more since I've been on the course.

"Much better. Are you okay?"

"Of course! I just wondered if you needed any help at your meeting with the bank about your loan. It's tomorrow, isn't it? I could come with you, if you wanted a bit of moral support?"

My good humour plummets with the memory of my earlier debacle. "Thank you, that's a nice thought, but it was today, actually." What the hell was I thinking, imagining I'd get a bank to lend me any money? I should have known better.

Her mouth forms a perfect circle. "Oh! How did it go?"

Oh God, I wish I'd never answered the phone. "They said no." Solemn faces now surround me. I kick myself for being such a downer. I want to get out of here. "Look, I'm at the pub, actually. Can I call you in the morning? I'll tell you all about it then."

Mummy's forehead furrows. "Yes, of course, darling. Have fun, sweetie. And say hello to all your friends from me."

I press the red button, guilty knowing the twinkle had all but faded from her eyes by the time we cut the call. There's silence around the table too. I am the very definition of a mood hoover. "I'm so sorry about that." I brush imaginary lint off my skirt. "I'm sorry I'm such a downer, I'm killing the mood. I'll leave you guys to enjoy the rest of the evening in peace." My chair scrapes back across the parquet floor as I prepare to stand.

Willow places her hand on mine. "Stop it, Claire." The touch is so unexpected, I freeze. She pulls her hand away quickly, then reaches into her bag for another antiseptic wipe. "Tell us what's going on in your head."

I hesitate, knowing she's applying what we talked about in class earlier.

Sarah pats my knee. "Go on, love."

I lean back in the chair. What *am* I really thinking? "I'm feeling bad about spoiling the good mood. I feel like I'm always moaning, and that people – all of you – must be wishing I'd go because I bring the mood down. My heart is beating faster," I say, noticing the thrumming tempo inside my chest. "I'm sweating a little. My chest feels tight."

Sarah leans towards me, forcing me to look at her. "You're having a stress reaction. It's like Alex said earlier, your mind's trying to cling to previous experiences. You're allowing yourself to misinterpret the situation, because it feeds the depressing narrative you've already written about yourself. In this case, we didn't even need to say anything. You attached meaning to our silence. I can't speak for anyone else, but my silence was only because I was trying to work out how best to support you. There was no judgement. No desire for you to leave. I want you to stay. I like being around you."

Willow and David murmur in agreement. "Why did the bank turn you down?" Willow asks.

Why wouldn't they? I'm a failure.

The words hover on the tip of my tongue. I pause, recognising what I'm doing... again. "Well... What I want to tell myself is that I'm a failure. At everything. So, why wouldn't the bank see that and not lend me the money? What they actually said was that I lacked collateral. To secure the loan."

"Didn't you get half the house?"

"Not yet. I will, when the divorce goes through. I was salaried in the business, so I'm fighting for a share of that too, but it doesn't look good. I resigned after what happened. They didn't force me to go. Ben and Bella were the company Directors."

Sarah frowns. "She stitched you up."

I nod, my cheeks heating with shame.

"That's not a criticism of you, love," Sarah says. "That says more about her. And him. But mostly her, I suspect. She's a cuckoo, slipping into your nest – in this case the business and your marriage. Now she's successfully pushed you out over the edge. I wonder whatever happened in her own life to make her that way?"

It's a very good question. I've never wondered what makes Bella act the way she does.

"The thing is, you can't keep beating yourself up for what's happened. And you can't worry about what might happen in the future. Events that may never come to pass. You can only focus on now. The only time you can actively change things is now. So, what do you need *right now*?"

I think for a moment. "I need someone to help me create a website. I need a site where I can showcase my work and give contact details to potential clients."

David laughs. "Well, that's easy enough. I'm a website designer. I'll do it." He hasn't spoken much all night. He seems content to just sit here with us. Until now.

I stare at him. "You are?" My voice wobbles a little as I attempt to moderate the note of surprise. With those arms, I'd assumed he was in construction or something. I should've known better than to judge him like that. I mean, I look like a fairly normal, fully functioning middle-age woman.

He laughs again, a low rumbling sound. "Yeah, I own an internet design company. I can do it for you. Just send me a spec, some links to sites you like the look of, any pictures you've got that you want to use and whatever page headings you think you want, with the text content, and I'll pull something together for you."

My eyes are prickling with tears. "Really? I mean, are you sure? I can pay you a little bit... then give you some more when the house money comes in. Things are a bit tighter since I packed in my job and until I get some clients."

He shrugs one shoulder. "Nah, just come and take a look at my home office. It needs redesigning. Give me some ideas for what I can do. I'll pay for all the materials. I've been meaning to do it for a while. I want to create a space I can meditate in."

My head tells me this is a gesture of pity. All my instincts want me to thank him politely and decline.

"Don't you dare," Sarah says, frowning at me. "I know what you're doing. You're about to turn him down. You think this is about him feeling sorry for you. Self-sabotage."

I glare at her. "What are you? A bloody mind reader now?"

"No, it's just exactly what I would do. It's easier to spot it when someone else is doing it. Say thank you to the nice man," she says, nodding at David.

"Thank you." I allow myself to feel a trickle of excitement and smile at David.

He smiles back, looking pleased with himself. His smile widens even further when Sarah sends him a massive, beaming grin of approval.

I'm still in a good mood when the taxi drops me off at home. No doubt assisted by the five vodkas I drank. It also helps the rain has stopped for what feels like the first time in weeks. My happy glow lasts until, through the window of my flat, I see Jack teetering up my ladder. The ladder is leant against the tree on the shed roof. The bloody idiot's climbing the ladder when it's on top of the shed.

I shimmy the sash window open and call, "What the hell are you doing? You look like the opening scene in an episode of Casualty."

A second after I do it, I realise I should have thought it through a little more. His head swings towards me, creating what I assume they mean by adverse camber when the ladder moves in the opposite direction to his body. He jerks back, trying to re-stabilise himself, but the ladder has little grip on the shiny, wet asphalt and collapses onto the shed roof. Jack follows it down, bounces once on the roof and then slips off the side, hitting the ground with a shriek of pain.

Jesus.

I'm running and trying to call *999* at the same time.

When I reach him, he's still flat on his back, arms raised as he tries to defend himself from the effusive pink-tongued licks being offered by the puppy. It's bouncing all around him. The creature's clearly delighted Jack's come down to play.

"Bertie, stop … Ow! Fuck." Bertie seems to have a hold of his ear now and won't let go.

"What is your emergency?"

"Are you okay? Do you need an ambulance?" I scan what I can see of him.

"I think I might've broken my ankle."

"Ambulance," I say to the operator. I'm too drunk to drive.

It's already half-past eleven. It's going to be a long night.

Chapter 8

"You didn't have to come with me." Jack's scowling. I want to laugh at him, but I know it will only make him more annoyed. He's in a terrible mood. From the pain, I imagine.

"Well, of course I bloody did. It was my cat's fault you were up the blasted tree in the first place." I glare at the kid beside us, who's just spent the last couple of minutes raking around inside his nose and is now examining his catch closely on the end of his finger. He lifts his gaze and looks around, as if he's wondering where he might wipe it. I definitely see him check out my coat as a contender. In the end, he pops the finger into his mouth.

"If Bertie hadn't chased her in the first place, I wouldn't have needed to be up the tree."

"What the hell were you doing up the ladder on the shed? I never do that. You just have to hold it close to her. She climbs down herself eventually."

He glares at me. "Eventually! I'd been cajoling that fucking cat for two hours before I attempted to climb up and get her."

Yeah, that was possible.

"If you hadn't shouted at me..."

"Don't blame me!"

He sighs, shoulders slumping. "I'm not. God knows how I'm going to manage with this." We both look down; his foot is already purple and twisted at a somewhat unnatural angle.

"It might not be broken." Liar, liar, pants on fire.

He rolls his eyes at me. "And Sukie might never climb the fucking tree again."

Touché.

I look at my watch. We've already been here more than two hours. Radiology is full to bursting with drunken revellers needing limbs X-rayed after falls.

He releases a long sigh. "Look, why don't you go home? It's late and I'm a big boy. I can look after myself."

I shake my head. "I've come this far, haven't I? I need closure. I'll stay until you get a diagnosis, at least. Then we can take it from there."

"Jack Wilton," a man calls from a doorway.

"Here!" I wave my hand then grab the wheelchair handles and push Jack into the X-ray suite. He's taken from me, and I'm sent back out into the waiting area. I eye the coffee machine, knowing nothing good will likely come from it. But it's after one in the morning. It's that, or nothing.

An hour later, with the bitter taste of whatever the hot brown liquid was from the machine still deadening my taste buds – not coffee, I know that much – we're back in a cubicle with a grim-faced doctor. "I'm afraid we're going to have to admit you."

"What! Why?" Jack and I chorus. Jack looks horrified.

"Your fracture is displaced. You'll need an operation to insert a metal plate to hold the bone in the right place, so it can heal properly."

"And if I don't?" All the colour seems to have drained from his face. His complexion's almost the same as the off-white walls. I examine the paint more closely; it probably started off as white but has yellowed over the years.

"You'll risk long-term problems with your leg if we don't operate. It's very straightforward. Nothing to worry about. You'll only be in for a few days. We can probably get you onto the list for the operation tomorrow, then a couple of days on a ward to get you up and about again. After that, you'll be able to go home."

"I can't stay in hospital. I have a puppy at home."

"I'm sure someone will be able to look after it for you. This is important for your long-term health." The doctor pierces me with a look that prompts me: *This is where you step in, lady.*

I steel myself. "I'll look after Bertie."

Jesus! What the hell am I doing?

Jack appears unconvinced. I'm not surprised. He's seen what a stellar job I've been doing with Sukie. "Really, I can do it."

Am I trying to convince him or me?

The fight leaves Jack, his body collapsing against the pillows. Or maybe it's the most recent dose of morphine kicking in.

"Don't let him climb the tree," he says, as the doctor calls for the porter to take him up to the ward.

"No tree climbing. Gotcha," I say, giving him a crisp salute. "Can I have your house keys?"

Jack scowls at me. "Why do you need my keys?"

"To collect Bertie. And his food, and stuff."

"Oh, yes. Right." He pulls the blanket aside, eyebrows knotting in confusion when he sees only his boxers. "Where have my trousers gone?"

"They cut them off you when they brought you in, remember?" I rummage about in the plastic bag all his possessions were stuffed into until I find them in the pocket of his shredded jeans. "I'll bring you in a new pair, if you like?"

"Keys?"

"No, trousers, you silly lummox."

His eyes are closed now. He nods, but I don't think he's going to have any memory of this conversation. He looks adorable. I shake the thought off, forcing myself into practical mode; now I think about it, he's going to need pyjamas and wash stuff too. I make a mental note to pop in and visit him with everything tomorrow, then wave goodbye to his nurse.

I'm more excited than I ought to be at the prospect of poking around his flat. Not in a kleptomaniac way, more in an 'I'm an interior designer and like nothing more than poking around inside other people's homes' way. I trot out of A&E,

twirling Jack's key around my index finger as I walk towards the empty cab stand. It flies off my finger, skittering along the pavement and coming to stop hanging over the edge of the storm drain.

I stare at it in horror. I was a millimetre away from yet more disaster.

The only other person in the taxi queue raises his eyebrow at me as I shuffle over and collect it. I promised Jack I was responsible enough to be trusted with his puppy, I need to start living up to that expectation.

The bloke in the taxi rank is still grinning at me. I smile back, because... well, I don't like to be rude. "You were lucky." He nods towards the drain.

I *hmm*, realising he saw my smile as an invitation to talk to me. Ben was forever telling me off for smiling at people and talking to strangers in lifts. I do it to be nice, and because I hate awkward silences. It has meant over the years I've had a few of these sorts of exchanges. He seems perfectly nice, though. No wedding ring on his finger, which is a good start. Maybe I should take everyone's advice and not shy away from meeting members of the opposite sex. I mean, I have to sometime, right? Maybe tonight's the night. Ben who? I'm feeling emboldened, although that may just be the residual effects of the vodka. I laugh, perhaps a little too loudly. "Yes, I already caused my neighbour to break his leg, I don't need to lose his house keys too."

The guy takes a step closer. He's nearly five feet away now and I can already smell the beer. And his breath. Up close, lit by the red glow of the A&E sign, he's a little less appealing. Sporting a black eye. He grins again, revealing a chipped tooth. "Bit clumsy, are you?" He takes another step towards me.

"Oh, no." I giggle and step away, jiggling on the spot, more from the fear of being alone in the dark with a complete stranger that's now shrivelling my insides and making me want to pee, than from any desire to sound or appear coquettish. I always want to pee when I get nervous. It was a nightmare when I used to have to do exams.

I crane my neck, hoping to catch a glimpse of an approaching taxi, but the road is depressingly quiet. It's nearly half past two in the morning and I'm standing here being chatted up by a man in a taxi rank. There's not another soul in sight. I contemplate going back into the hospital and finding Jack, but then I remember Bertie. He needs me.

"Uber!" I exclaim, as if I'm Archimedes discovering the displacement of water for the first time. I rummage in my bag for my phone and press the app. Five minutes, it tells me. I can do five minutes.

"So, what's a nice girl like you doing in a place like this?" my taxi rank friend asks, chortling at his grand display of humour. It's going to be five long minutes. I swear to myself I will never talk to random strangers again. Except I will, because I always do.

By the time the minicab sweeps in, I've discovered his name's Paul, he's divorced with one child. His partner and child live in Newcastle, presumably because it is a sufficient distance away his halitosis can't reach them there, and he was at the hospital tonight because he got himself into a fight. Barring the chipped tooth, black eye and three stitches inside his cheek, it seems he got away relatively lightly on this occasion. Last time he cracked a bone in his hand that kept him off work for six weeks – he works in construction. By comparison, Khaled, my Uber driver, has a PhD in Linguistics. He arrived as an asylum seeker from Afghanistan, but has been forced to drive a cab to earn enough money to keep the family fed. When the car pulls up outside the house, I'm exhausted. My hangover has settled into an earnest throbbing at the back of my head. I'm tired and I still need to pee. I nearly forget all about Bertie, until he yips as I pass Jack's door.

"Sorry, sweetheart, shoo... shoo. . ." I hook him away from the door with my foot as I attempt to squeeze inside before he escapes. He's a wriggling ball of fluff, with one dark patch over his eye. Very cute. I bend to stroke him, taking a second to look around the apartment. It's pristine, barring the trainer that's been chewed to pieces in the middle of the rug. "Need a wee? Me too." Surely Jack wouldn't mind me using his bathroom?

Assuming it's in the same place as mine, I head in that direction, by way of his bedroom. He has surprisingly good taste.

I don't know why I imagined he wouldn't. Even the bathroom is well fitted out, with some tasteful prints on the walls. I like it. I hoik up my skirt to shuffle my knickers down below my knees. He doesn't even leave the seat up. Amazing.

Bertie's whining on the other side of the door has me hastening to finish. I'm too late. He's already done the necessary right in the middle of the tasteful beige wool carpet outside the bathroom door. The trainer he chewed up obviously didn't agree with him, because the consistency... well, there is no consistency to speak of. And it smells like the devil himself arrived to deposit his business.

"You look far too sweet to produce anything that stinks like that," I tell him. He squirms in response. He's clearly feeling much better. On the plus side, I don't need to take him out in the dark now. There can't be anything left inside him after that. I'm beyond relieved because the wind's picking up again. Another storm brewing, perhaps? I find the kitchen towel, a cloth and some cleaning liquid and start scrubbing.

It's nearly half past three by the time I arrive back in my own flat with Bertie and all his bits and bobs. I swear, with his bed, food and toys, he has more possessions than Nicole's most recent child, Betty. After marshalling an initial hissing exchange, Sukie retreats to the top of the wardrobe. She's sending daggers my way, clearly seeing the arrival of this small bundle of barking mayhem as a further betrayal. "It won't be for long," I promise her, finally falling into bed at gone four. I've barricaded Bertie into the kitchen, which contains the least number of chewable surfaces. The lack of any doors that actually close properly in my flat might be something of a problem. With this last thought I close my eyes.

Chapter 9

"What the fuck!" At least, that's what I mean to say as needle-sharp teeth pierce the skin on my big toe. In fact, I suspect it's more like incoherent noise amidst much thrashing of arms and legs, until I manage to unlatch Bertie's teeth from my foot.

I squint at the clock. It's a few minutes past seven. I've had less than three hours sleep because I've already been up once to put Bertie back into the kitchen and clear up his pee. Sukie is watching me with what looks like a smug expression, still safe in her sanctuary on top of the wardrobe. I consider joining her until Bertie whines. Then I'm up and moving in a flurry of activity, for fear of what might come next.

Five minutes after opening my eyes I'm standing outside, holding onto the fence for dear life because the wind hasn't let up at all. As it whips through the thin cotton of my pyjamas, I yearn for something a little warmer over the top. Bertie's disappeared into a bush. I'm hoping he reappears soon, or at least before I develop frostbite, because I still want to try to meditate before I go round to David's. I'm always excited when I go to a new client's for the initial look-see. It's a bonus we're discussing the website too. Butterflies of excitement tumble and roll in my stomach.

I can't actually remember the last time anything other than aching sadness occupied that space in me. And regret. And self-recrimination for fucking up my life with Ben so spectacularly – Bella wasn't entirely wrong.

I should make the most of this feeling, because something will come along to fuck everything up again any day now. I know it will. It always does.

No!

I stop that damn thought right in its tracks, determined not to let my inner demons take me down today. I will not let them squash this small bud of hopeful optimism. I won't, not today. I flare my nostrils and suck in a deep breath of the chilly winter air. Then another. My mind won't clear. All I can think about is that it's bloody freezing out here. Perhaps I should continue this inside. "Bertie!" I raise my voice to be heard above the wind. "Come on boy. Breakfast!" That gets the desired result. Together, we scurry back indoors. I settle him with a bowl of food, hoping it will keep him entertained for a few minutes, and then sit down and attempt to meditate.

"You look lovely. Who's this?" David looks down at the small bundle wriggling on the ground beside me.

"This is Bertie," I say, pleased he noticed I'm not wearing my trackies. I've always liked to make an effort for my clients.

"Yours?" He grins, as if the idea of me looking after a small creature has to be a joke. Or maybe he's just amused by the way Bertie's attacking my shoelaces.

"No, he's my neighbour's. The poor guy had an accident trying to rescue my cat from the tree last night. He broke his leg."

It says a lot about how well I'm getting to know my class colleagues that David doesn't even laugh. Or look surprised in any way, really. "Website details first? Then design chat?" he suggests.

"Sounds good to me." I follow him inside to what is a large and surprisingly tidy flat. It's a bit boyish. No design. If I had to use a word to describe it, I'd call it functional or sparse, or utilitarian. It gives the impression he's not lived here all that long. Flatpack furniture has been assembled and is now lining the whole of one wall, but most of the shelves still sit empty. A packing box occupies another corner of the room, acting as a coffee table.

David looks down at Bertie. "Is he going to be okay?" The little sod has already taken hold of the TV cable between those needle-sharp teeth. I shove him off with my foot.

I'm not really made for this. Perhaps it's just as well I never became a mother. God knows what harm would have befallen any poor child cursed with me looking after it.

Stop!

I take a deep breath, then exhale slowly before taking another. I'm getting better at this. The breathing centres me, halting the spiral. I exhale a second time, letting my toxic thoughts recede. I haven't had a full panic attack for more than a week now.

The puppy's attacking my shoelaces again. I can't leave him alone for a second without him inflicting some sort of harm on himself or the furniture. It's why I couldn't leave him at home alone this morning. I need to work out how Jack does it or he's going to drive me round the bend. There has to be somewhere safe in the house we can leave him.

David frowns down at the demon. "We could put him in the kitchen while we work?"

The Gods are smiling on me for once. David's kitchen has a door that closes, and nothing at floor level he can electrocute himself with if – when – he bites through it. We should be good for a few minutes, or more, I hope.

David peers at his computer screen, looking like a man in his element, then turns to look at me. "So, have you got the web addresses of the sites you like the look of?"

I spend a good ten minutes showing him the website Bella and I created for the company. I led on the design of it and was rather proud of the result. I note she's taken my name and photo off the 'about us' section already. She's happy enough to keep pictures of some of my designs up though. What a bitch. It's like she's taken over my life; lock stock and husband.

I show David a couple of competitor sites I also like.

He leans back in his office chair, the structure creaking in what's obviously a well-practised move. "I've got the general idea. If you can send me the text sections on the different pages you want me to create, and maybe some pictures, I should be able to build something by the end of the weekend."

"Can you? That would be amazing." I look around again. "Is this the area you want me to design for?" It's big; we're clustered beside the desk, but there's a beautiful bay window down the other end of the room. South facing, it's full of light even at this dismal time of year. Not that he ever uses that end. I can tell. Boxes are stacked along the wall, piles of papers and magazines spilling out. All his time looks to be spent here if the three coffee mugs on the desk are anything to go by. My mind scrolls through some of the wonderful designs I saw for meditation areas as I begin to take measurements. He certainly has enough space to create something beautiful.

"I'll sketch some designs over the weekend, and send them over," I say, stretching my tape towards the ceiling. The coving is original and gorgeous.

David nods, watching as I finish jotting down the last couple of measurements in my notebook. Happy, I retract the tape measure, rummaging inside my bag to find its case.

"I'm worried about Sarah."

His words stop me in my tracks. I look up. David's staring at me intently, a deep v-shaped ridge now centred over his nose.

He's seemingly waiting for me to say something. "Worried? Why?"

He rubs a hand against the back of his neck.

I wait. He'll either tell me what's on his mind, or he won't. It's up to him. I can tell it's something important.

He gestures around at the room. "I've not lived here very long."

I'd kind of guessed that, especially after seeing the clutter he creates when he uses a space – like this office area – for a while. I just don't know the significance of the comment, or how it relates to Sarah. I nod. I don't know what to say, so I say nothing.

"I bought this place after I left my wife."

Okay, I wasn't expecting that. "You're married? Really?"

"Not anymore. I moved here from Reading when the marriage ended." He takes a deep breath. There's a rigid set to his shoulders, his eyes now fixed to the carpet. He doesn't seem to want to look at me as he says; "She was abusive to me."

I want to laugh. The idea seems ludicrous. This giant of a man, with arms and neck thicker than most women's legs being abused by a woman! And yet, looking at his hunched shoulders, his hands now rubbing at his face and neck, his complete lack of eye contact... it all suggests he's speaking the truth. What am I meant to say? "I'm so sorry." I wince, the words are not enough.

He grimaces. "I know how it must sound. A man like me being beaten up by a woman. She's half my size. But it wasn't just her fists. Sometimes she used weapons." He lifts his shirt to reveal a jagged red scar. It looks as if a surgeon has butchered his appendectomy.

"God, David. What happened?"

"Jealousy happened. It didn't matter that I never did anything to warrant that jealousy. She couldn't help herself. Saw things where there was nothing to see." He taps the scar. "This time a female client left a message on my phone and she listened to it. I was asleep. She attacked me with the bread knife. I was lucky, she didn't hit my liver or kidney. That was when I knew I had to leave."

Memories click into place. "That's why you struggle to relax. To meditate. You said at the meeting you worried about being attacked. I didn't realise you were being so literal."

He shrugs, as if it's nothing. "The wounds were bad, but the words were worse. That's why I'm worried about Sarah. I think Gavin's the same towards her."

I rock backwards on my chair. "You think he hits her?"

"I don't know if he hurts her physically, but mentally for sure. All the same reactions I used to have are there in her. The fear, the flinching whenever he comes close. She's a different person when she's away from him."

"I noticed that." Bertie yips from the kitchen, demanding my attention. "What do we do? I mean, what can we do? How can we know for sure?"

"If she's being abused, she'll be feeling overwhelmed by her fear. It'll be governing her every move. The terror he'll be violent again. Living like that – fearing for your safety – it's terrible."

We're talking about his own experience again. I can't help myself asking; "Why didn't you leave her sooner?"

He offers me a half smile. It doesn't reach his eyes. "I thought I was at fault. That if I could change my behaviour then somehow the abuse would stop."

"But it didn't?"

"No, it never does."

"You think that's what Sarah and Gavin's relationship is like too?"

He nods. "She's conflicted. She loves him but hates him at the same time. You've seen them at group. He abuses her with what he says, even if he's not hitting her. But I think he is. Or, he has."

It's hard to imagine anyone hitting that lovely girl. "She should leave him then."

He smiles, but it's the saddest smile I think I've ever seen. "It's not as easy as that. I was so ashamed. I lived in hope that my wife's good side would come back. She wasn't always bad, and it did occasionally. But never for long. Then there's money; I don't know how they're fixed financially, but if she's dependent on him then it's even more difficult."

I nod. "Why are you telling me all this?" My own anxiety has ramped up a notch. Just hearing about it has my stomach churning. I want to dismiss what he's saying, but there's too much about it that rings true.

"Someone needs to talk to her and get her to open up. She likes you. I'm hoping you'll do it. I think she'll confide in you. Maybe not straight away... but eventually."

Holy shit. He must be joking. "Me? I don't know if I'm equipped to help. I'm not a strong person. I'm barely hanging on myself most of the time."

He frowns. "You are strong – what are you talking about? Sure, some other people in your life have been shitty towards you, done some shitty things, but you're better off without them. That doesn't mean you're not strong. It just means they're weak."

Okay, now my brain's totally buffering. His utter conviction I'm a strong person is mind-blowing. Part of me wants to laugh in his face, but there's something in what he says. That the weakness lies more with the people who betrayed me. And then there's Sarah – my newest friend. "I'm not saying I will, but if the opportunity presents itself, what do I even say?"

"Be direct. Tell her you're worried about her, concerned about her safety. Listen to her. Reassure her it's not her fault. Be there for her. Don't judge her. She may not want to leave straight away. Don't criticise her for staying. Just let her know you're there for her."

This is a lot to take on board. My head is swimming.

He takes my hand. "Leaving takes strength and courage. She has to know she has people she can turn to for support. We need to build her self-confidence. I took a long time to get up the courage to go; in the end, it was her nearly killing me that pushed me out the door. We'll need to be patient. It may take time for her to recognise the problem. That's the first step. When she does, we can be there to help her."

Bertie whines from the kitchen. The urgent tone suggests I must move now or face the consequences. I move. But all the time I'm standing outside on the pavement, as Bertie sniffs about, I'm thinking about what David just told me. I remember Sarah wincing every time she moved last night. I also remember the heavy makeup she wore at the very first session. Was it covering a bruise? I hate the thought of it.

You can't help her; you can hardly help yourself.

The poisonous thoughts worm inside my brain.

I push them away, because if not me, then who?

Chapter 10

I'm still troubled by thoughts of Sarah and Gavin when I arrive at the hospital clutching Jack's wash stuff and pyjamas all bundled into an orange Sainsburys bag. I sprint for the hospital entrance to avoid being soaked by the misty drizzle that's settled in now the wind's dropped. It still takes too long; my hair, and any part of my clothes not protected by my coat, are saturated by the time I reach the hospital reception. I drip my way along hospital corridors until I locate the orthopaedics ward.

Jack's not long out of surgery. He winces, attempting to sit up, as I unpeel my coat and hang it on the back of the visitor's chair to dry. The pinched look around his normally smiling eyes suggest he's in pain, and understandably miserable.

No doubt the prospect of a long recovery ahead isn't helping.

He's probably blaming me for his accident. He must hate me.

Stop!

"Bertie's fine," I say, in what I hope he'll think is a confident and reassuring voice. I don't tell him I found Bertie with his teeth clamped around the bottle of bleach in my bathroom just before we left. He's a nightmare. I couldn't trust him to stay in his bed or the kitchen while I was out; given there were all manner of ways he could electrocute and/or kill himself, I brought him with me. As we speak, he's probably tearing up the inside of my car like a baby velociraptor. "Just out of interest," I say, in a voice that attempts to be offhand and disinterested but has Jack's head spinning towards me with narrowed eyes. I'm a little disconcerted, but soldier on regardless. "Just out of interest, where do you leave him when you have to pop out for a bit and can't take him with you?"

"In his cage, of course."

He has a cage! "Of course, and are you okay if I let myself into your flat and use it too?"

"What else would you do? Bring him with you?" He snorts, as if the very idea is preposterous. He must see something in my face, because he stops laughing. "You didn't bring him with you, did you?"

I nod, shame fixing my eyes to a spot on the tiled floor.

Jack looks around as if half expecting me to magic Bertie out of the Sainsbury's bag I brought his pyjamas in. "Where is he?"

"In the car."

"Dear god, you have to go, there'll be nothing left of it."

"I'm sure he'll be fine." I'm totally not sure he'll be fine. "How are you, anyway?"

"Sore. The morphine they gave me made me vomit green puke, and I have the prospect of weeks in a cast ahead. Then there's this place..." We both turn to look at the other patients. Jack brings the average occupancy age down by twenty years, at least. Worse, the man opposite is asleep in his chair, sitting with his legs splayed, wearing only his hospital gown. His meat and two veg make a very poor first impression. We both look away quickly. "How do you think I am?"

I take a breath and try again. "Can I get you anything else? Something to eat or drink from the canteen maybe?"

"No, really no. You've done enough." His words hang between us like Bertie's post trainer-eating wind.

"Well, okay then." I stand and brush more imaginary fluff from my skirt. "Do you want to let me know when you need picking up?"

"It's fine, I'll get a taxi."

There's not really much more to say after that.

He hates me, and I've overstayed my welcome.

"I hope you get home soon. Call if you need anything. Here are your keys – I took the spare set off the side." I bend as if to give him a kiss before remembering I don't actually know the guy very well.

He flinches back into his pillows.

I jerk away, heat blooming in my cheeks. Then literally run out of the ward, grabbing the corner of Old Man Turkey Lurkey's curtain as I go, so at least Jack doesn't have to stare at that for the rest of the afternoon.

I spend Saturday morning taking advantage of the overcast but dry weather, using the time to clean my car. There is now a large hole in the backseat's upholstery. There was also a rather runny poo to clear up. The smell has invaded the fabric, making me want to gag every time I get in. Apparently, bicarbonate of soda might work – although that guidance was for spilt milk. I've bunged a load on anyway on the off chance it'll do something to neutralise the stink. Meanwhile, I've been feeding Bertie hard boiled eggs ever since, hoping against hope it might bung him up a bit.

Just to top all of that off, I didn't get much sleep last night because, after locking Bertie in his cage downstairs, I was kept awake by his crying. The cage is in Jack's bedroom. Presumably, he prefers it when Jack's in the room too. Unfortunately, the contraption is far too heavy for me to shift anywhere on my own, so I'm stuck with a howling puppy until Jack gets home.

Nicole arrives as I'm fighting with Bertie for the chamois leather. She looks polished and perfect despite having two under-fives at home. I look down at my dirty t-shirt and leggings and the damp puppy who's just tipped the bucket of water over himself.

"Are you ready?"

"Ready?" I'm a little mystified what she's talking about.

"I knew you'd forget."

"Forget what?"

"We have hair, makeup and nails appointments this afternoon. To get us ready for Kate's fortieth tonight."

Holy fuck-a-moly! Kate's fortieth. I'd completely forgotten. Ben and Bella will be there too. I hadn't thought about it all week with so much else going on. "I'm not sure-"

"Claire Everett, don't you dare! I am not going to let you flake out on me. Not this time. You're in a good place. You're designing again. You're getting on with your life. You can do this. You can't hide away from all your friends for the rest of your days. I won't let you."

"But they're his friends too."

"So? He's the one who behaved like a shit-bag. You have nothing to feel ashamed of. If you spent some time with your friends, you'd know they're worried about you."

"Okay, okay. But what the hell will I wear?"

"We'll sort that out later. For now, put that terror wherever he's meant to go and get in the car." She opens the door of my mini, takes one whiff of its new interior fragrance and declares, "We'll take a taxi."

Four hours later, I've spent the last hour of that time staring into my wardrobe in despair. Nothing fits. I'm going to look like I've smuggled Bertie into the party under my dress.

Silence. Why is there silence? Where the hell is that bloody dog? It's all far too quiet for my liking. I look, but he's nowhere to be seen. I need to take him out before I put him in the cage for the night. I eventually find him facing off with Sukie. As I reach for him, he stretches his nose towards her, intrigued. She slashes him with one razor sharp claw, like a feline Freddie Kruger. Bertie yelps as blood immediately pools at the surface of the cut.

"That's not nice, Sukie," I say, picking a chastened Bertie up and tucking him under my arm as I pat him on the head. "We need to be kind to our guests." She stands on the chair, bunching her muscles to spring easily onto the table, then exits through the newly fitted cat flap, out into the garden. Five minutes later, Bertie and I are out there too. I'm huddling under an umbrella, trying to avoid the rain turning my newly straightened locks into triangular shaped frizz. A severe gust of wind grips the umbrella and rips it inside out. "Oh, bugger. Bertie!" The wind takes my shout and hurls it away in the wrong direction from the wayward pup who's still nose deep in the mud beneath the bushes. I stumble towards him, broken umbrella hanging from one hand as I push bushes aside with the other. "Bertie!" I scoop him up with my free arm, clutching his squirming body against my chest. His nose is covered in mud from the digging he's been doing. He proceeds to try to smear it all over my face as he 'kisses' me.

Nicole rings the doorbell at the precise moment Bertie and I arrive in the hallway in a sodden, muddy mess. I drop the umbrella and open the door. "Dear God," she says, when she sees me. "What the hell happened? You looked perfect when I left you."

"Bertie happened. Help me get him into his cage."

Together we wrestle the small hell hound into his prison. As soon as he looks up at me with his big brown eyes from behind his cage bars, guilt stabs me. He's pleading with me not to go. Not to leave him there alone.

"No!" Nicole says, as I reach to get him out again. "You haven't got any more time for that nonsense. He'll be fine where he is. He's got water, and you've fed him?"

I nod.

"Well then, let's go and see what we can do with... this." She waves a hand in my general direction.

Back in my own flat, I see what she means. I have streaks of mud all over my face, and my hair now looks as though I've had a bad 80's perm, but not everywhere. "Go and wash, again, and I'll redo your hair and makeup."

An hour later she's restored me to expected standards. My face is clean and made up and my hair is hanging straight to my shoulders. I'm wearing a black wraparound dress, all my lumps and bumps harnessed into place with underwear. I suspect sitting down will not be an option. Nor will eating. As we slide into a taxi, I regret not having made time to eat something earlier.

Of course, the first people we see as we pull up outside the house are Ben and Bella. I sit there frozen, my eyes drinking in all the small changes in my husband – *ex*-husband; he's lost a little weight, his love handles are less obvious over the top of his trousers, and his hair is cut shorter than I like.

Nicole opens the car door and tugs the arm of my coat until I start to move. Too soon, I'm huddled beside the car hiding beneath the hood of my parka. "Let's get inside and out of this rain," she says.

I move towards the house, one foot on the steps leading up to the front door. Then he laughs at something she says and reaches over to rub her belly. Pain slices through me and I gasp, clutching my chest.

Breathe. Deep breaths. In and out.

Don't have a panic attack.

Not here.

It takes a solid minute until the pain eases enough for me to move again as Nicole hovers anxiously beside me. We follow them inside, unnoticed, watching from the shadows in the hall as Bella unbuttons then shrugs off her coat, handing it to Ben to hang up for her. She looks perfect, slim everywhere but for the small bump in front. And she's wearing almost the identical dress to me. I want to die. Or run. "No!" Nicole hisses.

I turn, anxious Ben will hear, but they're oblivious, already wandering off towards the noise in the lounge. I'm left standing there like the ghost of Christmas Past watching her hand gripping on to Ben's forearm. He's smiling down at her.

Did he ever look that happy with me? I don't remember.

Did he look at me so adoringly?

He smiled quite nicely when I made him a banoffee pie once.

Were we happy together at all?

Nicole is in front of me now. Talking. Her lips are moving anyway, I'm just not hearing anything. All my senses are paralysed by pain. The pain of seeing them together, hearing their happy chatter, the smell of Ben's aftershave, their easy, familiar touches. Bile rises, acrid and bitter, to lay across my tongue.

The door opens behind us, a couple laughing as the blustery wind and rain buffets them into the hallway. It breaks me from my stupor. "Are you going to be okay?" Nicole whispers. That furrow is back in her brow.

"Yes." I decide. "Let's do this."

I mean, how much worse can it get?

Chapter 11

The answer is, a lot worse.

"What are you doing?" Nicole hisses, when I reclaim my fourth? Fifth? Eighth? Who knows, who cares, glass of wine, after bumping and grinding on the dancefloor with a man I met a little earlier. I can't remember what he told me his name was. I say dancefloor... we were the only people dancing, and the others only cleared out the way creating a space once we really started throwing shapes.

"I'm enjoying the party. I thought that's what you wanted?" I lean on the cabinet, as my head continues to spin despite me now standing still. My cheeks are hot, in fact my whole head feels as if it might explode from the heat. And my eyes seem to have developed a built-in time delay, arriving where I want to look a full second after my head gets there.

Nicole gives me her scary mummy glare. "You're making a bit of a show of yourself."

I wave her off. I've seen the looks I've been getting, but I'll be damned if I'll give a shit about these pompous pricks. Thankfully, Ben and Bella have kept to the other room. Not that I care anymore. I'm too buzzed to care. My dance partner waggles his fingers at me from the other side of the room. I giggle and wave back.

Surely he had more hair earlier?

"I need to go to the bathroom," I declare, shoving Nicole aside as I sweep my clutch bag up. My movements are expansive and clumsy, the floor now somehow uneven. I stagger sideways into a chest and knock a large vase over, spilling the flower water everywhere. "Whoops!" I laugh again, but no one laughs with me.

"Careful," Kate, the birthday girl, growls. She shoves me out of the way, leaving me to totter towards another group of people who hold their hands up in horror before I totter back again in time to see Kate begin blotting at the polished wood frantically with the absorbent cloth she's carrying. Once she's satisfied she's gotten rid of every trace of water she looks at me again. "Go powder your nose, for god's sake, Claire."

I do need the bathroom. I meander my way towards the toilet, taking care not to bump into anyone or anything else. Fortunately, no one's using the facilities when I arrive. I lean heavily on the door, concentrating hard as I work to slide the latch in to place. With effort, I take the last few steps towards the toilet, leaning over the bowl just as a wave of nausea hits. I projectile vomit directly into the pristine white porcelain.

Well, that was lucky.

Three more large heaves later and I'm feeling much better. I lean heavily on the sink, cupping handfuls of water to freshen my mouth and take away the acrid bite of bile and wine re-visited.

That'll teach me to drink on an empty stomach. Such a rookie mistake.

Nicole's words echo at the back of my mind; *You're making a complete spectacle of yourself; you're such an embarrassment, you stupid, fat bitch.*

Did she say all that? Maybe she didn't.

My head is spinning so I sit down heavily on the loo, reflecting on the (dis)pleasure of being reunited with all Ben and my 'old friends'.

Apart from Nicole and gyrating Jimmy, I've been avoided like the plague all evening.

Maybe they think divorce is catching? Or that, now I'm single, I might run off with their better halves.

I catch sight of my reflection in the mirror; my smoky eye makeup has migrated towards my cheeks.

Maybe not.

I peer a little closer.

I look a drunken mess.

A blast of wind rattles the window, rain pelting the glass like small pebbles. It sounds too solid for water, more like hail.

I push the blind aside and peer out into the darkness. It's chucking it down. The horrible cold and dark reminds me of the small dog waiting at home.

What am I even doing here?

A cold dark garden in the pouring rain or sleet sounds preferable to this new circle of hell. Maybe I should call a taxi and get out of here while I still have a shred of dignity left.

Who am I kidding!

I'm reaching for the lock to slide it open when a voice stops me. Ben. I'd know him anywhere. My hand freezes. His refined tones always thrilled me to the core. Very James Bond. Mummy used to say he could charm the knickers off a nun. He didn't use his skills to his own advantage though. He was just naturally charming. My heart pounds, thundering so loudly in my ears I miss whatever he says to the person he's talking to, even though they're standing right outside the bathroom door. I force myself to take some deep breaths and press my ear against the wood.

"Oh, you're not leaving so soon?"

This voice is louder. A woman? Kate maybe.

"We have to. Bella gets so tired now. We keep hoping this phase will pass and she'll be left brimming with energy again, like the books promise. But no sign yet."

A braying laugh. Definitely Kate. "Oh, I remember that. Parties were never much fun when I was pregnant. I became a glorified chauffeur. Still, it'll all be worth it in the end."

I bet he's smiling now. I imagine it, those dimples puckering in his slightly chubby cheeks. He was always so very desperate to have a child. I failed him.

"Thanks for the lovely party." There's a pause. "I'm so sorry about Claire -"

"You have nothing to apologise for. She's not your responsibility. She should know better. She's a big girl – quite literally these days!" *What a bitch.* "She's more than capable of taking care of herself." Her voice drops, making me strain again to hear. "She's a mess though. I think she's in there." The last words are little more than whispered hisses. I imagine her pointing towards the bathroom door. "Vomiting." The word is so quiet I almost miss it, even though I am pressed flat against the door now, my hot breath leaving condensation on the cool wood.

"This isn't like her, not the Claire I know."

"But did you really know her? Did any of us? Grinding herself all over that revolting man, like that. Julia's been sobbing in the kitchen all night. She'd been seeing Eric for a few weeks. I told her she's better off without him, if you ask me. Revolting man. Still, Claire should know better than to come on to another friend's man."

Julia is one of the sweetest, kindest people you could ever wish to meet. I had no idea the man I'd been dancing with was her plus one. Shame curls my toes.

I stop listening. I've heard enough. I examine my reflection again; a roll of fat has migrated above the line of my support knickers. I *am* a mess. These are not idle fact-less thoughts, these are simple truths.

Ben is far better off without me.

I want to run away.

No one would care. No one would even notice.

I grab a piece of tissue to wipe the tears from my cheeks then spot my clutch bag, lying on the floor beside the toilet. I have my phone and just enough cash for a cab. When I figure enough time has passed for Ben and Bella to have left, I sprint from the bathroom and head straight for the front door.

I'm regretting leaving my coat at Kate's once I'm back in the garden with Bertie. It's a filthy night. Even Bertie has no interest in hanging around. He does his business with unusual efficiency and runs back into the warmth.

"No, Bertie," I scold him, when he starts to cry as soon as I've locked him back into his cage and take a step towards the bedroom door.

He looks at me with his big brown eyes. Like chocolate puddings full of sorrow. He just wants someone to love him. I can relate. My heart melts a little. "Well, how about I lie here for a bit, until you go to sleep?" Jack's king-sized beast of a bed is lying there, unused. I can't imagine what harm it could do. Bertie will be happier and we'll both get a better night of sleep.

The bed is exactly as comfortable as it looks; big down duvet and soft, fluffy pillows that cloud around me when I collapse onto them. I kick off my shoes and wriggle out of the uncomfortable knickers, then slither between the soft fabrics.

"What the actual fuck!"

The Very Angry Voice sends me vertical as Bertie yips with joy beside me. I groan as my hangover announces its presence with a mallet-sized thump, clutching my head in the hope I will avoid it splitting apart and spilling my brains out over the pristine white covers.

"What the hell do you think you're doing?"

I peel open an eye. A very angry Jack is leaning heavily on his crutches in the doorway, glaring at me. A white cast encases his leg to the knee. I wonder, for a nanosecond, what he's doing in my bedroom. The unfamiliar furnishings around me prod my memory. "Bertie," I croak out. "He didn't like being left on his own."

"I don't care. Get out of my bed!"

I shuffle slowly to the edge and swing my legs to the floor. A trail of black eye makeup marks my migration across the pillow during the night. "I'll change the sheets."

"Don't bother. I'll do it. Just get out." Bertie punctuates the moment by urinating all over the cage floor. It runs straight out on to the carpet. It's after eleven, the poor thing should have been let out hours ago.

I look at the yellow lake, then back to Jack's cast. "Do you want me to -"

Jack makes a choking sound and his skin turns a mottled shade of purple. Hastily, I grab my bag, knickers and shoes from the floor, and scurry out, breathing hard by the time I've run up the stairs and let myself into my flat.

Given the awful weather, Sukie has chosen not to go outside to do her business. Instead she's crapped twice inside the flat. One perfectly positioned on top of the unopened bag of cat litter beside her tray, the other on the mat in front of the door. I step in the latter. It oozes up between my toes. Sukie meets my gaze with a flick of her tail

And now everyone hates me. Just as they ought.

Chapter 12

"Claire, answer this phone at once!" My mother sounds cross. She rarely gets cross with anyone. The last time I remember her being cross with me was when I was thirteen and bought joke teabags containing fart powder, then substituted them for her Yorkshire teabags. Her book club friends were terribly affected, apparently. I ignore the unsettled feeling I always get when I displease her. "To repeat this message, press one," the Vodaphone lady begins. I press two for delete. I've already had a hundred like it.

The phone beeps again, introducing the next message. "Claire, this is getting silly. I know you're embarrassed about the other night, but really, who cares? Kate was always an arse. They all are. So, you drank too much fizz. What does it matter? People only noticed because the party was more like a wake. Really, you're getting this completely out of perspective. Speak to me, please?"

I don't listen. I press delete and stay exactly where I am, where I've been all week; flat on my back in bed. I do pull the duvet up over my face, wishing everyone would just go away. My phone bleeps again. There's a third message on there.

"Claire? Sorry to bother you. We missed you at group this week. I just wanted to check you were okay. David mentioned he hadn't heard a peep from you all week. He's still waiting for your website content. Anyway, I hope we see you next week. We thought maybe we could have another little post session drink. Gavin's got to work again, so..." Sarah's words falter, fading off into an awkward pause. "I missed you," she adds quickly, before disconnecting. Okay, that one warmed my chest a little. I don't delete that one. In fact, I replay the message twice more.

Then, as my resolve weakens, I remind myself they're all better off without me. Even Sukie, who's taken to perching on the end of my bed now that the demon dog hasn't been seen for seven days in a row. The most I've done is get up to heat tins of baked beans and feed the cat. I'm running out of everything, so I will have to emerge from my cocoon at some point soon. I'm like an inverse butterfly, transforming back into an ugly caterpillar. I have no doubt I'll be one of the big hairy ones.

Every time I remember that night, I cringe.

Every time I think of Jack's face when he found me in his bed, I feel sick.

I don't blame him for throwing me out.

Two days ago, my mother and Nicole started knocking on the front door. I know they heard me. At least Mummy did. She got very shouty when I knocked the cat bowl off the side, but I still didn't answer the door. She tried to open it with a pin – she really needs to stop watching so many detective programmes. She didn't get in, but even if she had I've deadlocked it.

I just want them all to go away.

Today they've left me alone. Apart from the messages.

Wind rattles the windowpane. The light has barely risen above a grey gloom. I pull the duvet over my head, then uncover it again quickly when I realise how bad my breath smells.

I manage another two days of feeling sorry for myself before my phone starts ringing again. I wait for the voicemail message icon to show, then listen, expecting the usual tirade from Nicole or my mother. This time it's different.

A dog yips as a male throat clears. "Umm, Claire. Hi. Umm – Bertie, no, stop that! Let go! Umm, sorry about that. . . I'm sorry to bother you. I'm having a little difficulty; I wonder if you'd be kind enough to pop down and help me out?"

The message stops there. I play it a second time then stare at the phone in my hand, torn. The poor man is only in this situation because of my cat. The fact he's even spoken to me again is something short of a miracle. The least I should do is help him out if he's got himself into a pickle. He must be having a nightmare trying to manage Bertie with a broken leg. I've seen him out in the garden on the few occasions I've bothered to get out of bed, hobbling about after the puppy on his crutches.

But to go out there again, to face the world after my shameful behaviour. I don't know if I can. I don't think I should.

I twist my rings round and round on my finger. I still haven't taken them off. I should really take it off.

Maybe he's hurt.

It's this last thought that gets me moving. I pull a sweatshirt I've been using over the top of my pyjamas and shove my feet into slippers shaped like monster feet. It takes me a good few minutes to locate my keys. With a deep breath, I open my front door and pad down the stairs to Jack's apartment. I hear Bertie's claws clicking on the tiled kitchen floor as he scampers about inside. I knock, timidly at first and then a little louder when nothing happens, worrying all the while what I will do if he's hurt somewhere in the apartment and I can't get in. Did I give him back his keys? I can't remember.

There's the thud and click of someone approaching the door on crutches.

Jack's not bleeding on the ground then.

The door opens, and he's there. Looking handsome and whole and – barring the broken leg – healthy. "Claire." He pauses, sweeping his gaze over me. "Goodness."

Judging by his slightly stunned expression I must look like shit – I maybe should have thought to look at myself before I came down here.

"Come in," Jack says, holding the door wider.

I hesitate, before stepping into the now familiar lounge. Bertie runs to greet me, his little tail wagging. Unfortunately, Bertie is not alone. My mother and Nicole follow him out. I take a step away, back towards the front door, but Jack's blocking my path. I spin, nearly falling over my slippers. "You traitor!"

Jack holds his hands up, looking worried, as if I'm one of the escaped dinosaurs from Jurassic Park. He should be worried; I'm bloody furious. "I'm sorry I got you here under false pretences, but I did want to speak to you."

I stare at my big green monster feet. I can't even face looking at him.

"Claire, I want to apologise for my behaviour the other night."

I can't help myself; surprise has my eyes lifting if only to check he's not taking the piss.

Jack runs a hand through his hair. "I was incredibly rude. Your mum explained how Bertie had been crying all night when you tried to leave him, and how he shredded your flat when you left him in your own kitchen overnight. I completely understand why you slept in my bed. It really wasn't a problem at all. I was in a terrible mood when I got home. Painful leg, and all that. I shouldn't have taken it out on you. You didn't need to buy me all that new linen, let alone the carpet cleaner. I really am sorry."

Bertie is now trying to ravage my slipper. I shake my foot, hoping to dislodge him, but he's like a bloody piranha, clinging on as if his life depends on it. "Really, it's fine, you have nothing to apologise for," I say, taking a step to go around him, dragging the dog with me as I go. "I'm glad the stuff arrived okay." Good old Amazon. I'm almost at the door.

"Claire!"

I flinch at my mother's bark. She's worse than the bloody dog. Regardless, my back snaps straighter in Pavlovian response.

"Claire, sit yourself down this instant and talk to us. This can't go on any longer."

"I have nothing to say." I raise my voice a little to be heard above Bertie's growling. He's still hanging off my damn leg, determined to overcome the beast on my foot.

Nicole snorts. Jack is biting his cheek, looking like he's trying very hard not to laugh. Nicole gives up first and bursts out laughing. I turn to glare at her. "Oh, darling, I've missed you so much." She's still laughing as she wraps me in her arms and hugs me tight.

Next thing I know, I'm crying. My anger tips straight over into tears. I can't seem to stop myself. Somehow, they've manoeuvred me onto the sofa and I have Nicole one side of me, my mother the other, with Jack feeding us tissues as all the anger, mortification and shame I've been feeling erupts.

"It was so embarrassing. I'm so sorry you had to witness me making a show of myself," I say to Nicole.

"For goodness sake, you're not the first person to get drunk at a party. I might question your taste in men -"

"Blame the beer goggles."

"Well, anyway, after you left the same man cracked on with one of Kate's single friends from work. Julia caught them snogging on the terrace. She poured an entire bowl of fruit punch over their heads and told him to fuck off. I don't think I've ever heard Julia swear before. Kate had an absolute fit about the red wine they trailed back across her cream wool carpet. It quite put your water spilling incident to shame. Really, everyone's forgotten about you completely."

My mother dabs my cheeks with a new tissue, the contact of her skin with mine crackling with the usual static. "Now, sweetheart, you can't keep locking yourself away from the world every time you imagine you've done something less than perfectly. Stop trying to hate yourself into being lovable. You seem determined to look for evidence that you're worthless, whatever we say."

I do exactly that. Who is this wise woman and what has she done with my mother?

Nicole dabs my cheeks this time, because Mummy's set my tears off again. "Your mum's right. Life's not a competition. I know you feel that, because Ben ran off with that witch, it means there is something wrong with you, but that's poppycock. You're better off without both of them."

I hiccough a little sob, then blow my nose on the tissue Jack hands me.

"I get stuck in my head. I believe all the stuff the voice in there tells me and then I hate myself too much to do anything except sleep or eat ice cream."

"Well, that's progress," my mother says with a sad smile.

"Is it?"

Nicole and Mummy both nod. "At least you're recognising you're doing it," Nicole says. "You just need to remember all the wonderful stuff about yourself too."

I snort.

"Really. Let alone the talent you have for design, you are kind, loving, generous... need I go on?"

I wave my hand as if I'm trying to bat the words away, toes curling with embarrassment,

"Who came and looked after me the week I had flu?" Mummy says.

"Anyone would do that."

"No, darling." Mummy pushes a strand of my hair behind my ear, the same comforting gesture she made when I was little. "I have enough friends who only see their kids at Christmas – if they're lucky – to know." She takes a deep breath. "So now I'm going to look after you for a bit. We're going to Briar Hill for a week."

"A week! I couldn't possibly go for that long."

"Why? Might it get in the way of your daytime television schedule?" Nicole asks, one eyebrow raised. "Really, what have you got to keep you here?"

I think hard for a moment. "Sukie." It's the best I can do.

"I'll feed her," she volunteers.

"I have to get some designs done, and the content for my web page sent over. And I've still got a tonne of marking. I'm already very behind on what I promised."

"So, take your laptop with you. Simple," Jack says.

"Not you too." I glare at him. I'm not sure I've quite forgiven him for letting them ambush me. "I'm feeling a little bullied here."

"Good. We leave in two hours. Just do me a favour, darling, wash your hair before we leave, we could cook chips in that mop. And maybe some clean clothes, eh? And a quick brush of your teeth perhaps? Come along, let's get cracking."

I look down at my pyjamas, stained with baked bean residue. My right slipper is now completely mangled, and Bertie has set upon the other foot. I stand and slip them off. Bertie runs away with his prize, delighted.

As I allow Mummy and Nicole to lead me upstairs, Jack shouts, "No, Bertie, drop it!"

I smile to myself, knowing he doesn't stand a chance.

Chapter 13

Two hours later we're in my mother's car, winging our way down the A3, the grey, urban sprawl quickly giving way to green fields. I can't remember the last time I saw the countryside.

About halfway there I recall why I hate being driven by my mother. She sits in the outside lane of the motorway doing sixty-five, completely unaware of any traffic building up behind her. "So, I've booked us both on to the relaxation regimen." A car flashes us from behind, but my mother's oblivious. "That way, we get lots of treatments as well as the use of the facilities. I thought it would be good for us to have a complete rest." She chatters on as a BMW driver swerves around our car, undertaking us and making a wanking hand gesture towards my mother as he passes. Mummy waves back at him, smiling. "People are so much friendlier outside of London."

I slouch down in my seat, hoping no one can see me. Also praying it's not much further to go. My phone distracts me from the abuse of fellow drivers, vibrating with an incoming text. It's Sarah, responding to the message I'd sent earlier apologising for missing group last week and explaining I wouldn't be there this week either.

No worries, love. Glad you're okay. Sounds just what you need. Call me when you're back and keep up with the meditation. Sx

A little happier knowing I haven't alienated my newest friend, I settle back in my seat again, my eyes drifting back towards the passing landscape. Heavy grey clouds, bulging with unspent rain, wallow above the deep green of the countryside. Here and there I see fields with animals grazing.

The satnav instructs my mother to take the slip road and before long, we're zipping through a tunnel of trees, their leafless branches stretching across the road to block out the sky. "It's somewhere near here," Mummy says, peering at the screen and then at the road ahead. "Keep an eye out for the sign. It should be any minute."

"There." I point at the grand structure in front of us. It's almost impossible to miss. Mummy still manages to take the corner a little fast. We swerve into the driveway with a spray of pea shingle. The golfers playing on the course immediately beside the road look up alarmed, arms covering their heads. "Maybe slow down a touch," I suggest, when she appears determined to drive at sixty-five along the narrow, unmade driveway too. Golfers scurry away as fast as their club bags will allow.

She taps on the brake. "Yes, sorry, I get a bit heavy-footed when I'm in the car too long.

She swings into a parking space directly outside the front entrance. I suspect it must be a disabled space, but I'm too relieved to have reached our destination alive to say anything. The old place looks grand. Wisteria and ivy cling to the face of the building. I imagine the wisteria dripping with flowers in the warmer months, alive with the hum of bees, but when I open my door, I'm reminded this is not the summer. The cold wind blasts me after the warmth of the car interior. I grab my handbag, zipping up my coat until the collar covers half my face, hunch my shoulders up to my ears, and scurry towards the reception. My mother is hot on my heels.

A suited young man swings the door open. "Ladies, welcome to Briar Hill." We don't stop. Instead, we bundle past him into the warmth. I only pause when the door closes behind us.

"Good afternoon, ladies, may I take your names?" An equally smart and handsome young man greets us from behind a vast mahogany reception desk. I assume they must have a secret breeding centre for these men. They're too good to be true.

In a daze, I let them show us around the facilities; one end consists of sitting room after sitting room centred around a grand marble fireplace and decorated with old leather wingback chairs and nineteenth century antique French sofas. The other end's a complete contrast; sterile treatment rooms with stark white interiors populated with pseudo-scientific machinery and weighing scales. We're deposited in our respective rooms – complete with four-poster each.

"There's an introductory talk about Briar Hill and a group dinner if you're interested? It's in the conservatory at eight," my guide informs me.

I nod, knowing I have absolutely no clue where the conservatory is. Hopefully I'll find it by eight. Not that I'm in any way hungry. Butterflies have taken up residence in my belly. Excitement and nerves. I'm always anxious meeting new people, worried what they'll think of me. Funnily enough, the only place I don't feel that so much now is with the Mindfulness group.

I close down the negative thoughts – now sprouting in my mind like mushrooms after a shower of rain at the end of summer – taking some deep breaths and connecting myself to the here and now. There is nothing I need in this moment. Air fills my chest, rushing into my lungs all the way to the very bottom, before I exhale slowly. I take another. And then one more. I'm calmer by the time I blink my eyes open again. The emotion from my dark thoughts has faded.

I sweep the elegant silk curtains to one side and admire the vast expanse of lawns in front of me. This place is stunning. I'm very grateful to my mother for bringing me here. The flat, Ben, Bella, all the negativity and shame I've been so wrapped up in, feel a very long way away. Somehow that makes it all seem a little less important.

I flop down onto the bed, leaning against the cloud of cushions as I read through my programme. Tomorrow is all about relaxation. Two types of massage and a thermal bath. I think I can handle that.

There's a second sheet in my pack listing all the exercise classes available. I'm not planning to kill myself, but there are a couple I fancy the look of. As I'm here. I might as well, mightn't I? It might make me feel better – they say exercise does that. Gives you lots of endorphins that make you feel great afterwards. I could do with some of those. I haven't done any exercise in... When the hell did I last do any exercise? The only thing that comes to mind is the time Nicole dragged me to a spin class not long after she'd given birth to Betty. She'd been fine but I'd had to stop halfway through because I thought I was going to vomit. I'm starting from a low base then. What I need is something to ease me into it. Maybe the power walk, for starters? The countryside around here is certainly beautiful enough to warrant wanting to get outside into it.

I spend the rest of the afternoon humming to myself as I unpack my case and put all my things into the cupboards before clearing some of my marking. After a quick check-in with Nicole – Sukie is fine – I make my way downstairs for the introduction and supper. Mummy is already sitting at the table, chatting to three other women. They all look up at me with sympathetic eyes as I pull out my chair. I do sometimes wish my mother wouldn't share every detail of my life and medical history with complete strangers.

"Good evening." I smile at each person in turn, then whisper to my mother, "What have you been telling them."

"Oh, nothing, darling. Just how much you've been enjoying the Mindfulness classes. How they've helped with the panic attacks you've been suffering since Ben left."

Everything then.

I look around for the wine but find only water. It dents my optimism a little.

A woman wearing a white coat launches into a lecture on healthy eating for wellness. I pick up the pen on the pad they've provided, trying to appear interested. After about ten minutes the woman beside me reaches over and pats my hand. "Don't worry, dear. It's not as grim as they make it sound. The food is really quite delicious." I look down at my notepad. I've drawn my own version of Edvard Munch's The Scream. Repeatedly. At least twenty of the little faces staring out at me all over the page.

It certainly sounds bad. The food they serve here is no sugar and low carbs. I'm doomed. Those are my major food groups. Along with alcohol. Oh, and caffeine. Both of which are also on the not recommended list. I'm not sure I'm going to survive a whole week of this.

"It would all be much easier if I looked like Kate Middleton," I say, pointing towards the cover of the *Hello!* magazine left in the middle of the table.

"But you know, not one of us is perfect. Not even Kate, I'm sure. The sooner we can learn to accept that about ourselves, the happier we'll be in the long run."

I rock back in my seat. "Mummy, where did you learn all this? And why are you only telling me now?"

"Life, darling. And you didn't need to hear it before. Or maybe you just weren't listening to me. Anyway, as you get older you realise most of what you spend your youth obsessing about is really very pointless. Being happy and healthy is all that matters in the end."

"Hear, hear," a couple of the other guests echo around the table.

"Which is why we're here, of course." Mummy beams at me and I can't help smiling back at her. I reach for my glass and only remember it's water, not wine, when I take a big sip.

Having woken early, I'm determined to start the day the right way with some exercise. This is the first day of the rest of my life, I've decided. So today it starts with a power walk. It's a walk. How bad can that be? The morning is overcast, heavy grey clouds once again blocking any sign of the sun, but it is at least dry for the first time in days. I figure this walk should help me get into a more positive mindset before I face whatever they serve for breakfast. I'm not very hopeful based on the food talk last night.

There are only two other women waiting on the wooden benches outside the reception area, both decked out in very sporty leggings and tops, over bodies that look well-exercised and toned. They look like the sort of women Bella would be friends with. I tug at my own tracksuit bottoms, grabbed from Primark for less than a tenner, and pull my oversized t-shirt down to cover my bottom. The first jangle of alarm tingles through my arms and legs.

I can walk, I'm just being silly.

The girls start warming up when the instructor approaches. "Hi!" He beams at me, showing off a set of very bright, very white teeth. They co-ordinate with his trainers. "I'm Carl." He sticks out his hand, and I take it reluctantly, wondering if it's too late to back out of this. "Have you ever done any power walking before?"

He's so polite. One look at this body must tell him there is not much walking, let alone power walking, happening in my life. "Umm, no. But I like to walk."

Liar.

"Great." He smiles again. "So, we set a fast pace, but don't worry, I can track between the two groups if you get separated. If you choose to turn back that's fine, but just let me know. Otherwise, we'll do a quick warm up and then set off."

I follow him through a series of stretches, my body protesting the unfamiliar movements. I've already developed a light sheen of sweat on my skin before Carl announces we're ready to go. The three of them take off across the lawn like rabbits at a greyhound track. It's Usain Bolt's pace if he needed the toilet. Badly. I force my legs to move faster but seem to be taking three steps to every one of theirs, and I'm still falling behind. I spend the first ten minutes cursing my mother for giving me short legs.

By the second ten I realise this has all been a terrible mistake. I'm scurrying along uneven ground, not daring to lift my eyes from where I'm putting my feet for fear I'll twist my ankle out here in the middle of the Surrey wilds. I think they have adders in this part of the world, although maybe not at this time of year. Still, it could be dangerous to be alone. I force my legs to move even faster, breaking into an occasional jiggly jog whenever I lose sight of them. I wish I'd thought to put on a sports bra, but I didn't think I needed one for walking. Wrong. The ladies are now a good fifty metres in front of me. "We like to run up the hills," one of them calls back to me in a jolly hockey sticks lilt.

I try to smile at her, but I fear it may have been more of a baring of teeth. They sprint up the hill as I trudge along behind, my pace slowing even further as gravity pulls against me. "Everything okay?" Carl calls back, cupping his hands around his mouth to amplify his voice over the ever-increasing distance.

"Perfect," I say, through gritted teeth. I'm clawing air into my lungs by the time I make it to the top of the hill. There's no sign of the chatty Cathys.

"I sent them off on an extra loop," Carl informs me with a yet another smile. The peace and quiet lasts no more than five minutes before their yammering can be heard again.

"This is my favourite bit," one of them says, letting out a braying laugh. "Cardiac Hill." I think she's joking. It turns out she's not. "More than one person's had a heart attack trying to get to the top of this," she tells me jovially.

By the time I get to the top I have tunnel vision, a red mist reducing my ability to see more than my own feet. I want to curl up and sleep in a bush. And maybe die. Death feels preferable to this, right now. "That's it, you're doing brilliantly," Carl says. He's circling me like a sheepdog, nipping at my ankles every time it looks like I might stop. "You've done better than most people. Most the guests turn back when they realise how fast we walk."

I'd forgotten that was even an option. Why the hell didn't I turn back?

The other ladies are still chatting. "Do. They. Ever. Stop. Talking?" I gasp in slow stilted words to Carl between attempts to suck air back into my lungs.

He laughs. "No, I'm afraid not."

"Dante missed out a circle of hell."

"I love your sense of humour. You remind me of-"

As expected, he names an overweight female comedienne. I grit my teeth and force my short, fat legs to pump a little faster.

Chapter 14

I look down at my bowl of breakfast and try not to shudder. Chia seeds, apparently. It resembles frog spawn. And after placing a small amount on the end of my tongue, I discover it tastes like it too. "Morning, darling," Mummy says, waltzing into the room with a joyful smile. She's wearing her Briar Hill monogrammed towelling robe, like me. She pats my cheek. Static cracks against my skin. "Why, you're glowing already, darling, whatever are you having for breakfast? I must have some too."

"I'm glowing because I went on the power walk this morning." My raspberry complexion has yet to revert to its normal milk white.

"Oh, was it good?"

"No. It was horrific." I spoon in another mouthful of frogspawn, gag, then give up, pushing my bowl towards her. "Want a taste?"

She takes a small amount onto her spoon, tasting it gingerly. Her nose wrinkles. "Goodness, that's an interesting flavour. It must be terribly good for you." She looks up at the waitress hovering at her side. "Umm, I'll have the scrambled eggs and mushrooms, please," she says.

"Good choice," I say, wondering if she might let me steal a spoonful.

Another pair are shown to the table next to ours, also wearing their robes. A mother and daughter duo. Judging by the blue bands on their wrists they're on the eating regimen. That's even more hardcore than the generally healthy food we're being offered. The daughter huffs at the reduced menu offered to her by the waitress. Chia seeds are their only option. Poor them. No wonder she looks a little out of sorts.

"Hello," Mummy says, sticking out her hand. I cringe. She's the parent I inherited my tendency to talk to strangers from. "I'm Daphne, and this is my daughter Claire."

"Eleanor," the lady says, taking hold of my mother's hand. "And this is Catherine." She and I share a smile as our mothers make terribly polite chit-chat. They have the weather fully covered before Eleanor grinds the conversational gears. "It's a terrible curse to have an overweight daughter, isn't it?" She gestures towards Catherine, then sweeps her hand around to include me. "I mean, I've never let myself weigh a dot over nine stone. Girls these days just don't take care of themselves. It's no wonder Catherine's still single. At thirty-two! At least yours is married." She nods towards the wedding rings I still haven't taken off. "In our day that would never happen. Still, hopefully we'll shift some inches whilst we're here. Don't eat all of that, darling," Eleanor says as they slide a dish of Chia seeds in front of Catherine.

Not much chance of that, I'd imagine.

Mummy fixes her face into a polite smile, but she's clearly appalled. Worse, Catherine looks mortified.

Catherine digs her spoon into the gelatinous mass of frog spawn in front of her, manages one mouthful and then pushes it away.

"Thank you for not being like her," I say to my mother when our companions finally make their apologies and disappear for treatments.

"That poor, poor girl. What time's your first treatment?"

I retrieve the schedule from my dressing gown pocket. "Ten thirty. I've got my health check, and then a full body relaxation massage. It sounds gorgeous. What about you?"

We spend the next half hour exchanging information about our appointment times. I'm not really sure why. There's no way I'm going to retain the information about my own appointments, let alone Mummy's. On the plus side, it means I get to sit down for a little longer. My legs seem to have the muscle strength of blancmange since I got back from my walk.

I stagger from the breakfast table, weak with hunger, and make it as far as the lounge where I collapse into a chair. I could kill for a latte, but the only drinks on offer are herbal teas. I settle for lemon and ginger, but it's a poor substitute. My head is throbbing. I'm not sure if it's dehydration after my walk or caffeine withdrawal. Just at the point I don't think it's possible to feel any worse, and am considering going for a lie down, my name is called for my treatment.

"My name's Amanda and I'm going to do your assessment today," the blonde tells me. She must be in her late forties but possesses the body of an athlete, clad in a crisp white coat with her name embroidered in blue on the pocket. I'm mesmerised by her high ponytail as it swings back and forth as I follow her at a brisk pace along the corridor. "Just in here." She holds the door open to a brightly lit room.

"Pop your clothes off and then jump on the scales."

Do I have to? I haven't weighed myself in ages. Years even. Reluctantly, I shrug off my robe before walking towards the scales like the condemned man to the gallows then step on. I stand there in my bra and knickers and discover that, as well as my pounding head, wobbly legs and aching hunger, the numbers flashing in front of me are nausea inducing. How did I ever let it get so bad? No wonder Ben wanted nothing more to do with me.

The nice lady places a sympathetic hand on my shoulder – when did she walk over? How long have I been standing here? I burst into tears.

Somehow, after nearly a packet of tissues, we make it through the session. I hear nothing of the advice she offers, about managing to calm myself down just enough to leave the room at the end.

Even the calming wave of essential oils that rushes out to greet us when I walk into the semi-darkened room for my second session isn't enough to distract me. "If you can take off your robe and bra, I'll be back in just a moment." The therapist sweeps out the room again, leaving me alone with my dark thoughts. When she returns, I spend the entire hour trying to hold in my stomach. Not relaxing in the least.

I bump into Mummy in the corridor, looking pink-faced and a little oily. She takes one look at me and pulls me into a hug. "They weighed me. I didn't realise how bad it had got," I choke out in fresh, heaving sobs. "No wonder Ben left when he did."

"Don't be ridiculous, darling. Anyway, Ben's a fool. I've told you this already."

"How did I let myself get into this state?"

She pulls away from me, looking stern. "None of this," she waves her hand at my body, "is as important as what's up here." She taps my head. "Until you change that, there's nothing else likely to change. You're a beautiful woman, Claire, regardless what size you are, but you need to believe it. If Ben didn't make you feel loved or lovable, then I'm sorry to say he probably wasn't the right man for you in the first place. Even during our worst arguments, I never doubted your father loved me. Size and shape had nothing to do with it."

I sniff. "I don't believe many men are quite like Daddy. Ben certainly wasn't." I'm not sure I've ever admitted to anyone there were times when my husband disappointed me. Even sometimes hurt me with what he did or didn't say.

"No, I don't suppose he was. Your father was one of a kind. A bit like you." She runs a hand over my hair, smoothing my disobedient curls back into place. "Just be happy, my darling. If you focus on that, the rest will come."

I sniff again. She's right. Getting depressed about my situation is not going to help me make myself the life I want. I nod.

"Good. Well, as Marjorie says, as long as you're alive, there's more right with you than wrong with you. Right. I'm off to aquarobics." And with that, my mother strides off down the corridor.

The rest of the week passes in a blur of walking – not power walking – Pilates and carbohydrate-less meals. After feeling like something someone has chewed up and spat out the first three days, I perk up on day four. And, after only one small blip when I found myself contemplating licking my arm after applying some apricot body lotion, by the time we get to the final night I'm sorry to be leaving. The difference is not just in the slight loosening of my jeans, but also in my mindset, because in between all my treatments and classes I've had time to think. To really think. To evaluate myself and my life. To make a choice; carry on feeling sorry for myself and killing myself with food, or choose to live again, even if it's not the life I'd planned. I think I choose life.

So, having made that choice, I've managed to send David the spec for my website, finished the last of my marking and started the designs for both David's office and my other client's new home. The space and time to think and create has been more healing than almost anything else. And I've been meditating.

"I can't wait to get the hell out of here," Catherine says to me in a low voice. She and Eleanor have ambushed us and asked if they can share our table. We're eating our last dinner: a two-course meal of soup followed by beetroot and bean burgers that I'm rather enjoying. Her mother is watching us from across the table with a beady eye.

"Oh, haven't you enjoyed it then?" I ask.

"Hell, no. I'll be stopping at the first McDonald's I get to once they let us out."

I laugh but can't help feeling sorry that she's missed the point of this place entirely.

Catherine leans in closer, cupping her hand over her mouth as if she's afraid her mother might lip read whatever she's about to say. "A couple of the others and I are thinking of slipping out to the pub later. Do you fancy joining us?"

"Umm, probably not. Thanks, though. I've got some work I want to get done." It's a lie. I've finished all the work I have for now, but while I don't plan on becoming teetotal, if I'm going to drink all those calories I'd rather do it with people whose company I enjoy. Catherine has been a blot in an otherwise pleasant week; constantly complaining about the food – or lack of it. I'm relieved when she makes her excuses and slips away from the table. Her mother immediately stands up and follows her.

"Trouble brewing there," Mummy says, watching them go.

"Catherine's her own worst enemy though," I murmur.

"True, but telling her off isn't helping. She already hates herself. Instead of showing her love, her mother's probably chasing her down the driveway. It's an awful shame and it's damaging that young woman terribly."

I stare at my mother. She's become the emotional equivalent of Yoda. I don't know what I'd have done without her. "Thank you," I say.

"For what, darling?"

"For bringing me here. For giving me love, when I couldn't love myself. For being patient with me. It's helping." I brush a tear away from my cheek with the back of my hand.

"I can see that, my darling. I can see you properly again. And it's my pleasure. You don't ever have to thank me. You're my daughter. I'd do anything for you." Now we're both crying. A waiter approaches the table and then swerves away at the last minute on seeing the state we're both in.

Can't blame the man, really.

Perhaps it's the stillness of the day, or the appearance of the sun for what feels like the first time in weeks, but my heart is lighter the next morning. I sit on the patio, waiting to be called for my final health check and treatment, letting the weak winter sun seep into my bones as I breathe deeply, feeling the aliveness of now.

"How can you have gained two pounds?" Eleanor shrieks at Catherine as they emerge through the patio doors into the garden, shattering the silence. I look away because Catherine doesn't need an audience. She has enough self-hatred to deal with. I know how exhausting the weight of that can be.

Maybe that's why my mood's lighter. I've let some of it go. The voice in my head has been quieter this week. I've spent my time doing things that give me energy. I've loved myself a little more.

"Claire Everett?"

I smile at the therapist, standing to follow her into the little room. "Final health check?" she says, smiling at me.

"Yes." I glance at the scales.

"Jump on when you're ready, lovey."

This time there's no fear. No desperate removing of jewellery in the hope it might lose me an extra pound. There is only acceptance.

I've lost five pounds.

Was that what all my grief and misery weighed? No wonder I felt so burdened down by it all.

"What changed? What made the difference?" Mummy asks later, as we're pulling away. "Can you hold on to that feeling, do you think?"

I pause before I answer. I've been trying to work it out myself. "I think I made peace with myself. I made peace with now. I stopped trying to change what might happen in the future or tear myself apart with the guilt of what happened in the past, and just started to focus on what I can do right now." What I don't say – what I realised in the shower this morning – was that I haven't given Ben or Bella a single thought since I first stood on the scales. If that's not progress, I don't know what is.

"I'm proud of you, darling."

"I'm bloody proud of me too."

Chapter 15

I slip back into life at home easily. But it's different than it was before. I'm different. And I'm not the only one who seems to have noticed. "You're so much calmer," Sarah says at my first return to group. It's good to see her, so I pull her into a hug despite the scowl on Gavin's face. He's back tonight too. I find myself wishing he wasn't.

"I feel calmer," I say, squeezing her hand as I release her. I do. The tension that's been coiled inside me these last months has relaxed and unwound a little. My head is clearer. As if I've taken my first deep breath of clean air. As if I've let all the angst go. And this new clarity has made a difference elsewhere too; my meditation sessions are more peaceful. They're less of a task to be endured so I have something to talk about at group, and more something I find myself looking forward to.

I'm also working on my business full time. I've given up the marking. It's only baby steps, but I've made great progress on both of my design commissions. "David said he loves what you've designed for him," Sarah says, smiling. "I can't wait to see it."

Gavin's face twists into a sneer.

"Yeah, well, you should see my awesome website. That guy is amazing."

Gavin drags her away after that. He makes sure she doesn't work with either David or me for the rest of the session.

"You don't need to buy me a drink, it must be my turn," I say later at the pub, as David pulls out a chair for me at our usual table.

He waves his hand dismissively. "Put your purse away, this is my treat." He strides towards the bar where he's served almost immediately, despite Willow and Colin having been standing there waiting for the last five minutes.

"Shame Sarah wasn't able to come," I say, as he places my drink down in front of me.

David frowns. "Did you see the difference in her?" He picks up his pint and takes a long draw.

I sip on my fresh lime and soda. "I did." To be honest, it was hard to miss. The formerly outgoing, vibrant woman sat in subdued silence while Gavin put on quite the performance. He was loud to the point of obnoxious, rolling his eyes and laughing openly at comments other people made. Even Alex, whom I've never seen become ruffled by anything, wrinkled his brow once or twice.

David leans forward in his chair, lowering his voice. "Have you had a chance to speak to her yet?"

I shake my head. "No. Not so far. I've not really seen her since I got back from my meltdown. Not until tonight, and Gavin wasn't letting her out of his sight for a minute."

"Exactly. Will you, though, if you get a chance?"

Willow and Colin have finally been served and are approaching the table.

"Yes," I say rapidly. "I'll ask her round to practise meditating."

David sits back in his chair, looking relieved. "Thank you."

"You don't have to thank me," I murmur. "She's my friend too."

"I know, I'm just worried about her. I want to help, but it'd only make it worse if he saw me and thought I was sticking my nose in."

"Make what worse?" Willow asks, picking up on the tail of our conversation.

"The choice of paint for the meditation area Claire is creating for me," David says smoothly. He's more practised at this lying business than I gave him credit for. "The design is so beautiful, I don't trust myself to choose the paint. I think Claire should do it." It's a smooth save, although I'm not sure Willow is convinced.

"How are you?" I ask her. She's been very open with the group that she started therapy recently.

"Ups and downs," she says. "Sometimes I think I'm making progress, then other times my anxiety is just… overwhelming, making me a virtual prisoner in my own home."

How awful. "It sounds terrifying," I say.

"It can be. It's all the more infuriating when you have idiots like Gavin, feeling the need comment how they have a 'touch' of OCD too. Like, the fact they can't walk past a wonky picture without straightening it or just *have* to keep a tidy drawer is the same thing as what I experience. I wish that were all it's about, but it's only the tip of the iceberg. It's like saying you have a touch of schizophrenia or are a little bit pregnant."

"More like a touch of stupid, in Gavin's case," I say.

"More than a touch. He's terminal," David adds.

We raise our glasses in silent agreement. I meet David's eye and nod, resolving to help my friend the first chance I get.

"Bertie, slow down!" The panicked shout greets me as I'm opening the front door. I'm just in time to see the puppy spring down the front steps, yanking against his lead. Still on crutches, Jack wobbles, struggling to manage his balance, the stairs and Bertie's forward momentum. I lunge and grip the back of Jack's shirt, tugging him back to upright, just before he topples headfirst down the steps.

"Holy shit," he says, face white with fear. "That was a close one. Thank you."

"I figured you weren't intending to take a dive off headfirst."

"No, I've had my quota of bone breaks covered for this year, thanks."

I smile, taking hold of the lead from him, as Bertie continues to scamper around his legs, tying them both up in knots. I unwrap them slowly before offering the lead back to Jack.

"Can you hold on to him for a second while I get myself down?" He surveys the stone steps with wide, fearful eyes.

I take pity on him. "Of course." I grab the puppy and lead him, now squirming with excitement around my own ankles, down to the pavement where we turn and wait for Jack to join us. Bertie is bouncing, beyond delighted to be outside, as Jack makes painfully slow progress down the steps. It's dangerous for him with no rail to hold on to. "Where were you planning to go?" I ask, when he reaches the bottom. He's a little out of breath just after that.

"It's such a lovely day, I thought we might take a short turn around the park. Bertie's a little bored of the garden. So am I, to be honest." He winces. "But I might have overestimated my ability a tad." He looks down at the dog and then back up at the steps towards the house. "Maybe I shouldn't -"

"I was going for a walk myself. If you can stomach a bit of company, I'd love to join you both. Perhaps I can hold on to Bertie for you, while you manage those crutches?" Truth is, I need to get out the house to stop myself from Facebook stalking Ben and Bella. It's an old, bad habit I don't want to slip back into. I've been doing so well since Briar Hill. Today a post from Bella came up on my timeline, showing off their new nursey. Of course, she's designed the life out of it. I had to force myself away from my computer. Anything to do with the baby is like crack for me. I don't need it in my life right now. Or ever.

Jack's relief is obvious. "Would you? I don't want to be a pain. If you were planning to do something else, don't let us stop you. I'm sure we'd manage."

"No bother, it really is quite lovely today."

It is. The sun may be weak, but the brilliant blue sky, without a cloud to be seen, is heartening, nonetheless. The wind has dropped to a gentle breeze, cool enough to remind us it's not too long until Christmas. It catches Jack's fringe so that it flops across one blue eye. I resist the urge to push it back behind his ear. Inappropriate. Instead, I zip my coat a little higher, stuffing my hands into my pockets so they can't cause any mischief. "Shall we?" I say.

We walk in a comfortable silence, Bertie scampering ahead on his retractable lead once we reach the safety of the park. The poor hound's been kept locked up a fair bit since Jack hurt himself. I really should offer to do this more often.

"I'm sorry," Jack says to me suddenly.

I look around, expecting something or someone horrible to jump out at me. I find nothing. "For what?"

"For letting Nicole and your mum sneak up on you by pretending to need your help. It was sneaky."

"Oh, that." I consider his apology. "It was sneaky," I agree. "But I probably needed it."

He's silent for a minute or two, as if trying to work out what to say next. We amble past another couple walking their dogs, exchanging nods and smiles. "You're looking much better," he says finally.

"A little less fat." I laugh, while inwardly berating myself for putting words into his mouth.

He looks confused, glancing down at me momentarily. "No... I mean, yes." His skin pinks up across his cheeks. "Maybe. I mean... I didn't mean that. I mean, maybe you have lost weight, but what I meant was, you look happier. Less sad. More content."

More content. That's a good description of how I'm feeling, actually. I nod. "It did me good to get away. Some things clicked a bit in my head, I think. It's a process, but at least I'm a bit more in control of where I'm going now, rather than stuck in a runaway car with no brakes."

"I'm glad. Anyway, I wanted to say I was sorry for deceiving you."

I pat his arm. "Really, don't worry, it was done with the best intentions." Bertie chooses that moment to do his business.

Jack rummages in his pocket to retrieve a bag. I contemplate letting him struggle to pick it up himself, but the sight is too pitiful as he props the leg in the cast out like a stabiliser, wobbling on the remaining leg as he tries to bend far enough forward to reach the pavement. I imagine the smallest gust of wind might tip him straight into it. "Give it here," I say, taking the bag from him. I insert my hand, so the plastic shields my skin, before scooping it up. It's warm. I shudder, looking around for the nearest poop bin.

"They're over there," Jack says, pointing back to where we came into the park.

"There must be another one." I scan the hedges, looking for the anything that resembles one of the red bins, dangling the small bag from one finger and keeping it as far from my nose as I can manage.

"No, there's one at that entrance." He points to where we came in. "Or the other is over there." This time, he points towards the opposite end of the park, where the second entrance is.

"Well, that's rubbish, no wonder people hang their bags from trees and bushes and then forget to take them home again. Who wants to carry this around on their walk with them?" I hold up the bag.

He reaches for it, crutch dangling off his wrist. "Give it here, I'll carry it," he says, crooking his fingers at me to hand it over.

He leans heavily on his crutches. "How do you plan to carry it?"

"I'll hook it on here." He points at the hand hold on the crutch. My face must express some of my doubt because he adds, "It'll be fine."

"Sure it will," I say, watching how the bag bangs against the metal crutch with every step. He grumbles under his breath. He's starting to look a little tired, his face pale and pinched with what I imagine is pain. "What do you do for a living?" I ask, to distract from the fact I've steered him on to the return route home. Bertie's still exploring everything within sniffing range. He could probably carry on for another ten laps of this park.

"Accountant."

"Huh, you don't look like one," I say without thinking. What I mean is, he doesn't look like Ben. What is it with me and accountants?

He grins. "I'm going to assume that's meant as a compliment. To be fair, your flat doesn't look much like an interior designer's home either."

I grunt. I can't dispute that. "I wasn't intending to use it as a showcase."

"Good job."

I nudge him gently with my elbow, being careful not to make him lose his balance. He sways a little but stays upright. The poo bag swings outwards with the motion and then smashes back against the metal crutch pole. It's one bash too many and the plastic bag splits, spilling Bertie's dogshit all down his plaster cast.

Both inside and out. I stare down at it, horrified, then drag my eyes upwards to look at him.

He's staring down at his leg, eyes wide with shock. Then the smell hits us full force. He closes his eyes, before opening them again to look at me. "I don't suppose you could give me a lift to the hospital?"

"Of course." I feel terrible. Is this my fault? He looks pretty pissed off. I scratch about for anything I might say to cheer him up. "On the plus side, my car already stinks."

Really? That's the best I could manage?

"Awesome." Jack rolls his eyes, a dejected look on his face as he trudges home behind me.

Fortunately, he stays a few paces downwind.

Chapter 16

"And you haven't seen him since?" Sarah calls through to the kitchen. We've just completed our meditation, and I've filled her in on my walk with Jack.

I emerge with a bottle of wine and two glasses. "It was all fairly mortifying at the hospital. Poor thing."

I pour two large glasses of wine, handing one to Sarah, before settling myself onto the sofa beside her.

She chuckles. "So now you think he's hiding from you?"

Sukie brushes up against Sarah's leg, scent marking her, before jumping onto the seat cushion between us. She considers us both for a moment. I hold my breath as she pads on to my lap, curling up and closing her eyes. I'm statue-like, unable to believe she's actually sitting on me for the first time in... well, ever. I really want to stroke her, but her tail twitches as soon as my arm moves. I freeze again, my hand now less than an inch from her mahogany fur. As if she senses it, her back and fur shudder. I withdraw my hand again and force it underneath my leg. Sighing, I turn my attention back towards Sarah, trying to remember what she asked me. "Yeah, he's hiding from me. I feel so bad, like everything that's happened to him is my fault somehow."

"Everything is not your fault, that's just your thoughts spiralling again. Why does it have to be anything to do with you? Maybe you haven't seen him because he's really busy with work?"

"Maybe." I take a sip of my wine, trying to avoid disturbing the cat. It's no use, she jumps off as soon as my leg muscles twitch.

"How can it be your fault? It was his dog's mess. Didn't you say he insisted on carrying the bag? You're not in the habit of sabotaging dog poo bags, as far as I know, so how can any of it be your fault? Stop being so self-obsessed."

I laugh. She's right. I take another slug of my wine. "True." I sit back in the chair. I won't get a better opportunity to talk to her than this. "So, what about you? How are things your end?"

Her eyes dart towards the door as if she's concerned someone might be listening, or maybe she's looking for an escape. Then her gaze shifts towards her phone on the coffee table. Gavin's already texted her four times in the hour since she arrived. Twice during our meditation. As if he really is listening in to our conversation, the phone lights up again with another text, vibrating against the table. Sarah jumps, reaching forwards quickly to pick it up, then palming it. "Fine, thanks," she says, with a quick glance down at the screen.

I take a deep breath. Her shoulders are hunched around her ears despite our relaxing meditation session earlier. There's also red, raw skin around what's left of her fingernails, they're chewed nearly to the bone. It's now or never. "Look, forgive me. The last thing I want to do is make you feel uncomfortable."

Rain patters against the window. She wraps an arm around herself, pulling a cushion onto her lap. "Then don't."

This conversation is going downhill fast. "Okay, fair enough. I just wanted you to know I'm worried about you, as a friend. Same as you were worried about me when I was having a moment a few weeks ago. It made a difference to me knowing that. I needed to tell you that if, or when, you want to talk about it, I'm here. Any time. Whatever you need." I reach across, taking care not to spill my wine, and squeeze her arm.

She looks at me then, tears pooling in her eyes. "Thank you," she whispers.

I can do no more.

The wind has picked up again, rattling the windows in short, shivery bursts. I watch as a crisp packet is tossed into the air. It summersaults three times before dropping back down to the pavement. At least it's stopped raining. I button my coat all the way up to my chin just to make sure the chilly wind won't be able to penetrate, then slip out the apartment, hurrying down the steps and out the front door. I'm meeting with Bella. And maybe Ben. I don't know for sure. But it's okay, because both my solicitor and theirs know all about it this time.

I spent longer than I ought to have getting ready, but as I pull the front door closed behind me, I'm feeling good and surprisingly calm. My solicitor and I had a long talk about the folders of designs; he'd made it clear that given the weak footing I'm on already, it might be seen as a gesture of goodwill for me to hand them back over. I thought I'd be devastated, but actually I'm fine about it. Funnily enough, I've barely looked at the things since the day I took them from the studio. Partly because they've been with my solicitor until I collected them from him, but also because I've started a new one.

When I picked the files up last night, I couldn't wait to look through them, but the designs didn't inspire me at all. They seemed drab and predictable. Old fashioned, even. I'm much more excited about what I'm doing now. My new book is bulging with ideas and clippings and it feels good to be drawing a line under what I did before. My brain has been buzzing with thoughts of the cherry red and white Marmoleum floor tiles arranged in a chequerboard pattern I plan to use for my latest client's design. It's kind of like starting afresh – fresh eyes, maybe. Like my life is one big raisin I'm finally taking the time to look at. I'm feeling inspired, which is just as well because I already have more new clients. Sarah and David and Nicole and Mummy have all been talking me up to their friends. Whatever the reason, it's all rather exciting. I'd forgotten the buzz I get from a new project.

It's a brisk twenty-minute walk before I'm pushing the door of Starbucks open and welcoming the blast of heat that greets me. I'm early, but that was on purpose. It gives me a chance to settle in a bit before they arrive. "What do you want?" the girl behind the counter asks me without altering her bored expression.

I'm tempted to have a caramel latte. It's that sort of weather. But I've been off the caffeine since my week away, and it seems a shame to go back to it now when I've been feeling so good. "A peppermint tea, please."

She curls her lip. "Anything else?"

I gaze at the rows of cakes and pastries but realise I'm not actually all that hungry right now. "No, thank you. That's all."

"What's the name?"

"Claire."

She scribbles something that vaguely resembles Claire onto an empty cup, as I meander my way over to the collection counter. It's lunchtime, the panini pack are all in for the hour, and there's not a lot of space. I used to be one of them, not so long ago. This was the closest coffee shop to the studio. "Claire!"

I smile at the young man holding out my cup, taking it from him as I scan the surroundings for somewhere we might all sit. I spy a small group of people just getting to their feet, and spring into action. I hover beside them until they feel uncomfortable enough to hurry, then as soon as they leave, I collapse into the leather armchair, placing the folders on the seat beside mine and my cup on the table. "Are any of these free?" someone asks moments later, pointing at the three empty chairs surrounding me.

I blow on my tea. "I'm sorry, I'm waiting for some..." My voice trails off as I lift my gaze and take in the sight of the startlingly attractive man standing beside my table. A flush rises from my chest up to my cheeks.

He smiles.

Now, my synapses are misfiring all over the place, making speech momentarily beyond my abilities. A small gurgling noise comes from my throat. I attempt to turn it into a cough.

Bella and Ben choose that moment to walk in. She looks like she's been sucking lemons. Ben trailing behind her, looks harassed. Bella clocks me at my table and barks an order to Ben, who trots off obediently towards the counter, as she makes a palaver of squeezing past tables until she reaches mine. "Did you choose a table in the corner deliberately, because you knew it would be hard for me to get to?" She clutches her belly, making sure we've all noticed her bump.

"Please, do sit down," my mystery companion invites her, pulling out a chair.

Bella looks at him, and then down at the chair as if she suspects he's done something horrible to it. "I'm sorry, who are you?" she says, overcoming her suspicion and slumping into the seat.

"A friend of..." he peers surreptitiously at the side of my cup "…Claire's."

Bella snorts, as if the very idea he might be my friend is implausible. She glares at me. "Really, Claire, if you think you're going to make Ben jealous by bringing a fake boyfriend along, then you're dreaming."

"I'm sorry." My unknown companion holds his hands up, stepping in before I have a chance to respond. "I was the one who saw Claire sitting here and came over." He looks at me and grins. "It was good to meet you, Claire. Call me." He bends forward and scribbles a mobile phone number onto the napkin in front of me. Then gives a puffing Ben, who's just stepped up to the table, a grin before bending to kiss me on the cheek and walking off.

Ben drops the tray onto the table with a clatter, spilling some of Bella's latte onto the accompanying pastry. He turns to watch the stranger depart. "Who was that?"

"Ben! Watch what you're doing, will you?" Bella grabs her latte and mops at the liquid on the plate with a napkin. She holds up the slightly soggy pain au chocolat and crams half of it into her mouth.

I pinch my arm, just to make sure I haven't slipped into some waking hallucination for a second, but no, they're still both there; Bella's still devouring her pastry, and Ben looks... well, he looks a bit worn out, actually. "Are you okay?" I ask, before thinking about what I'm saying. Last time I saw him look this bad he was coming down with appendicitis.

"He's fine," Bella says. "A night out with Martin." We exchange a knowing look. She shakes her head, perhaps only now remembering we're not actually still friends. "Where are the files?"

I pass them to her. She takes them and begins leafing through the pages.

"You look well," Ben says to me softly.

"I feel well." I can't really say the same to him, so I keep quiet.

He casts a nervous eye towards Bella, but she's too wrapped up in the folders to pay attention to us. "I hear you've started designing again. I'm glad."

I settle back into my chair, taking a sip of my tea. "I have. It's been great actually; I've got a few new clients."

"Who?" Bella's hawk-like gaze lands back on me.

I take a deep breath before responding. "Oh, no one you know. New people to me, that's all."

She frowns. "Well, I'm glad you saw sense about these," she says, hugging the folders to her chest. "They're company property."

"Are they all there?" Ben asks quietly.

"Yes." She looks away, so she misses his *I told you so* look.

"Bella was convinced you'd tear out some of the pages to keep for yourself." He laughs, but the sound's a little brittle.

"You're welcome to them." I offer Bella a smile. It's true, she is.

She raises an eyebrow and peers at me. "What are you up to?"

"Nothing." I hold up my hands in surrender. "Really. I've started a new book. You're welcome to this stuff if it's helpful. I don't mind."

"You've changed your tune. What's going on? Are you finally on the happy pills, or something? You seem different." She pauses to look me up and down. "You've lost weight."

She makes it sound like an accusation. I smile, recognising she's damaging herself more than she's damaging me with her paranoia. "I'm just feeling a bit more myself again. Thank you for asking, though." I push my chair away from the table. "Well, if that's everything, I'll make a move." I down the last few mouthfuls of my tea, before shrugging my coat back on.

"You're leaving already?" Ben says, reaching out a hand to me.

I smile at him. "I'm meeting a new client in an hour." I pocket the napkin with the phone number, because why the hell not? Then smile at them both. "Lovely to see you again. Bella, you look wonderful," I say, with a nod towards her bump. It might still hurt a little that she's the one having Ben's baby, rather than me, but I can't be sad about the fact he is finally going to be a dad. "You'll be a great father," I whisper, when I bend to kiss him goodbye. His familiar scent of Lynx body spray and Ben washes over me, bringing some sorrow in its wake. But it's only that; just the sadness of an ending, not the chest-wrenching pain of heartbreak. I pat him on the shoulder, then bend to kiss Bella. "Keep well," I say, and mean it.

Chapter 17

I stare down at the words carpeting the floor around us. All the feelings we have printed onto squares of paper and laid out for others to see. Ashamed, anxious, jealous, resentful, frightened, vulnerable. Those are just mine. Placing them there and looking down, I recognise them for what they are; the feelings derived from all the negative thoughts I've been bombarding myself with. I stand a little apart from those feelings now. Which doesn't mean I don't still feel those things sometimes, only that I recognise them for what they are when I do. And now I have a few more tools to help me manage them.

I peer down at Sarah's words: dread, frightened, scared, ashamed, forlorn, upset. Her words make me want to cry. She sees me looking at them and offers me a sad smile. What can I say? Nothing. In the end, I just reach over and take her hand, squeezing it in mine. If nothing else, at least she'll know she's not alone. She smiles at me again, just a slight curl of her lips, but it doesn't reach her eyes.

"You okay?" I ask her later, as we make our way towards the pub. We're walking slower than the others. It means we've dropped behind a little, giving us the space to talk. She nods but doesn't speak. "I can't believe we only have one more session left of group. I'm feeling a little forlorn at the prospect of it all finishing."

"Me too."

Gavin isn't with us tonight. Even so, Sarah's quieter than normal. She's been withdrawn all evening. "We'll still keep on meeting though, won't we? You and me, I mean. And maybe David?" I look over when she doesn't answer. "Won't we?" I ask again, less certain now.

"I want to."

There's a 'but' in that sentence. "But Gavin doesn't want you to?" I guess.

She shrugs. "He thinks you're all a bad influence on me."

I watch her carefully. "What do you think?"

She shrugs again. "Maybe he's right. Things have been worse between us since we started coming to group. He says I'm not being myself."

"Or maybe you *are* being yourself. Maybe you're just not being who he wants you to be." We walk on in silence as I let her digest my words. What if she decides she wants nothing more to do with me? "Look, all I know is my life is richer for having you in it. I value your advice. I'd be very sad not to have you in my life anymore."

"Same here," Sarah says in a small voice.

I'm so relieved to hear her say it, I hug her; pulling her small frame tight against my chest. I stop when she gasps with pain. "I'm sorry," I say, releasing her and backing off. "Are you hurt?" Now that I really look, her eyes are shadowed and sunken-looking. I don't know why I didn't notice it sooner. She has one arm wrapped around her side now, protecting her ribs.

"It's nothing," she says with yet another shrug. "I fell. I'm such a klutz."

Rage sears through me at the obvious lie. "Really? We're going with that, are we? I fell? What a cliché."

The anger I'm feeling towards Gavin barbs my tongue. Any common sense I might have possessed flies away with the wind rattling the branches above us. "You know, I went on this course because of the panic attacks I was having. But what I learnt was, I was inflicting most of the damage on myself. I was the cause. My own thoughts are a form of abuse, only I couldn't recognise it until Alex and you and David pointed it out to me. You don't have that problem. Your problem is that Gavin is actually abusing you. With his words and now," I say, waving at her hunched form, "physically."

Even as I'm vomiting the words out, I know I'm getting this all wrong. But I can't seem to stop myself. My breaths are coming faster, spurred on by my anger. "I'm telling you to your face so that we both know exactly what is going on here. So, you can recognise it for what it is: abuse. Because we both face a choice now: we can walk away from this class and carry on exactly as we were… I don't know about you, but panic attacks, depression and diabetes are about all I have waiting for me if I do. Or I can make a change. Try and recognise the abuse I inflict upon myself so that instead of letting it crush me, I can fight it."

Sarah's staring at me as if I'm a wild animal. Maybe I am. I have a burning need to make her see the truth of her situation. I drop my voice. "It's abuse, Sarah." She pulls away, but I carry on, "Your husband is trying to crush you, because he's seen you starting to break free. He wants you exactly where you were: depressed, miserable and completely under his thumb. You face a choice too; you don't have to do what he says. You can choose something different. I know it won't be easy – none of this changing stuff is – but that doesn't mean we shouldn't try." I stop, chest heaving.

Her eyes are wild, hair buffeted by the wind, but she pulls herself to her full height and faces me. "But he's my husband. I love him and he loves me." As if that answers everything.

I shake my head sadly. "That's not love. A wise woman once told me you can't hate your way into being loved. Him telling you what a failure you are won't make you more successful. Telling you you're worthless or unlovable won't make you feel any more worthy or loveable. Hitting you won't make you into who he wants you to be. We all have to learn to love ourselves first, that's what we've been learning on the course. Please don't let him convince you otherwise."

Sarah's crying now. She wipes her nose on her sleeve, scrubbing at her cheeks with the back of her hand. "You make it all sound so easy."

"It's anything but, I can promise you that. But you won't be alone. You have friends."

"I can't afford to walk away from my marriage."

"Can you afford to stay? What happens next? Cracked ribs when you express an opinion he doesn't agree with? A black eye when you chat to someone and he thinks you're flirting?" We both glance at David's burly form retreating into the distance. "What point is too much? Where is the line exactly? I don't know, Sarah. You tell me."

I should shut up now. I should have shut up five minutes ago. I've gone too far.

She bristles, stiffening as she pulls away. "No, you don't know, do you? You've got a failed marriage behind you, a husband who shagged an older woman to get away from you. No relationship, no proper job, no children, no prospects beyond a future in a mouldy flat in South London and repeated panic attacks anytime someone points out how tragic you are. And you think you're the right person to give me advice on my relationship? Well, forgive me if I choose not to listen to you."

She knows every one of my vulnerabilities. Her words strike exactly where she knows they'll cause the worst damage, picking at my pathetic heart like a falcon pecking away at a pigeon's heart.

She's right. What the hell am I thinking offering her advice? Who do I think I am? What am I even doing here?

I wrap my coat tighter around me to keep the chill off. It can't protect me from the icy numbness that's creeping through my veins now, as my breathing quickens into short, shallow gasps. "I'm sorry," I say, taking a staggering step away from her, almost as if I'm punch drunk. My head is swimming with dizziness. "I'm sorry," I say again, turning now, shoulders hunched. It's too late to protect myself though. I walk away, the urge to run pressing at me. Somehow, I manage to keep my pace steady.

"Claire," she calls, but I don't turn. I don't stop. I keep on walking.

"Claire, good timing," Jack says, smiling down at me as he hobbles out the front door with Bertie on the lead, just as I'm coming up the steps. The puppy squirms with delight at the sight of me.

I ignore them both, walk straight up the steps and through the front door, then run up the stairs inside to my apartment, where I rip off my coat and collapse on the sofa.

All things considered, the fact I only stay locked up in my flat alone for an hour should be thought of as progress. I have Jack to thank for that. Or maybe Bertie. I was just contemplating making myself a double round of fried egg and bacon sandwiches on thick white bread, having finished my first bout of crying and intending to use crap food as a consolation for all the nasty feelings still swimming around inside me, when a clatter and shriek has me running to the front window. I get there in time to see Jack bounce down the last three steps outside with Bertie's lead wrapped around his crutches. The dog in question appears delighted to have him on the ground again, if his jumping and licking are anything to go by.

It's Jack's deep groan that gets me moving. I'm running downstairs and out the front door before I have time to remember I don't want to see anyone, terrified he's broken yet another bone. "Jesus Jack, are you okay?"

"Bruised pride, and possibly coccyx, but otherwise I'm okay, I think," he says, groaning as he tests parts of his body a little gingerly. He reaches out a hand towards me. "I could do with a hand up though, if you wouldn't mind?"

"Of course." I stick out my hand and brace myself as a counterweight to his, so he can pull himself back to standing. He hops a little awkwardly on his good leg as he tries to manage both the leash and his crutches. "Here," I say, reaching for the lead. "Give Bertie to me."

"It's no bother," he says, holding on stubbornly.

The lead is still wrapped around his crutch; he is seconds away from toppling for a second time. "Listen, you bloody stupid man, let me take the damned dog before you break the other leg and end up with a catheter and needing bed baths." I snatch it from him with a loud huff.

"I didn't want to be a nuisance."

"Oh, for goodness sake!" I make another exasperated noise, bending to reel Bertie in as I unwrap the lead from around his crutches.

"Still, bed baths don't sound too bad," he says, a slight smile lifting the corners of his mouth.

"I'd let Bertie give them to you. With his tongue. After he's eaten something unspeakable from the back garden."

"Oh, that's just nasty. There's no need for nastiness."

I grunt, remembering Sarah's earlier comments. I can't afford to lose any more friends today. "You're right. I'm sorry."

He tilts his head and looks at me. "Sorry? Why are you sorry? What the hell are you talking about? What's wrong with you, woman?" He's staring as if I've transformed into something with green spots, then peers a little more closely. "Have you been crying? Who's upset you?"

"It's nothing," I say, setting off up the steps, dragging Bertie along behind me. I pause at the top and wait for Jack to join us.

"It's not nothing, not if someone made you cry." He wraps an arm around my shoulders and hugs me against him. "How about I open a bottle of wine and you tell me all about it?"

I sniff. "If you're nice to me I'll probably cry again. Which will piss me off, because I hate the fact I seem to be crying all the time these days."

"Most of the time we've spent together, you've either been crying or drunk. At least this way we can combine the two," he says consolingly. I let him steer me indoors and park me on his settee before he hobbles off, returning with a bottle in one hand and two glasses in the other. He's dispensed with the crutches and seems to be managing to weight-bear relatively well.

"Look at you!"

He grins. "I know, it's not nearly so painful. Hopefully next week they'll take the cast off and I'll get given one of those Beckham boots. Then I can take the bloody thing off and finally have a bath."

"Already? That's quick," I say as he twists off the bottle cap and pours us both a generous glass of pinot.

He shakes his head. "Quick? It feels like the last three weeks have been a bloody lifetime. It can't pass quickly enough as far as I'm concerned. Anyway, cheers." He raises his glass and clinks it against mine. "So, tell me? Who's been mean to you? At least I know it isn't me this time." He hesitates, "Is it?"

There is serious doubt in his voice. I giggle, taking a long sip of my wine. The mellow fruity flavours melt against my tongue. This is a lot better than the sandwich I'd planned for myself. I release a long breath, as I consider what to tell him. "A friend on my course is having some trouble at home."

"Relationship trouble?"

"Yes... but serious." I take another sip of my wine for courage. "Her husband's abusive to her – at least, I believe he is. Whenever he's around she's like a different woman. A mutual friend pointed it out to me and asked me to speak to her – you know, just to let her know we were there for her, if she wanted us. Today I tried to, but it didn't go quite as I planned." I take another sip. "I got cross when I realised he'd hurt her – I thought the emotional abuse was bad enough. But the fact he hurt her so badly she was holding her ribs and winced when I hugged her, pushed me over the edge. I said all the wrong things. What I meant to say was that I care about her, that I'm here if she wants to talk. Instead I put a wall up between us when I suggested she should leave him. That she shouldn't put up with it."

Jack's listening intently. His eyebrows furrow now. "And she took it badly?"

I sigh. "You could say that; she took every shitty detail she knows about my life and threw it in my face. She was right. Who the hell did I think I was, trying to sort her life out when my own life is a crock of shit?"

"You're someone who cares about her. That's enough. That's all she needs to know for now. You can't rescue her or boss her into making a decision to get out. You can only be there whenever she wants to talk. And she will."

He sounds so certain. I wish I could be that sure. "Do you really think so?"

"Absolutely. I'd say you touched a nerve. Right now, I bet she's gutted about the stuff she threw at you."

I stare at him. I imagine Sarah's beside herself for the horrible things she said. I know in my heart she didn't mean them. She's a good person – she wouldn't want to hurt me. Not really.

"Do you still want to help her, if you can?" Jack asks.

I blink at him. Do I? "Yes, of course," I decide.

He nods. "Then send her a message. Tonight. Let her know that you're still her friend. Let her know that you're there for her, if she needs you. Tell her it's not her fault. That's all you need to do."

I stare at him. Can it really be that easy? I fish my phone from my pocket and send her a text. *I'm sorry I overstepped the line. You're a good friend – I don't want to lose that. Whenever you need me, whatever for, I'm there for you. No more judgement.*

I receive a heart emoticon back almost immediately. And just like that, my mood lifts. "You're amazing," I tell Jack, as I hug him goodnight. I step away quickly when his delicious smell has me yearning to rub my face into the crook of his neck.

When I do, he has a pink spot on either cheek. They're rather endearing.

"Goodnight Claire," Jack says, his voice husky.

"Goodnight," I squeak, and run up the stairs.

Chapter 18

"Ben?" I shiver in the icy air rushing straight up the stairs, rubbing my eyes and squinting to make sure I'm not imagining him on the doorstep, but no, it's him. In the flesh, standing at the front door. He looks unshaven, a bit of a mess in fact, bundled up against the cold in a big, black coat. I don't blame him; the temperature feels like it's dropped another five degrees. The heavy dark clouds, just visible from where I'm standing, look like they might dump snow rather than rain. I look at Ben more closely. He really does look terrible. I immediately start to worry. "What's wrong?"

"Can I come in?" He casts a furtive glance over his shoulder.

Of course, I'm the other woman now. If anyone we know should see him coming to see me at – I glance at my watch, squinting a little as my still-sleepy eyes struggle to focus on the small numbers. "Bloody hell, Ben, it's half past six in the bloody morning! What are you doing here?" What with the few glasses of wine I'd put away last night, I hadn't been intending to get up early today. With my only meeting scheduled for this afternoon, there was no need for me to see anything much before nine o'clock.

He ignores me, running up the stairs and pushing inside. He walks quickly into the lounge. I follow, somewhat confused. "What's going on?"

He's looking around, as if searching for something, striding from room to room. It doesn't take him long to complete the tour. "Where is he?"

I scratch my head. "What? Where is who?"

"The guy." He juts his chin out, something he always used to do when he was being particularly bloody-minded about something. He did it a lot. And then I used to tell him to *wind his neck in*. It usually distracted him from whatever was working him up – something I'd done to annoy him, more often than not. "Don't tell me you let him fuck you and then leave? Jesus, Claire, I thought you were better than that."

Any warm feelings I've been having about our past dissipate like exhaust fumes from a van that just failed its MOT, leaving only poison behind. "What the hell are you talking about?" I demand, flicking the switch on the coffee percolator, anger now pushing the last fuzzy traces of sleep from my brain. It's too early for this shit. I need coffee. Peppermint tea isn't going to cut it this morning. "Who were you expecting to find here?"

He glowers at me. "I saw you, Claire."

Nope, no clearer. "Saw me? Saw me what?"

Ben huffs. "Last night. I saw you walking in with a guy. He was all over you." I can't imagine what he's talking about, until he says, "And he had a dog. You know Sukie hates dogs. I can't believe you could be so inconsiderate."

Realisation dawns, like the last two pence piece in the penny pusher game at the arcade that suddenly shoves the clump of coins over the shelf. He means Jack. He saw me helping Jack in. I'm about to set him straight when another thought strikes me: What the bloody hell has it got to do with him?

"So?" Ben says, arms crossed over his chest, fingers drumming on the tops of his arms, his feet planted wide. It's his *I'm waiting* stance. It always pissed me off when we were together. Made me feel like an errant child.

I take a deep breath, separating my emotions from my response. "Why are you really here, Ben?"

He makes some explosive puffs of breath, sounding like the coffee percolator, his cheeks reddening alarmingly. "Who the bloody hell was it?"

Two more deep breaths. "I can see that you're angry Ben. But whoever it was has nothing to do with you. I have nothing to do with you." My voice sounds calm. I am mostly calm. There's just a flicker of excitement that he still reacts like this when he thinks I've been seeing someone else. I tamp it down. He's living with Bella. They're having a baby.

"Well, of course it has something to do with me. I'm your bloody h-" He stops talking, suddenly aware of what he was about to say. He huffs again, then slumps down into a kitchen chair, wincing with the movement, saying nothing. His teeth are clenched, a small muscle flickering just above his jawbone. I recognise the signs. He's buggered his back again. He does it all the time.

I finish making the coffee, adding the creamer and two sugars to his that I know he likes. I bought them out of habit, even though I use neither. Bella used to tell him off for all the sugar he added. I swirl the creamy contents until they dissolve, wondering if she still does. She was probably right, to be fair.

He looks up as I hand it to him, his expression hangdog. "Thank you." He takes a sip, and smiles. "You remembered."

"We were married for fifteen years, Ben. What did you imagine? That I'd erase all my memories of you?"

"I wouldn't have blamed you." I make a vague noise in agreement. It would certainly have made those early months an awful lot easier. "I haven't seen you in ages," he says.

"You saw me at the café a couple of days ago."

"You haven't come round to the house though. You always used to come round."

I laugh. "You filed a restraining order against me! You shouldn't even be here. Does Bella know where you are?"

He flushes again, and I have my answer.

I sigh. "Why are you here, Ben?" I ask a second time, pulling out the seat opposite him. Sukie chooses that moment to nose her way into the kitchen, finally deigning to get out of her nest on top of the wardrobe. She sniffs around Ben's ankles. He reaches down to stroke her, but she gives a quick flick of her tail and moves beyond his reach, choosing to rub herself against my calves instead. I get to my feet again to chop up some of the fresh chicken I cooked for my lunch yesterday. She's just earned it.

We watch her eat, in silence. When she finishes, she hops up onto the table and saunters out through the cat flap. "She looks well," Ben says.

"She's getting there," I agree.

"I wasn't sure how she'd do... away from me, I mean. She was always quite attached to me."

"She was," I agree. "But she moved on. She had to. She's more resilient than you gave her credit for." I'm not sure if we're still talking about Sukie.

Ben frowns. "I'm sorry, Claire."

"What for? Waking me up at the arse-crack of dawn or wrecking our marriage?"

"Both... but mostly the latter. I was stupid."

"Yeah, well, there's no point living in the past. We have to live in the moment – that's the only thing we can change. The choices we make now are all that matter. I'm not sure your choice to come round here was a good one. You have a baby on the way. Bella needs you."

He lifts his head and stares at me. "She doesn't need me. Not really. Not like you did. She's so bloody self-sufficient. She has all the pasta and rice in little glass jars. Not a plastic bag in sight. Everything is organised within an inch of its life. I miss the beautiful chaos you brought to our life."

"Erm, thanks, I think?"

He reaches out and places his hand on my arm. "Seriously, Claire, I miss you. Seeing that bloke flirting with you the other day at the café. Then seeing you with someone else last night... the thought you'd moved on... it made me feel sick."

Anger swirls inside me. How dare he emotionally manipulate me like this! Tugging on my heartstrings. "You have no right to say this stuff to me anymore, Ben. We're getting a divorce. You left me, remember? You're living with another woman. She's having the baby you always wanted. Whether Bella lacks the chaos I brought to your life, or not – and I'm still not sure if that's a good or a bad thing, frankly – that baby is going to need you. So, you need to grow up, and start making choices that aren't all about you for once. You're hurting people. I won't be one of your victims this time."

He stands, wincing with the movement, pushing his chair away from the table and walking towards me, only stopping when he's close enough his breath warms my cheek. "Admit we were good together. I know you miss it too. You don't really want to get a divorce."

He leans towards me as if he might kiss me. I jerk away. "What are you playing at?" I place the table between us. "I think you should leave."

"Claire -"

"No, Ben. Are you going to leave Bella? Are you going to walk away from that baby when it's born?"

He hesitates for too long.

"Exactly. I think it's time you went back to your pregnant partner. It's time you man-up to the choices you made. The same as we've all had to."

He winces again as he pulls his coat back on. "I'm sorry. Again."

"You should be," I tell him, opening the door. "Oh, and get your back seen to before the kid arrives. You need to be able to play with it. You're turning into an old man."

He grimaces, but nods before descending to the front door. As he reaches for the handle, Jack's key rattles in the lock. Bertie's prancing around at his ankles. Jack looks up at me and smiles, then towards Ben who's glaring at him.

"Everett," Jack says, throwing another quick look in my direction.

"Wilton." Ben makes his name sound more like a growl. They face one another in a silent standoff.

I didn't know they knew one another. Accountancy's a small world, I guess. I should probably intervene. I don't. Instead I close the door on the pair of them and go back to bed. And I don't drink the coffee.

Chapter 19

I'm still angry with Ben when I wake up the next morning. How dare he come around here thinking he can just waltz back into my life! The worst thing is, I'm tempted. I'm such a loser.

"You need to move on." These are Nicole's pearls of wisdom when she pops in with the kids for a cup of tea. "You're fair game all the time you're sitting here on your own. Find someone else. That'll show him what's what."

"Nice idea, but in case you haven't noticed, men are hardly falling over themselves to ask me out," I say, herding Betty away from Sukie, who looks like she's about to pull the same Freddy Krueger trick she pulled on Bertie.

She grunts at me. "How does one meet people these days? All my friends are married. What about the people on your course? Or failing that, a dating app?"

I rest my head in my hands. "Oh, dear God, has it really come to this? How depressing."

Nicole slams her hand down on the card game she's playing with Mathilda. "Snap!" Mathilda bursts into tears. It's the third time in a row she's lost to her mother.

"Don't you think you should let her win once in a while?" I say, passing Mathilda my phone to distract her. I flick CBeebies on for Betty. This flat is no more fit for under-fives than it is for puppies.

Nicole shrugs. "It's character building. No, what you need is to make a concerted effort to meet someone new. It's not like it's possible to bump into handsome men in the street these days, they're all too busy staring at their phones. It's difficult to meet new people. You'll have to make an effort and put yourself out there a bit more. Kiss a few frogs." She pauses for a minute, thinking furiously. "What about the hottie downstairs? He's perfect."

"Jack?"

She nods enthusiastically.

I shake my head. I can't say the thought hasn't crossed my mind. He is perfect. But I don't want to ruin things between us. I'd be bound to cock things up and then I wouldn't have him as a friend anymore, and the thought of that... No. What I need is a handsome stranger.

A memory stirs. I wander towards the coat hooks and rummage through my jacket pocket, pulling out a somewhat creased paper napkin. Thankfully the number's still visible; His name is next to the number. Chris. "There was this guy," I say, waving the napkin at Nicole.

Her eyebrows lift in surprise. "Who's that?"

"A guy I bumped into when I met up with Ben and Bella the other day. He was nice. Defended me when Bella started to get Bella-ish." From what I recall he was rather pleasant to look at too. Now that I think about it, he's pretty perfect for a first stab at dating again.

"Well, what are you waiting for?" she says, wiping a slug of green mucus from beneath Betty's nose. The girl produces more of the stuff than any other child I've met. "Give it a go. But make sure you leave me his number in case he turns out to be a serial killer. I think you're meant to tell me where you're meeting too."

"What so you can turn up and embarrass me? I don't think so."

She rolls her eyes at me. "No, so we can check the CCTV footage if you disappear."

I run a hand through my hair. "Thanks for the motivational talk, I'm feeling well up for it now. Anyway, you're getting a bit ahead of yourself; he probably won't even remember me."

She waves a hand. "Oh, don't be such a Negative Nelly, get on with it. Call him. This could be the start of the rest of your life."

I hold my hand up. "Please, stop. You're making me feel nauseous." It's no lie; the thought of speaking to this guy is turning my guts to water. "Do I have to call him? Can't I just text?"

She thrusts my phone at me. "Call him. Right now. What have you got to lose?"

I think for a second. "Umm dignity, pride, self-respect?"

"Oh, shush. Get on with it."

I enter the number and press dial before I lose my nerve. "Hello?" A male voice answers almost straight away, giving me no time to prepare.

I didn't expect an actual live human to answer. I mean, who answers their phone to unknown numbers these days? That's what voicemail is for. I'm not ready for this. I'm about to end the call when I catch sight of Nicole glaring at me. She'll never let me live it down if I don't go through with this. "Oh, hi..." I squeak. Hell, could this be any more embarrassing? "I'm not sure if you remember me, but we met in Starbucks the other day." Shit, what do I say if he doesn't remember me? Maybe he gives his number to hundreds of girls in Starbucks every day.

He laughs, a warm, rumbling sound. "Claire, wasn't it? I do remember. You were meeting that bad-tempered woman – she was a... character." I appreciate the hesitation. "I'm glad you called. I wasn't sure if you would."

"You are?" I sound like I've been sucking on helium balloons.

He laughs again. "Yeah, I am. What can I do for you?"

Oh, God, what now? Nicole's gaze sears into my back. "Erm, well, I wondered if you might like to go for a drink sometime?" Oh, my freaking god! I just asked him out.

"I'd really like that. I'm actually free tonight. But how about we have dinner instead of just drinks? There's an Italian a block down from that Starbucks I met you at. Do you know it?"

I do. Ben and I enjoyed more than one supper there after working late at the studio. I haven't been in months though. "I know it," I say slowly.

"Mummy," Mathilda's bell-like voice chimes. There's a sharp intake of breath at the other end of the line.

"You have a daughter?" I get the feeling he's using the same tone of voice he might if I had confessed to keeping poisonous snakes as pets.

"She's not mine." I grimace at Nicole, who raises one eyebrow in return.

There's a brief silence, then: "About seven then?" he suggests.

I grunt in agreement before I have time to second-guess myself. Then I disconnect the call.

Nicole whoops, grabbing Mathilda by the hand and leading her towards my loo. "We'll start with the preparations when I'm done here," she declares.

"Just make sure you wash your hands," I call after them.

A few hours later my hair is straight, my body contorted into underwear I may not be able to remove on my own, and I'm feeling about as good about myself as it's possible to. The restaurant's close enough for me to walk. It would be quicker to take the tube, but I decide I need some exercise. I've done hardly anything since Briar Hill. Halfway there, I'm very glad I talked Nicole out of the three-inch heels she'd suggested for me.

Standing outside underneath the awning I hesitate, willing myself the strength to walk in. What if he's not there? I spin the rings on my left hand. Nervous habit.

Shit! I'm still wearing my wedding and engagement rings.

I slip them off my finger and slide them into a compartment inside my bag, leaving my finger bare. I stare down at the dents left behind. Then, before I can second guess myself, I push inside.

I smile at the owner, eyes scanning the tables for my date, spotting him in a corner. Already here, that's a good sign. I lift my hand and wave to show I've seen him, weaving my way past the other diners.

"Hi," I say, smiling as a flush of heat rushes to my cheeks. "It's nice to see you."

Chris grins. He has a nice smile. Good teeth. "Nice to see you too. I wasn't sure you were going to come in." He nods towards the window. He must have had a clear view of me dithering outside. My cheeks heat again. "Do you want to sit down?" he says. When I nod, he stands and pulls out my chair for me. "Are you happy to share a bottle of wine? Red if that's okay?"

I nod again, feeling a little shy now that I'm here. What the hell was I thinking? What are we going to talk about?

"So, Claire, apart from the fact you like peppermint tea, I know very little about you. Tell me about yourself."

I clear my throat. He smiles again. He really is very good at making me feel at ease. For a first post-marriage date this could be a whole lot worse. "Well, I'm an interior designer," I say. I think I surprise him, because his eyebrows lift a little. "I've started my own company. It's only small, but I'm enjoying the work."

"And have you always worked in interior design?"

"Since university. I love it. What about you?" I'm intrigued to know what this guy does. He looks fit; something that keeps him active, I'd guess.

"I'm a fireman."

We pause as the waiter arrives and hands us both a menu, placing some breadsticks in the middle of the table. I use the time it takes Chris to choose a bottle of wine to calm my thundering heart with some deep breaths. A fireman! Holy hell. I grab a breadstick for want of something to do, nibbling along its length like a beaver.

"Hungry?" he asks with a grin.

I've already demolished the first breadstick and am reaching for a second. Oh, no! I don't want him to think I'm greedy... But what am I thinking? He's seen me and I'm clearly not a picky eater.

Stop! What am I doing?

He's staring at me now, as if I'm some sort of a puzzle to solve. "Yes, I like my food," I say. I might as well tell him how it is.

"Good," he says, grabbing a breadstick of his own. "Me too." He demolishes the thing in three bites. "What do you fancy?" he says, lifting the menu.

"I like the lasagne." I don't need to see the menu to choose, I know it by heart.

He lowers the card to look at me, head tilted to one side. "So you've been here before then?"

"Yes. I used to work in a studio just around the corner. I like it here; the food's great."

He rocks back in his chair. "I can't believe I never noticed you before. I come here all the time." Of course he does. The fire station is just up the road from the studio. I resist fanning myself with my menu as I contemplate what he might look like in a uniform. Nicole will positively pop with excitement when she hears. "I normally notice any good-looking woman sitting on their own."

"Yeah, well, maybe you didn't notice me because I was here with my husband." At this his eyebrows nearly vanish into his hairline, eyes dropping to my left hand. Perhaps he sees the dents there. "My ex-husband," I clarify, taking a third breadstick.

I watch him out the corner of my eye as the waiter comes to take our orders. Chris seems to have taken the news reasonably well. At least, he hasn't run off yet. He's watching me. I squirm a little under his gaze. When the waiter leaves again, he sits back and crosses his arms across his chest. "How long ago did your marriage end?"

"Nearly ten months."

"And are you happy about it?"

How to answer that? There's no point in lying – not if we want to have any sort of chance of developing a relationship. We're too old to mess about. "I wasn't, to begin with. He left me for another woman. But they're having a baby now and so that's that. I'm ready to let go. I'm making a new life for myself. It's been a process – it's still a process – but I'm getting there."

He smiles at me, a gentle smile that reaches all the way to his eyes. "Thank you for being so honest. I appreciate it. I'm glad you're getting there."

The next half an hour is more pleasant than I expected. He's easy to talk to. A widower, I learn. His wife passed away from cancer nearly five years earlier. I take another bite of my lasagne, reflecting how lucky I am to have bumped into this man. What twist of good fate led me to the café at the same time as him? The food is delicious and he's better company than I ever hoped. A kernel of hope buds inside my chest as I listen to him talk about being a fireman, his face animated.

Taking a long sip from my wine glass I place it carefully back down on the table. Smiling my best smile, I peer up at him from under my lashes. "So, what are you looking for in a relationship? I mean, what's important -"

He holds a hand up. "Sorry to interrupt," he says, reaching forward. "It's just, you've got a little bit of lasagne in your eyebrow."

I take a moment to process this. It's not a phrase you hear every day. I mean, where am I meant to go from here? I hastily scrub my eyebrow with my napkin. He's right, there is lasagne in my eyebrow. More than a splash. I excuse myself from the table and retreat to the ladies where I hastily text Nicole. She calls me straight back.

"How's it going?" she asks without any preamble. "What's he like?"

I sigh. "He's lovely. Really nice. A fireman."

She squeals with joy. "A fireman. Holy hot fire hydrants, Claire! You've hit the jackpot!"

"Yeah, well, maybe."

She makes a frustrated noise. "What are you talking about? What's not to like? Let's recap on what you just said; he's lovely, he's a fireman, he's single, he's a fireman, you're single... He is single, isn't he?"

"Yes, he's single. His wife died of cancer five years ago."

"Oh. Sad. But still... what's the problem?"

I sigh again. "He just had to stop me mid-sentence to tell me I had lasagne in my eyebrow."

Nicole is not often lost for words, but she's quiet for so long I have to check to make sure we haven't been cut off. Then she snorts, muffled laughter now obvious despite her having placed her hand over the phone. "I can hear you," I hiss, as another woman in the cubicle next to me starts laughing.

"Oh, I'm sorry, babe. It's just that's... that's. . ." Another loud snort, "Fucking awesome. I mean, what a perfect first date story to tell your kids when you're older."

I sniff, a little mollified now I'm thinking about it in those terms. "I'm going back to the table," I say, mustering what dignity I have left.

"Maybe just have coffee rather than risk a pudding," she says, not bothering to hide her snorts of laughter now. "Call me later. I have to hear part two."

Chris looks up when I approach the table, the corners of his mouth lifting a little. "Are you okay? I was about to ask if there was a window in the ladies you might've bunked out of."

I grimace. "I was just trying to regain my composure after the lasagne incident."

"What's a little food in the eyebrow between friends?"

I grin, despite my embarrassment. This guy is really quite adorable. I'm probably done with trying to be coquettish though. I pull out my chair, hand resting on the back. A thought strikes me. "So why are you still single then?" I ask, deciding it's time to get straight to the point. There must be something wrong with him. He's too good to be true.

"Ouch. Straight in there! You don't mess about, do you?" He lets out a deep breath. "I normally leave this sort of conversation to the second or third date. What makes you think there's something?"

If I could raise an eyebrow, I'd be arching it right now. "I mean, look at you… There must be something."

He grins. "I like you, Claire." There's a pause, his face sobering, and then, "I don't want kids. At all. Turns out that's a deal breaker for a lot of women. They either finish with me straight away or, worse, hang around for a bit hoping they can change my mind."

I sit down heavily. "I can't have kids. I tried with my ex-husband. It never happened."

Chris' expression brightens. "See – we're a match made in heaven."

I shake my head. "But I still want them one day. Even if I have to adopt." I didn't know it for sure until this moment, but now I'm certain. I meet his gaze. "I guess that's a complete no-go for you?"

He nods, his expression sad.

I lift the bottle of wine and re-fill our glasses. "Ah, well, at least we had a nice dinner. We might as well finish this. And I think I will look at the dessert menu after all."

Chapter 20

Three days later, I'm still a bit down in the dumps. Worse, I'm now second guessing myself about Ben. He's been texting me. Just little reaching out texts, but still. Three times I've constructed a text back to him. Three times my fingers have hovered over the send button. Three times I've deleted it before I sent it. But it was a close-run thing the last time. I don't trust myself with a fourth test of my resolve. Nicole is away with the kids for a week at Center Parcs, so I don't really feel like disturbing her with yet more of my tedious mental anguish. And, despite the brief text exchange with Sarah, there's been nothing since. I'm feeling a little forlorn. I've been working every hour, just to avoid giving myself any headspace to think about the debacle with Chris. The experience has made me long for the easiness I had with Ben. That's not good.

I pick up my phone, then put it down again quickly. I've been playing this game all morning. Worse, anxiety is crashing over me in waves; the fear he might not want me now even if I do change my mind. Fear of what might happen if I call him. Fear of being alone. Fear of not being good enough – of only being his bit on the side while he lives his best life with Bella. Fear of being unlovable. Fear of another lasagne-in-the-eyebrow moment if I do try dating again.

I need to do something to pull myself out of this ever-decreasing circle of anxiety and self-recrimination. I'm not sure what, but something. Alex recommended some techniques for when stress, anxiety and depression threaten at group last week. It might help if I remember where my bloody notes are.

I spend fifteen minutes hunting for my workbook. Normally, I'd call Sarah, but I can't. We're still not really talking. Not like we were. Instead, I turn the flat upside down. Then I find what I'm looking for in my car. I really need to sort my shit out.

I collapse onto the sofa and open the book to week seven.

Do something pleasurable.

Do something that gives you a sense of satisfaction.

Act mindfully

They make it sound so easy. I start with what I know: a meditation session to get me in the zone. It helps. I'm calmer afterwards, feeling more grounded again once I've finished. I choose cooking a nice meal for the 'something pleasurable'. I'll combine that section with the 'do something that gives you a sense of satisfaction'. I'll walk to Sainsbury's and get the stuff for dinner and post the divorce papers back to my solicitor on the way.

I've been putting that off for days now. I'm finally convinced I must make the break. I can't change everything that's happened between Ben and me over the last year. All I can do is make a good choice for me now. And being married to a man who left me for another woman, one who is now having his baby, is not a good choice. If he couldn't respect and love me enough to be faithful last time, what hope is there that he'll manage it second time around? The fact he seems willing to be unfaithful to Bella, despite their impending parenthood, does not inspire much confidence. No, I deserve better. I *choose* to deserve better.

I grab the papers, and before I overthink myself, I scribble my signature everywhere my solicitor has indicated I should.

There. I've done it. I've actually bloody well gone and done it!

The momentary euphoria passes. Next thing I know, I'm blubbering like I did the first time I watched Titanic. Three soggy tissues later, I determine I can't afford to wallow any longer. This way lies panic attacks and comfort eating.

I stuff the paperwork into an envelope, press on a stamp and write the solicitor's address across the front, leaving behind large blots of ink everywhere my tears have fallen. Grabbing my favourite recipe book from the shelf, I scribble down all the ingredients I'll need for my favourite pan-fried salmon recipe, then grab some shopping bags from the drawer overstuffed full of them – because I constantly forget to take one with me – before pulling on my old coat and scarf. It's a bit tatty but it's warm. And it's not like I'm out to impress anyone.

I grab the letter from the side and leave the flat, trotting down the steps before I change my mind.

Thick grey clouds squat overhead like broody hens, but it's not raining – or even snowing – yet. It's cold enough for me not to want to hang around though, so I set off at a fast pace, attempting to ignore the chill by tucking my chin into the wool encircling my neck. I can't ignore the bite of aching cold against my cheeks and fingers, choosing to stuff my hands into my pockets and leaving the envelope tucked beneath my arm.

Why the tears? It's the right decision, there can be little doubt about that. I thought I'd come to terms with it weeks ago. Alex said tears can be the outward manifestation of our fears. A physical response to the inward mental assault of fear and self-doubt. Or am I just mourning? The ending of my marriage. The loss of love. Maybe it's a bit of both.

I choose a route through the park, knowing there's a post box beyond the exit on the other side. It's in the right direction for the shop too. Halfway across, I pass the café. I haven't eaten since... maybe I haven't eaten. I pause long enough to buy myself a banana before continuing my march to the other side. I've eaten it in three bites and am left holding the skin out in front of me to avoid smearing the banana slime all over my coat. The park is quiet today, perhaps the cold is keeping some of the regulars inside. It crosses my mind to drop the skin in a bush. It's biodegradable after all and my hands are certainly regretting having the envelope and the banana skin to hold, but I don't. I know there's a bin beside the post box.

Instead of worrying about the cold, I focus on another pressing matter: what am I going to do about Sarah? I can't leave things as they are, but I don't want to provoke anything by reaching out to her when Gavin might be around. I need to be patient, wait for her to come to me. If nothing else, I'll see her at group on Wednesday. It's our last session. That thought makes me very sad.

I smile at a woman and her daughter handing out leaflets advertising a sale at Hair Today Gone Tomorrow – a local hairdresser's. I've never been there; I always found the name a little threatening. I reach the bin, deposit my rubbish and then stand in front of the post box. This is it... the point of no return. I raise my hand and look at the banana skin. Banana skin? Where the hell is my letter? I look back across the park, in case I dropped it on the path, then down to the cracked pavement. I walk once around the post box, and then stare at my empty hand for a full minute. And then it comes to me. The bin. I posted the letter in the bin.

I stare at it, half hoping it might spit the letter back out. It's the kind of bin that only has a small opening at the top where you post the rubbish. Stops it blowing out again, I suppose. Or maybe it's to stop terrorists popping their bombs inside? The cracked pavement and large recycling containers daubed with graffiti suggest otherwise. No, they'd not get much mileage from blowing up this bin. Although, if I had some explosives, I'd put them to work right now. Who knows why they put lids on bins nowadays, but it's bloody typical of my luck that this one has one. There's almost no space at the top to reach inside. I mean, why would most people even want to? There's a lock on the front that whoever comes to empty it presumably has a key for. I contemplate waiting until that person turns up, but I have no idea how often they come. It could be once a week, for all I know. And it's bloody cold. What the hell am I going to do?

I step closer, the pungent stink of rot and decay leaving its tang in my nostrils. I resort to breathing through my mouth. There's nothing for it, if I want to get the letter out, I'm going to have to force my arm into the small gap and hope I can bend it sufficiently to reach inside.

I crouch down, pushing up the sleeve of my coat up to my elbow as I take a deep breath and insert my arm. It's tight. My arm's a little too wide. It quickly becomes wedged as my fingers grope about in nothing for a moment. I twist a little and my fingers brush against something solid... Too solid to be my letter. I register slimy wetness on the back of my hand and gag. Who knows what people have put in here. I gag again, forcing my arm further inside. The only way this can get worse is if my arm gets stuck.

"Mummy, what's that lady doing?"

I look up to find the leaflet lady and her daughter both staring at me.

"Don't stare darling, it's not kind. You never know what hard times people might be up against." The woman offers me a sympathetic smile. "Do you want me to fetch you a cup of tea and something to eat?" she asks.

I know she means it kindly, but the fact she's assumed I'm homeless is a bit of a kick in the teeth. Maybe I shouldn't wear this coat again. Maybe I should buy myself a new one. "Oh, that's terribly kind of you," I say. My voice sounds horribly prim – like Mummy's when she's trying to impress someone posh, "but really, I'm fine."

The woman raises an eyebrow. To be fair to her, I am on my knees with my arm inserted inside a park rubbish bin. I must look anything but fine.

"You see, I posted my letter in the dustbin instead of the post-box," I say, as if it's the sort of thing that happens all the time. I laugh, but there's no return smile, no rush to reassure me that they quite understand and do it all the time themselves too. The laugh sounds more like a donkey's bray, shrill and slightly manic. My fingers brush against something papery, I grip it and tug it out. "Aha!" I shriek as I wave it towards them. It's one of their leaflets. They both step away. The leaflet's covered in something... I don't want to think what because it smells so bad. It must look like I'm offering it back to them. They both take another large step backwards. The woman has a tight hold on her daughter's hand now. I suspect I've segued from harmless homeless person who deserves some sympathy, to unpredictable deranged woman who fishes about in rubbish bins for the fun of it. And I still don't have the letter.

I reinsert my hand, because after all I've come this far and what else do I have to lose? It takes another five minutes, but finally I locate my letter lodged against the far side of the bin, flush with the wall. The woman and her daughter have long gone, so I'm unable to vindicate myself. I retrieve it, relieved to find it relatively unscathed, then sit there for a few minutes, back against the bin, somehow immune now to the stink. I daren't pull my sleeve back down, because some unknown substance is smeared all over me.

"Hi, Claire," Jack calls. He waves.

I contemplate pretending I haven't heard him, that maybe I am someone else and he's mistaken, but he's been walking along a straight path towards me, Bertie on the lead beside him, and must have been watching my antics for some time.

Instead, I wave a bin-juice smeared arm back at him. "Morning," I call cheerily.

Then I get to my feet and go home, no longer having any sort of appetite for salmon. I don't post the letter.

Chapter 21

"I'm going to miss this," Sarah says, wiping away the tears spilling onto her cheeks with the back of her hand. She's crying with laughter, not sorrow. I've just finished regaling the group with my most recent exploits. There was a fair bit, what with my date and the letter. There's not a dry eye in the house. Even Alex has given up trying to look professional.

It takes a good ten minutes of our precious last session before they've collected themselves again enough that we can continue. David leans towards Alex, unusually intent. "I have a question for you; how do we remain mindful without this meeting every week to keep us focussed?" It feels like he's pulled the words straight out of my mind. Exactly what I've been worrying about all week. We're not alone. There are numerous nods around the room.

"Thank you for asking that, David. It's an important question. You're right, it takes effort and practice to remain mindful. You'll need to keep it up in some way. If you can't find the time to practise with others, then think about how you use your life at home or work to bring gentle attention to what you're doing, so that you do that thing and nothing else. Maybe you can use the phone ringing, or laughter, or a train passing to be the natural bell of Mindfulness – to bring you into the moment." His soft gaze sweeps across the group. "When you listen to someone, can you listen without agreeing or disagreeing, or planning what you're going to say next? When you're talking, can you say what you need to say without embellishing? Nothing more. It takes effort, but it can be done. And hopefully you can help one another."

God, I hope so. Staying mindful and not slipping back into my old habits will take some serious effort on my part. I'm under no illusions. I have an empty tub of cookie dough ice-cream to prove it after the bin debacle. But it wasn't a weeks' worth of food. I may still be a long way from being cured, if such a thing even exists, but I am better than I was. I see what I'm doing to myself now. I recognise it for what it is, and I don't judge myself as a failure as quickly as I used to. I hope I can course correct with the techniques I've learned. That feels like monumental progress. Alex offers me one of his beautiful smiles when I share my thoughts with the group and my chest warms a little.

I avoid Sarah on the walk to the pub. I've learned that lesson, at least. Everyone is coming, for once. Even Alex. Well, everyone except Gavin, who didn't turn up tonight. But to be honest, I think we were all glad about that. It was fine at group – David, Sarah, and I working together just like normal – but now we're outside, it feels awkward again. I steal looks at her whenever I think she's not looking. She must be doing the same, because at least twice I've caught her staring back at me and we've both turned away quickly. It's like being back at school. I was never very good at making friends there either. Or, at least, holding on to them. It's one of the reasons I loved Ben so much; he was one of the very first people I met who just seemed to really like me.

David's tried to reassure me I've done nothing wrong; he's been running between us like a Border Collie losing control of its flock, but despite his efforts, it feels like something is broken. Whatever it is, it's left me with a weight in my chest that's impossible to shift.

"I think we should celebrate completing our course," Jennifer suggests, once we're all seated around the largest table in the Font and Firkin. She raises her glass and we all drink to ourselves.

"I'd like to make a toast," Sarah says. All eyes swing towards her. "To Willow – the bravest person I know. You recognised you needed some extra help and you went out and found it."

"To Willow," we echo. She has reported making good progress with her treatment. Most importantly, she's still going to her sessions every week because she really wants to get better. She still wipes the top of her glass or bottle with an antiseptic wipe, but she looks less anxious. I've noticed her and Alex talking a fair bit, their heads bent close. He gives her one of his special smiles – she definitely gets more of them than the rest of us – wrapping an arm around her shoulders, looking pleased. They make a cute couple. I have no idea if it's like dating your doctor, and totally not allowed. He'll be good for her – kind and accepting. She'll blossom even faster with that sort of support. She's never going to be cured, but she can hopefully learn ways to manage her condition. And I'm sure she can be happy.

"Most knowledgeable person is Jennifer," Colin says, raising his glass towards her. "I'm totally coming to you if I need to remember something. You're like a human Google search." Jennifer turns the shade of a raspberry but looks very pleased with herself as we all raise our glasses.

"Funniest person is Claire," Willow says. "I don't know what I'm going to do without your stories every week. The world will be a little greyer without you in it. I'll have to stay in touch for the updates," she decides. There are lots of laughs and murmurs of agreement.

"Hear, hear," David echoes. "Today's was a doozy. There's no way I'm ever going to forget you. I'll be dining out on some of your stories for years to come."

"To Claire."

"Great, I'm the class clown," I murmur. "That sounds about right."

"It's a gift, Claire," Sarah says. "It makes you a joy to be around. You made this course what it was. Your honesty, your willingness to put it all out there, warts and all. It made the rest of us feel able to as well. Without you I wouldn't have got half of what I did from the last eight weeks. I owe you a debt." She raises her glass to me again. Our eyes meet and I find myself barely able to see her through a sudden blur of tears. Those words mean... well, everything.

David reaches over and squeezes my arm. And, just like that, as Sarah and I stare at one another, the weight lifts from my chest.

“Claire,” Alex calls as we’re making our farewells. It’s raining. No one really wants to hang around outside for too long, but no one wants to be the first to leave either. “Have you got a second?”

He walks into the now-empty snug, bathed in the red glow given off by the still-burning embers in the fireplace. Bemused, I follow him to one of the small tables and sit down. “Everything okay?” I ask.

“Everything’s fine.” He reaches over and pats my hand. “I wanted to echo some of what they said at the table earlier. You did make this course special, Claire. You don’t know what a gift that is, being able to make people laugh. But I also know some of it masks your own unhappiness. I sense you think that if you laugh at yourself first, it won’t hurt when other people laugh at you. It’s a deflection, to stop people seeing how much you’re really hurting inside. Let them in, Claire. It’s okay to have those feelings. Sharing them will help you to process.”

For the second time tonight I'm on the verge of tears. He passes me a tissue from a packet he's stored up his sleeve. Can this man really be any more perfect?

"The other thing I wanted to ask was, why didn't you post the letter?"

"What letter?"

"The letter you put in the bin. The divorce papers."

I shift a little, uncomfortable now. "I don't know. It just felt like maybe it was a sign from above that I should think again about it."

He looks at me in that way of his; the one that pierces through my outer veneer, straight into the vulnerable parts at my centre. "I can see why your thoughts might lead you to that conclusion. But they are only thoughts. There are no facts there, other than that you posted your letter into the rubbish bin."

I run a hand through my hair. "Maybe." Do I really believe it was a sign from God? I don't even go to church, so that's not likely. But still, I haven't touched the letter. It's sitting on the side at home. And I did send Ben a text, telling him it was lovely to see him. Maybe Alex has secret psychic skills and has been reading my mind.

"You're strong, Claire. You don't need someone to look after you. You're exactly who you need to be and more than able to live whatever life you choose to lead. Don't let anyone tell you any different. That's all I wanted to say, really. I just felt it needed saying before I left." He pushes to his feet.

I stand more slowly, a little taken aback by the conversation.

There's no one left in the main bar other than Willow. She looks shyly up at Alex from under her lashes as he reaches her table and holds out a hand towards her. She takes it, letting him pull her to her feet. "I'll see you soon, Claire," Willow promises.

I look around. "Did Sarah leave?" I ask. She doesn't have a car. How is she getting home without Gavin?

"Yeah, David offered to drop her off."

Chapter 22

The incessant ringing of the doorbell sucks me from deep sleep. It's still dark outside. Too dark for doorbells to be ringing. Sukie agrees. She jerks up from the space between my legs, where she's taken to sleeping, and leaps onto the wardrobe. Outside, it's still raining, the pitter-patter on the windowpane amplified with every gust of wind. It's been raining solidly for the last four days.

The doorbell rings again. Should I answer it? Who the hell comes around ringing doorbells at – I glance at my watch – three am? Someone must have died. I grab my dressing gown and hurry to the intercom. "Hello?"

"Claire? Oh, thank God!"

"Sarah? Is that you?"

"Can I come in?"

"Of course." I press the release button then open the door to my apartment. She runs up the stairs towards me looking bedraggled.

"I'm so sorry to bother you at this time," she says once she's inside, dropping the small bag she's carrying onto the ground. "I didn't know where else to go."

"You're always welcome here," I assure her, leading her into the lounge. "Do you want a cup of tea?" I flip on the light switch, "Or something stron -" My words dry up. Her face is black and blue. One eye completely swollen shut, the other all shades of pink and purple. "Jesus, what did he do to you?"

"Oh, it's not too bad..."

"Don't! Don't say that. Don't defend him for doing that to you. Do you need a doctor? Should I take you to the hospital?"

"No," she says quickly. "Not the hospital. He'll look for me there. Anyway, I'm better than I was."

I look at her more closely. The bruising doesn't look fresh. It wasn't done this evening. "When did he do it?"

"Wednesday. After group."

"What on earth for?"

"Because he saw David drop me off."

I process that in silence for a moment. "Okay. What do you need from me? What can I do?"

"I need a place to stay for a bit. Somewhere he can't find me."

"You've left him?"

She nods wordlessly.

I pull her into a hug, her small body trembling beneath the wet clothes. "You can have as long as you want. Now, get yourself into the shower. Have you got anything dry in there?" I nod towards the small holdall by the door.

"Not much. I didn't have long." She looks miserable. Second-guessing herself now by the looks of things, hugging herself tight.

"No bother." I disappear into my bedroom and sweep up a clean pair of fleecy pyjamas, my spare dressing gown and the monster feet slippers Jack bought me to replace the ones Bertie ate. "Here." I thrust them all at her. "There are clean towels in the airing cupboard. Help yourself. I'll put the kettle on."

Ten minutes later she emerges from the shower with her hair wrapped in a towel. The dressing gown swamps her. I laugh. "I'm sorry, I think I'm a size or two bigger than you."

"It's lovely and warm," she says, flapping her arms at her sides, looking uncertain.

I take charge. "Sit down and drink your tea. Then we can get some kip and work out everything else in the morning."

"Thank you. I mean, after everything I said to you, I wouldn't have blamed you for slamming the door in my face."

"You don't have to thank me." I push the mug towards her.

She takes a sip, hands trembling.

"You don't have to thank me," I say again. "That's what friends are for. I'm here for you, however long you need me."

"Thank you," she says again. "Really. I didn't know where else to go. I couldn't stay there anymore. Gavin was so angry all the time. Wouldn't even let me leave the house. I've never known him to be that bad. It was as if seeing me with David set something off in him. I mean, he's hit me loads of times before, but I really thought he might kill me this time." A tear rolls down her cheek and plops onto the dressing gown.

I reach for a tissue and hand it to her. "I'm proud of you for deciding to get yourself out." I want to say more. I want to tell her to go to the police. But I know I need to tread gently. This is a big step she's taken.

She scrubs at her eyes with the tissue, tears coming in earnest now. "I wouldn't have bothered you, but I had nowhere else I could think to go. Mum and Dad are convinced he's the best thing since sliced bread, so if I go there, they'll be straight on the phone to him. It was only when I really thought about where I could hide from him, where I had people who would be on my side, I realised he's isolated me from all my old friends. I can't remember the last time I saw any of them. We have dinner with some of his work cronies and their wives once in a while, but that's about it. The rest of the time we stay in, just the two of us. Until the course I didn't see anyone. He hated that I used to go to the pub afterwards with you."

I squeeze her hand. "He was trying to make you weaker, by keeping you isolated. But you're strong. You saw what he was doing, and you got yourself out. You took control. That's incredible. You know what Alex would say: make the best choice for you right now. That's all you can do, and you did exactly that. You confronted the issue head on and got yourself out. I'm so proud of you."

"I wasn't that brave. I crushed up eight sleeping tablets and put them into his Shepherd's Pie."

"How did you avoid eating any?"

"I told him I wasn't hungry. It wasn't much of a stretch – I've been vomiting up a bit of blood since the other night, so I haven't been able to keep much down."

"Jesus, Sarah, do you hear yourself? That's crazy, we really need to get you to see a doctor."

She nods, looking tired, it's as if her head's too heavy for her body. "Not the hospital though. He'll look for me there."

"Not the hospital," I agree. I have no great desire to bump into Gavin.

She drains the last of her tea. "He'll come looking for me tomorrow. I don't know if he knows where you live, but if he does then you can expect a visit."

"I don't care. We'll cross that bridge in the morning. I'm proud of you," I tell her again, hugging her close. She's so small and fragile, it's a wonder she's not more broken than she is.

We pull apart. "I'm happy to sleep here," she says, patting the sofa.

"Nonsense. I spent fifteen years sleeping with Ben. Assuming you're not suffering from terrible flatulence?" I look at her. She shakes her head. "Then, I think we'll be fine sharing my bed. That's if you don't mind?"

"I don't mind." She smiles her first smile.

I show her into the bedroom. "I'll take this side," I suggest, pointing at the side closest to the wardrobe. "Sukie's been known to take a swallow dive from up there every once in a while. You've probably got enough injuries to be going on with." This time a little giggle escapes Sarah – no doubt at the memory of what happened the last time Sukie jumped on my face. Warmth blooms inside my chest, pushing away a little of the chill prompted by thoughts of what Gavin's done to her.

I lie awake most the night, listening to her breathe and wondering how the hell anyone could hurt her. She deserves better. If I have anything to do with it, she'll get it.

"Claire... Claire!"

Gavin.

The voice sends a shiver through me. We've had nearly a week of peace, but we both knew it was too good to last. I turn to face him. He was clearly waiting for me to come out of my apartment. "Oh, hi." I attempt a smile, but I'm not sure I get away with it. My face feels tight with tension. I have no doubt it looked more of a grimace.

"Have you seen her?"

I decide to act dumb. "Who?"

He frowns, some of the nice-guy act slipping for a second. "Don't play silly buggers with me. Have you seen my wife?"

"Sarah? Is she okay?"

His lip curls a little. "You know perfectly well if she's okay, or not. Where is she?"

"What do you mean, where is she? Is she missing?" Okay, my voice sounds high and totally false. I need to get a hold of myself before I give the game away. I resist the urge to look up at the apartment window, for fear she might be looking out and Gavin will see her.

Gavin steps towards me. I've never thought of him as a big man before. Certainly he isn't compared to David, but as angry as he is and at close proximity he's threatening as hell. He drops his voice, sending a shiver of fear cascading down my spine. "Don't fucking mess with me. Tell me where she is. Is she with him? That fucking lumpen piece of shit?"

This time I don't have to act my confusion. "Who? What? Look, I really don't know what you're talking about." I step away from him, wanting some space. He follows me. "I need to go, I'm late for a client." The client is David. I have to finish off the last of his meditation space. I also agreed with Sarah I'd tell him what happened. Warn him in case of exactly this.

"Just tell me, is she with David?"

I flinch. It's like he plucked the name straight out of my brain. "Why would she be with David?" I need to get away from here, but the idiot's standing directly in front of my car. "Can you get out my way, please?"

He doesn't. He steps closer. He's not bothering to hide his anger at all now. He leans into me, his hot breath singeing my cheek. "I swear to God, Claire, if I find out she's with him, I'm going to kill the fucker. You tell that shit-stain from me, he's a dead man."

I swallow, mouth dry. "Are we done here?"

He clamps a hand around my wrist as I try to walk around him. "If I find out you knew something and didn't tell me, I'll be back for you too."

I shake my hand free, my own anger bubbling to the surface now. I refuse to be another of his victims. "I'm not your wife, Gavin. If you hit me, I'll call the police. If you threaten me again, I'll call the police. Back away this minute or I'll start screaming."

He must realise he's gone too far because his aggression level drops a notch. He shifts to what sounds like pleading now. "I just want to know where she is. I love her."

Those words only serve to amplify my anger. The bloody cheek of the man. Was he planning to love her to death? I can't help myself, the words spill out of me. "You love her? You're joking, aren't you? Maybe you should've thought about that when you were punching her in the face or cracking her ribs. If she's left you, then I'm glad. I saw the bruises, same as everyone else. If she's had the guts to get out, then good. I won't lie; I wanted her to leave you. You're a sick man. You need help." My chest is heaving by the time I'm finished.

Gavin's face is now scarlet with rage. "You think you're so much better than me, but you're not. No wonder your husband ran off with someone else. Couldn't wait to get away from your stuck-up, priggish, fat arse. I should do him a favour-"

I've had enough. More than enough. I cut him off mid-sentence, "You have five seconds before I start screaming."

His hand lashes out and gabs me around the throat. Any tighter and I'll be struggling to breathe. "We were happy until you lot started dripping poison in her ear."

"You might've been happy," I gasp out between breaths as my fingers try to claw his hands away, "but she never was. Let go of me!"

"Claire, are you okay?" It's Jack. He's behind us. He must have come out of his apartment.

Gavin drops his hand from my throat.

I stare Gavin straight in the eye as I say, "I'm okay, thanks, Jack. Gavin was just leaving." I make sure Jack knows the shit's name in case something happens to me. "I think we're done here. Will you get out of my way now, please, or do I have to call the police?" I sense Jack still standing on the steps behind us. He's watching Gavin like a hawk, prepared to intervene if need be.

Gavin steps away. "I'm going." He drops his voice to a whisper. "But I'll be watching. Oh, and tell Sarah from me, she'd better hope I never find her, because the mood I'm in... if she thought it was bad before, she's seen nothing yet."

I shiver. "Get some help, man, for everyone's sake," I say, shoulder barging him out of my way. Hands trembling, I unlock my car, get inside and immediately re-lock the door.

Gavin strides away without bothering to look back, fists clenching and unclenching at his sides. Jack watches him leave, then turns towards me in the car. "You okay?" he mouths through the glass.

I nod, but it takes at least five minutes before my hands have stopped trembling enough that I can drive away.

Chapter 23

"Hello, darling," Mummy's voice calls out as I let myself back into the apartment. I'm out of breath. Thankfully there had been no sign of Gavin waiting outside, but I'd sprinted from the car to the house anyway just in case.

Mummy's sprawled on the sofa, having made herself very at home. "I wasn't expecting you," I say, bending to kiss her powdery cheek. I receive the usual static shock. "Fuck!"

"Language, Claire. Really, I've taught you better than that".

Sarah's expression's bemused. People often look like that when they meet my mother for the first time. I should have warned her really. "So why are you here?"

"No reason really." My mother is a terrible liar. She tugs her ear whenever she fibs. Daddy used to think it was hysterical. Her fingers are tugging at the lobe right now. She catches me watching her.

I raise an eyebrow.

"I'd just been for lunch with Marjorie and thought I'd pop in to see how you are. She mentioned she saw Ben leaving the other morning."

There it is. The truth explodes like a bomb between us, a cloud of unvoiced, unanswered questions hanging in the room for a good thirty seconds afterwards.

"Well? Are you going to explain yourself?"

"No," I decide. "It's really none of your business."

"Claire, you know this is a terrible idea. I was sure he'd come crawling back at some point, I just didn't think it would be quite so soon. You're not strong enough yet, so I need to be strong for you. Ben's no good for you, and deep down you know it too."

"I know no such thing. He was perfectly good for me for the last fifteen years."

My mother purses her lips. "No, he wasn't actually. Anyway, you deserve someone who treats you better."

I'm really not in the mood to get into this right now. Sarah's head is toing and froing like she's watching a Federer-Nadal match at Wimbledon. Distraction is my only hope. "So, you've met Sarah then?" I push away any guilt I ought to feel at throwing her under the bus.

Mummy smiles over at my friend. "Oh yes, what a charming girl. We've been having a perfectly lovely chat since I arrived." Sarah grins at her.

"Cup of tea?" I offer them both. "Or something stronger? Vodka maybe? Or brandy? I think I have a bottle somewhere."

"Darling, it's only half past five. It's a little early to start drinking, don't you think? Have you got a drink problem?" She peers at me, as though the truth might be written into the whites of my eyes. I guess if I was in liver failure, it might be.

I wave towards the window at the inky darkness beyond. "It's dark, isn't it?"

"It's barely ever light at this time of year. If that's your yardstick, I'm definitely worried."

"Bah! So, do you want a drink?" I look to Sarah for some support. After my altercation with Gavin earlier, I really need something stronger than a cup of tea. My hands have been trembling all afternoon. It wasn't helped that David wanted to come storming round here once he heard what had been going on. And that was before I told him about being door-stepped by Gavin. At that point he became off-the-scale angry. He's always appeared to be the gentlest of giants. I've never believed him before when he said he needed to manage his anger. I do now.

I suppose his concern for Sarah's wellbeing was really quite touching, but I was totally over violent confrontations of any sort. It was only my pleas that I couldn't cope with a murder being committed at my address for fear of the landlord evicting me, that persuaded him to hold fast. That, and I've promised to suggest to Sarah that she stay with David for a bit, since Gavin doesn't appear to know where he lives. I still have to break the news to her. That's another good reason why I need a stiff drink.

"I'll have a cup of tea. I can make it," Sarah offers.

"Oh, no, you won't." There's no way I'm letting her leave me alone with my mother. She'll never let go that little factoid about Ben being here at the crack of dawn. "Sit down. My guests don't make their own drinks."

"I don't think I count as a guest if I've stayed here a week," Sarah insists.

"I didn't realise you were staying here," Mummy pipes up, doubly interested in her now.

It's my perfect excuse to escape. I leave Sarah trapped, forced to explain to Mummy why she's living with me. I'm surprised it hasn't come up in their conversation before I got home. That leads me to believe Mummy can't have been here all that long or she'd already have wormed it out of Sarah. With a quick apologetic smile over my shoulder, I send up a prayer of thanks and scuttle into the kitchen alone, leaving them chatting behind me.

I emerge five minutes later with a tray containing three steaming mugs of tea and a plate of biscuits. One of the mugs – mine – has an additional slug of brandy inside. Medicinal, of course.

Mummy pounces on the tray as soon as I put it down, handing out the cups with no attention given to who gets which. I watch with dismay as she hands me a virgin mug of tea and keeps the brandy one for herself. I swear the devious mare knows exactly what she's doing. When she says *cheers* before taking a long slurp, I'm certain.

There's nothing for it but to tell Sarah the bad news. I grab a fortifying chocolate digestive – because if ever there was a time for stress eating this is it – demolish it in three bites, then before I have a chance to lose my nerve, announce, "Gavin was waiting outside the house this morning." Biscuit crumbs spray from my mouth in my haste to get the words out.

Sarah's complexion drains to milk white. Her mouth opens and then closes again. Physically, she appears to shrink a little. I hate the impact this man has on my friend

"Is Gavin your husband?" Mummy asks in a gentle voice, reaching across to take hold of Sarah's hand.

Sarah manages to nod. Her eyes are brimming with tears now.

"And did he give you those bruises?" She nods towards Sarah's eye. It's still yellowish in places, even after all this time.

Sarah nods again. Now tears do spill over onto her cheeks.

"David wants you to go and stay with him. He was quite adamant about it," I say.

"Who's David?" Mummy asks.

"He's a friend from our course."

"I don't think..." Sarah's voice is little more than a whisper now.

"Staying with a man won't help things at all," Mummy says in a matter-of-fact voice. "If your husband finds you there, it will only make matters worse."

Sarah nods. "If he's found me here then I won't be safe. Neither will you. I can't risk anyone else getting hurt."

"He doesn't know you're here. He just suspects I might know where you are," I say.

"How was he?"

"Cross. He already suspects you're with David. You're right, Mum, it'll only make things worse if Sarah does go there and Gavin finds out."

"I need to think about where else I can stay. I can't stay here -"

"Don't talk nonsense. Of course you can. I'm big enough and ugly enough to stand up to your bully of a husband."

"You don't know what he's like."

"Oh, I think I've got a fairly good idea."

"This is silly. I won't let you put yourself in harm's way because of me. I'd never forgive myself if something happened to you.

"I'm not letting you -"

"Enough, both of you." Mummy drains the last of her tea, smacking her lips appreciatively when she has finished. "The answer's very simple."

We both look at her; I imagine my expression must be as blank as my guest's.

"Sarah can come and stay with me. This bully of a husband won't have the foggiest where she is because no one will know, except for you, Claire darling. But you barely come to my house, so it's not like he's likely to follow you round there at all."

"That's not fair, I..." I struggle to recall the last time I went round to Mum's. When was it she had the flu? Last Christmas? That's nearly a year ago. The rest of the time she's come here.

"Oh, really, Mrs Lane, I couldn't be such a nuisance to you," Sarah is protesting.

"Nonsense. I'd enjoy the company. And please do call me Daphne, dear. Anyway, you'd be doing me a favour. I'm living in a three-bedroom house all on my own. I rattle around in there, to be honest. I've even considered selling up and moving somewhere smaller. Marjorie's bought herself a lovely little bungalow down on the coast. She's moving to be closer to her daughter. I thought a bungalow might be a nice idea for me too. Help me keep my independence for longer."

What the actual hell! "But you can't sell!"

She looks at me, blinking. "Why ever not?"

"Because... because that's our home. And if you move to the coast, you'll be so far away! I need you."

"Bless you, darling. I love you too. I wasn't thinking about moving to the coast. Just to a bungalow somewhere around here. Anyway, that's a decision for another day. For now, what do you say?" She looks at Sarah. "Will you come and stay?"

She looks at me. I nod. "Well, if you're quite sure you don't mind?"

"Not at all. I'm excited to have the company. Shall we shake on it?"

Sarah grins and sticks out her hand. Mummy takes it. There's a crack of positive ion exchange and Sarah grunts with surprise. I guess that seals the deal.

Chapter 24

Somehow, we manage to get Sarah out under cover of darkness without any problems. She climbs into Mummy's car carrying her small bag of stuff and I watch them drive off, feeling a little guilty that Mummy is probably over the limit, having serendipitously had a double shot of brandy in her tea. I don't relax until Sarah's text arrives to let me know they've arrived safe and sound.

It turns out to be by far the best solution for everyone. Sarah has a room and bed all to herself, as have I. More particularly, Gavin's taken to stalking me daily now. Several times Jack has appeared in the nick of time to see him off when Gavin's been harassing me by my car. I'm not sure what I'd have done without my neighbour on a couple of those occasions.

Plus, Ben's been round more than once. It would have been beyond awkward if Sarah had been there too when that happened. I'm not really sure why he's visiting me. I've reiterated the points I made the first time – mainly that he's expecting a baby with another woman – but the message hasn't yet sunk in. Worse, I quite like it. Even Sukie has taken to sitting on his lap when he's here, the turncoat.

He's waiting for me when I pull into my normal space. "Where have you been?" he asks as soon as I get out the car.

"Seeing a client." I'm tired. The client I spent the afternoon with is one of my more challenging ones, but if I get this one right she's hugely well connected, so it's worth putting the effort in.

"Claire!"

I groan, recognising Gavin's voice. I really don't need this right now.

"Who's that?" Ben asks, craning to see into the deepening darkness.

"My friend's ex." I turn to face Gavin. "What do you want?"

He looks terrible, his face black and blue. "Did you walk into a door?" I can't help making the dig.

Gavin isn't amused. He clenches his fist and takes a step closer.

"Hey, back off there, buster," Ben says. He sounds so ridiculous saying it, I have the totally inappropriate urge to giggle. He's also a good head shorter than Gavin, so he looks a little silly trying to face him off. I suspect if he knew quite how much damage Gavin has the potential to inflict with those fists – albeit to women – Ben might be a little warier. Time to rein in Scrappy Doo.

I place a hand on his shoulder. "It's alright Ben. He was just leaving, weren't you, Gavin?"

"Where is she?" Gavin spits at me.

"I've told you before and I'll tell you again: I don't know. A long way away from here, if she has any sense. You need to back off and leave before I call the police. This is harassment."

"I think we should call the police now," Ben says. His voice is higher than normal and clipped, making him sound more than a little pompous. He's rising up on to the balls of his feet as if to make himself taller as he waves his mobile around.

Gavin frowns down, looking at him the same way I look at yappy dogs. "Who is this prick?" He bumps his chest against Ben's, who bounces back a few steps. "Hold on, did she call you Ben? Are you the ex? The one who ran off with an older woman?"

Shit, how embarrassing, Gavin knows all about my marital woes. This is really not the time or place to get into this. "Just go home, Gavin. Sarah's not here."

Ben's face is flushed pink. He's staring at me now, itching to ask how it is that this guy knows all about his love life. But I don't want to get into all that right this second.

"Maybe you should sort out your own life out before you start interfering with someone else's," Gavin says, clearly taking some pleasure in our joint discomfort.

I huff. "If you're quite done, I'm going inside for a hot bath and a glass of wine." I walk around Gavin. I can't resist throwing back, "Same time tomorrow then?"

"Fuck you too, Claire. I hope you go to hell."

"Yeah, well, see you there." I run up the steps with Ben close on my heels. He's positively vibrating with rage.

“How the hell does that man know who I am?” he asks as soon as we’re through the front door.

Jack chooses that exact second to walk out of his apartment. Because, of course he would. He sees Ben with me and frowns. He chooses to ignore Ben and looks straight at me. “Was that prick giving you hassle again?”

I sigh. “Yeah, it’s fine. He’s gone.”

Jack frowns. “This isn’t a joke anymore. It’s getting to be serious, Claire. You need to report him before he hurts someone.”

“Someone else, you mean. And it was never a joke, by the way.”

“I know that, I’m just worried for you.”

That comment warms my heart a little.

“Umm, I don’t mean to interrupt here, but what the hell has any of this got to do with you, Wilton?” Ben glowers at Jack. “I think you should keep your nose out of my wife’s business.”

Jack barks a laugh. “Seriously, Claire. After everything you’ve been through, you’re going back to this? What the hell are you thinking?”

Warm feeling well and truly gone, I scowl back at him. “I’m not thinking anything. I’m too tired to think. In fact, I’m too tired for any of this.” I wave my arms in the direction of the pair of them.

“Yeah, well, your life is pretty exhausting,” Jack says huffily.

"Tell me about it," I say, the second before he slams the street door.

"I don't know why you're bothering to talk to that loser," Ben says, following me up the stairs.

I swing round to look at him. "And I don't know why you're even here. Haven't you got a pregnant partner at home?"

He flushes deep pink. "I need to talk to you."

I sigh. "I'm really tired. It's been a hell of a day." I push my key into the lock and open the front door, sniffing gingerly in case Sukie has resumed her dirty protest. But ever since I had the cat flap fitted, she's been cleaner. Today is no different. She trots into the hallway to greet me, rubbing herself against my leg when I bend down to stroke her, before sniffing at Ben's. He's followed me inside. I'm too tired to fight him. "What do you want?"

He follows me into the kitchen, watching as I dish up a plate of food for Sukie. She purrs as I put it down for her. I can't resist stopping to stroke her again. "She didn't used to like you," he says.

"I know." I straighten, turning to face him finally. "Was that really what you wanted to talk about? The cat?"

"What? No! Of course not. I wanted to know why you signed them. I thought we were thinking about things first."

Okay, I'm confused now. "Signed what? What are you talking about?"

"The divorce papers. My solicitor called to tell me he got them this morning. I thought we were... I don't know. It just all seems so final." He runs his hand through his hair. "I didn't think we were there yet."

"What the hell are you talking about? The divorce papers are..." I stop. The brown envelope is gone from the side where it has sat ever since my aborted attempt at posting them. It has crossed my mind that I really ought to post them a few times, but I haven't been able to bring myself to take that final step for some reason. There's no doubt I've enjoyed the last few days with Ben. I walk to the sideboard and peer over the side to check they haven't fallen down the back. Nothing. "Where the hell has it gone?"

"What?"

"The letter. It was right here. I didn't post it."

"Well, someone did. My solicitor had it on his desk this morning."

"But how?"

"Could someone have picked it up and posted it for you?"

I run a hand through my hair, trying to get my brain to think. Too much stress doesn't help. My heart is racing now. I ought to breathe, but I'm too fazed. What do I know as fact? The solicitor has received the divorce papers. I'm getting divorced. But how? "Sarah wouldn't have posted it; she knew what was inside. She knew they were too important to me," I say.

Ben looks confused, he doesn't even know who Sarah is.

A thought hits me, like a mallet straight between the eyes. "Mummy." She was so annoyed I was seeing Ben again, I wouldn't put it past her at all to pick up the letter, slip it into her tote bag and post it. Sarah could have told her what was inside. "That snake!" I exclaim.

I grab my mobile out the top of my bag. "Did you post it?" I say, before Mummy's halfway through her usual *hello, darling*.

"Post what?" she says. She knows exactly what I'm talking about. She's even a terrible liar on the phone when I can't see her. If I could, I know for a fact she'd be tugging on her ear lobe.

"You know what I'm talking about." The anger is burning inside me now, red hot. It bursts from me in angry verbal spurts. "That was not your call to make. What I decide to do regarding my marriage is *none* of your business. It's *my* marriage, not yours. You have *no* right to interfere in it. None at all."

There's a little sniff from her end and then in a smaller voice, "He's no good for you, Claire. You know that as well as I do."

"I know no such thing. I hate you for doing this." I end the call and promptly burst into tears. Ben gathers me into his arms, soothing me with quiet words of reassurance, that we can stop the divorce at any point we want, that nothing is set in stone even now at this late stage. I let his words rush over me, feeling protected for the first time in a long time. So when he presses his lips gently to mine, I don't stop him.

Chapter 25

I wake to find I'm unable to move my legs. I assume Sukie's to blame, her big, fat body draped across them and preventing me from moving thanks to the excessive amounts of chicken she insists I feed her. But no, Sukie's watching me from on top of the wardrobe. A loud snore alerts me to a second human presence in the bed. Ben.

I sit up quickly, grabbing the duvet to cover myself while I check whether or not I'm naked. I'm not, thank God. I'm still wearing my ugliest flannel pyjamas. Memories roll back into place. We nearly had sex! We had almost-sex. Lots of kissing and dry humping like teenagers. What the hell had I been thinking? Well, I wasn't thinking, that much is clear. Then I recall the argument with Mummy.

The hissy fit I threw over the phone wasn't my finest moment, but I still think she was out of order taking the decision out of my hands. It was mine to make, not hers. Then the comforting and the kissing and... Dear God, I nearly had sex with a married man. Well, not a married man, because he's still married to me. Or is he? The signed papers are with the solicitor. Are we divorced now? I'm not sure. Either way, I nearly had sex with a man who has another significant other. A significant other who is expecting a baby with him. What the hell was I thinking? My breaths shorten. I'm a stupid, selfish bitch. I wasn't thinking about anyone other than myself last night, and now I've nearly inflicted terrible harm on at least two other people. Bella and myself. Three if I include the baby. Because nothing good can come of a relationship started under those sorts of circumstances. Even with what little happened, I'm ashamed of myself. Waves of panic ripple over me, threatening to overwhelm me.

Stop!

Breathe.

I draw a long, deep breath then release it slowly, clearing my mind every time the thoughts about what might have happened as a result of my actions – what might still happen – start to overwhelm me again.

Breathe in.

Breathe out.

In.

Out.

Slowly, the panic recedes.

"What are you doing?" Ben asks.

I open my eyes and find he's staring at me with eyes bloodshot from lack of sleep.

He rubs at them blearily. "I dreamt I was in a pit of snakes and I didn't know how to get out of it, only that they were close, and I was in danger. Then I woke up and realised it was you hissing."

"I was breathing. Meditating."

He snorts. "Meditating! You? Really? Since when?"

"Since... well, it doesn't matter." For some reason I have no desire to share anything about my course with him. I especially don't want to share why I needed to take it in the first place. He has a low enough opinion of me already without adding panic attacks to the mix.

Ben glances at his watch and grimaces. "I'd better go." He jumps out of the bed and begins pulling on his jeans.

"Why? Where were you meant to be?" It's Saturday. He must have made up some sort of story to explain his absence.

"I'm meeting the lads for a round of golf. Up in Lincolnshire."

More pieces fall into place. "Is that where she thinks you are now? In Lincolnshire with Mark?" Jesus, could this get any more sordid? My anxiety is replaced by self-loathing. I'm as bad as her. "So, what is this then? Did you just fancy a little romp on the side? Is she too pregnant now to feel like having sex? Am I your Plan B? Sorry I didn't roll straight onto my back and spread my legs for you."

Ben flushes a little and my stomach lurches with the grim realisation I may have hit somewhere close to the truth.

"For god's sake, Ben. What the hell has happened to you? When did you become such a shit, and when did I become such a fool to nearly fall for it twice over? I think you should leave."

"It's not like that. I didn't intend for this to happen. I didn't come around here expecting... I didn't intend to stay..."

"What? You wouldn't have had sex last night if I'd been up for it? Isn't it bad enough you've been kissing another woman behind Bella's back?"

"I'm not sorry, even if you are. I know that probably makes me a bad person, but I'm glad it happened. You didn't seem to be complaining all the time I was kissing you either."

He's right. Shame shrivels my insides. "No. And now I have to live with the consequences of my choices. I'm not very proud of myself right now." I run a hand through my tangled nest of hair. "So, tell me something: why bother to come around here at all to have a go about me sending in the divorce papers? I mean, what is it to you? Why are you even bothered? You'll have to divorce me at some point so you can marry Bella."

He screws up his face. "I don't know if I want to marry Bella," he says, pulling on his t-shirt. "I mean, I'm happy about the baby – of course I am – but I don't know if we're really compatible as a couple in the long term. Not like you and I were. With you it was just... easy. I didn't have to think about it. Bella is bloody hard work. When I do see her, we seem to spend most of our time rowing. Fortunately, that's not all that often. She's always busy; work's taking over her life. Not just during the week, she's at it all weekend too, forever organising some social event or other, claiming they're good for networking with clients. I hate the bloody things." He sits down heavily on the edge of the bed to pull on his socks.

"You know me," he continues. "I like nothing better than slippers and trackie bottoms at the weekend. When I tell her I don't want to go to the bloody things she kicks off – tells me I'm not being supportive. But seriously, I can't honestly think of anything worse. It's bad enough having to do that shit during the week for work. It's too much to be expected to do it all weekend too. God only knows what's going to happen when the baby arrives." He throws his hands up in frustration. "I can only imagine it'll all be ten times worse because she'll be off out gallivanting, and I'll be the one left holding the baby."

I'd been enjoying hearing him bitch about Bella's shortcomings, but that last comment stirs my ire. "I always knew you were selfish, Ben, but this takes the biscuit. Are you really resenting the fact that you might have to look after your own child? What did you imagine it was going to be like, having one, for all those years we were trying?"

He faces me, standing to button up his jeans. "Well, I thought we'd look after it together. Not that you'd be gone ninety percent of the time and I'd have to look after it on my own. In fact, I know it wouldn't have been like that because you wouldn't have wanted to be away from your own child. Not like her. She's already booked the poor kid in at a nursery. From seven until seven. And she's only planning to take a month off after it's born.

We'll barely see the poor thing. Especially if we're out doing stuff at the weekends too. Maybe I can arrange to meet it for a drink at the pub when it's eighteen."

I can't fathom not wanting to be home with my baby were I lucky enough to have one.

Ben's really into his flow now. "It's just not what I imagined when I thought about becoming a dad. I know that's what some people choose, and that's fine for them, but I hate the idea. The only option I can think of is to look into taking some paternity leave." He lifts his gaze to mine. "You agree, don't you? It's not right to do that to a tiny baby."

I say nothing, but he takes my silence for agreement. "See. That's what makes you who you are. It makes you the woman I love."

I shake my head, trying to clear away the impact those words still have on me. I've wanted to hear them for so long. Dreamt of him saying them more times than I can possibly count and wept buckets when I realised it wasn't real. But not now. It's far too late.

"So, let me get this straight. You think that because you might have to be a full-time parent to your own child, that you don't think you can see yourself marrying her. In fact, what you'd quite like is to have the mother of your child home looking after it, with me as a standby mistress when she's too knackered for sex, and then you can pop in to see your kid when it suits you. Preferably when it's asleep, I imagine."

He sits back down on the bed beside me. "No. Not at all. I want this baby. I do. I've always wanted a baby, we both did. You know that. What I don't want is a baby with Bella."

I flop back against the pillows. "Bit of a problem there then."

"But don't you see? We can make it so that you and I bring up this baby. Sure, Bella will be part of its life some of the time, there's no getting away from that, but if the amount of work she's piling on to make up for that client she lost is anything to go by, then she'll barely be around much. She can't afford to be. Not and stop the business from going under. That's where we come in." His eyes are bright with excitement now. "You and I can bring up this baby." I start to object, but he raises his hand. "No, just wait a moment. Think about it. It's the perfect solution. Isn't this what we always wanted? I mean, I know you'd prefer a child of your own, but isn't this the next best thing? It would be fifty percent ours. And I know you'd be the best mother this child could ever wish for."

And there it is. His whole fantasy life laid out in front of me; Him, a baby, living together as husband and wife again. Everything I ever wanted. Except there's his mistress to negotiate childcare with. And the fact that he was unfaithful to me. And her, come to think of it. Because knowing he'd been kissing and dry humping someone else would be enough to break Bella's heart.

What the hell am I even doing considering it? Because I am considering it. "Ben-"

He holds a hand up. "No, don't say anything yet. Don't decide quickly. This is too important. Think about it before you do. It deserves that much, at least." He bends over to tie his shoelaces, then leans forward to kiss me. I let him. It's all so familiar, it seems like the natural thing to do. "Think about it," he says again. "I've got an appointment with Doctor Hammond on Wednesday about my back; if it's okay with you, I'll come around afterwards to see what you're thinking. Would that be okay?"

I nod, and he smiles. "Have a nice time with Mark," I call as he sees himself out. It's exactly the kind of parting we'd have had before – except some of those times he wouldn't have been meeting Mark. Some of those times he'd have been creeping off to see Bella. The thought leaves me feeling queasy.

By mid-afternoon I've cleaned the whole flat from top to bottom. Sukie's retreated up the tree to protest my excessive use of the hoover, especially when I insisted on hoovering her nest on top of the wardrobe, so now I'm up on the shed with the ladder to retrieve her. My remarkable productivity levels have all been displacement activities in order to avoid thinking about Ben's offer. That, and because the alternative would be eating a week's worth of groceries. I tried to meditate, but my mind just couldn't unplug from thoughts about Ben and babies.

"Be careful," Jack calls from the back door. He's propped against the doorframe, watching me, wearing his new Beckham boot. No crutches.

"I'm very experienced," I reassure him, jutting out a practised hip to balance the ladder on, as I try to coax Sukie down; "Come on, you little rat bag," I croon, "I've put the hoover away for another month or so. You can come home. Come down now." She watches me from her nest in the branches, ears twitching at my little noises of encouragement.

Rain drops pitter-patter onto the shed roof beside me. The wind's picking up again too. "Come on," I call, "You don't want to get caught out in the rain." It seems she agrees with me because just as the intensity increases from occasional spots to a steady drizzle, she tiptoes onto the first rung. It takes her another five minutes to reach the shed roof, by which time it's raining in earnest. She leaps onto the fence, runs along the panels and then onto the flat roof and up, into the apartment window before I've even climbed down off the shed. "You're welcome," I call after her. Ungrateful madam.

Jack is waiting for me by the back door. "So, Everett spent the night then?"

I cringe a little, knowing how bad this looks. "Yes," I admit. I don't bother to tell him we didn't have sex, but for some inexplicable reason I do feel the need to make an excuse. "I received some bad news, he was just there at the right time when I really needed some company."

He frowns. "What bad news?"

"My mother posted my divorce papers off without my knowledge."

He's silent. As if waiting for something more. "That's it?" he says eventually.

"What do you mean, *that's it*! It was an outrageous thing to do when I wasn't mentally or emotionally ready."

"You were going to post them yourself the other day. What's the big deal?"

Who does this man think he is? "But I didn't. And then I couldn't. I wasn't ready. I needed to post them when I was ready."

"And so, because of that, you fell back into bed with the same man who cheated on you. That makes sense."

Anger and shame loosen my tongue. "Not that it's any of your business, but I fell into bed with my husband."

"Uh-huh, the husband who's expecting a child with the woman he had an affair with. Really, I knew you could be a bit dippy sometimes, but that takes the biscuit for stupid decisions."

Hands on my hips, I turn on him. Dippy, for God's sake! I'm bloody offended. "For your information, he doesn't want us to get divorced – he wants us to bring up his baby together –

that's why he came round in the first place, because his solicitor rang to say he'd received my papers. The ones I hadn't posted but my interfering mother had."

"Yes, well, I can see why that's what he wants. To have his cake and eat it and all that. But what do you want, Claire? Or do your needs always come second to making sure that Ben gets what he wants? I mean, can you really be happy with a man who only ever puts himself first? I have no doubt you loved him. Maybe you think you still do. What's less clear to me is whether he loves you enough to put what's right for you first."

It's pouring now, but I'm stuck in this garden until Jack decides to move out of my way. Bertie's barking for attention back in his flat. I cross my arms. "I'm not sure at what point my life became any concern of yours."

He produces an indignant grunt. "Well, you've done a pretty good job of inflicting your life's woes on me recently. I didn't think today would be any different. Or is it that now you've got Ben back to run around after, all the rest of us get pushed to the wayside?"

"Look, I appreciate your concern, I do, but I need to make these decisions for myself." My landline starts to ring upstairs in the flat. No one ever uses my landline except Mummy. "My phone's ringing, I need to go."

I push past him and run up the stairs, tripping over Sukie who's lying just the other side of the door and narrowly avoiding knocking myself out. "That's evil," I tell her, reaching for the phone at the very moment it stops ringing.

I grab for my mobile instead. I have three missed calls, all from my mother. I guess she wants to make friends again. So do I. I could really do with talking all this Ben stuff through with someone. I press the recall button.

A man answers. "Hello."

I'm confused, pulling the phone away from my ear to make sure I've pressed the correct number. I have, it's definitely Mummy's number. "Who's this please?"

"Is that Claire?"

"Yes, speaking."

"It's William here. I'm a friend of your mother's. Look, I'm terribly sorry to have to tell you this, but Daphne was taken ill in the early hours of this morning. They think it might have been a heart attack. Sarah's gone with her to the hospital. She's at St George's."

Chapter 26

This is not the same part of A&E I visited with Jack. No waiting on a seat with countless families and couples with their broken bones, cuts and scrapes. Instead, I'm rushed through into a different area, one that's filled with machines that bleep, manned by serious-looking medical professionals. Mummy is wired up. Looking small and terribly frail, cannulas adorn both creases of her elbows waiting for the next time they need to draw blood or inject drugs. Above her head a heart monitor bleeps continuously, counting the steady beats of her heart. Sarah is sitting at her bedside, holding Mummy's hand, her head bent over as Mummy sleeps.

I watch them for a few seconds, comforted by the machine's ponderous count. Then, when I've reassured myself she really is alive, I whisper, "Sarah."

My friend stirs slowly. She looks incredibly tired, wearing dark purple shadows under both her eyes that have nothing to do with her brute of a husband for once. How long have they been here? Were they here when I was still having almost-sex with Ben? When I was cleaning the flat? Rescuing Sukie? Arguing with Jack? How long? "You're here," she says. "Your mum will be pleased to see you."

"What happened?"

"Daphne wasn't feeling all that well last night. Not very hungry – she rarely is – but worse than usual, even. I was worried about her. I nearly called you then, but I figured you'd need a night to cool off after your row with her. Anyway, I heard a crash very early this morning. She said she'd needed a wee. Had a funny turn, next thing she knew she was on the floor. I called 999, I didn't know what else to do. We've been here ever since."

I pull out her folder of medical notes, can't understand a word and put them back again. "Why didn't you call me sooner?"

Sarah runs an agitated hand through her hair. "It was all a bit of a rush. We left our phones at home. William found out from her neighbour what had happened and came in to see if we needed anything. I gave him the keys to the house and asked him to call you. He promised he would, but couldn't get into your mother's phone to get your number to begin with, and she was too out of it to remember her access code. She got there in the end, but it took a while. I'm sorry, mine was dead – I've deliberately powered mine down since... well, you know."

I nod, grabbing a chair and pulling it up beside the bed. "Well, I'm here now. How is she?"

"Hanging in there. It was touch and go for a while, but she seems to be getting a little stronger. Seeing you will be just the tonic she needs." Sarah pushes herself slowly to her feet. "They're taking her up to the ward in a minute. They want to keep her under observation… mentioned something about probably needing to do an operation tomorrow. They were waiting for you to get here to tell you the details." She presses a soft kiss onto my mother's forehead. "I'll let you go up with her, if you're okay here alone for a bit? I'll pop home, if you don't mind? I need a shower and at least an hour of sleep." She looks back down at Mummy. "Tell her I'll be back in later with her nightie and wash bag. She's been complaining about the hospital robe, worried someone might see her bottom."

I smile at her. That sounds like the mother I know. "I don't suppose anyone is looking. But thank you. Thank you for being here for here when I wasn't." I choke out the words over the ball of emotion that's wedged itself within my throat.

Sarah pats my shoulder. "She's a tough cookie."

I only nod. I want to ask her if this is my fault. If the horrible words I said to her yesterday have caused this. I'm not sure I'll ever be able to forgive myself, even if she can. What the hell was I thinking? Shouting at her like a spoiled brat. Guilt churns in my stomach, threatening to bring back up my porridge from earlier.

I reach for Mummy's hand, smiling as the familiar crackle of static bounces between us. It's enough to wake her, tired blue eyes blinking into focus. "Hi," I say, feeling a little shy. "How are you feeling?"

"Hello, my darling. Oh, not too bad. I'm sorry about all this bother."

"No bother." I smile and pat her arm. "How are you doing?"

She runs a hand over her face. “Oh, a little more ragged than I’d like, but hanging on.”

A nurse bustles into the room. “Oh good, you’re awake again.” She looks across at me. “And who’s this then?”

“My daughter,” Mummy says, looking at me with pride. It chokes me up again, so anything I might have wanted to say is now impossible unless I plan to start blubbing. She needs me to be strong, not fall to pieces, but I’m failing at the first hurdle.

The nurse smiles at me. “I’ve been hearing all about you, Claire. It’s lovely to meet you at last. I’ve been looking after your mother since she came in.”

“Thank you,” I murmur.

“Not at all, it’s been my pleasure. We’ve thoroughly enjoyed her company.” She looks at Mum. “But all good things must come to an end, Mrs Lane. I’m pleased to say we’ve got you a bed upstairs, no waiting in corridors for you. The porter should be here in a minute, and then we’ll take you straight up. Get you settled in, so you’re a bit more comfortable than on this old thing.” She pats the plastic mattress on the trolley.

“Can you stay for a bit?” Mummy asks me, a small wrinkle in her brow.

I’m horrified she thinks I might be rushing off somewhere when I’ve just arrived. Can she really believe I think so little of her? “I’m not going anywhere,” I promise.

She smiles, looking pleased. “Thank you, darling.”

"Don't thank me, I wouldn't want to be anywhere else. I'm only sorry I didn't know sooner. I'd have come straightaway."

"Oh, yes, there was a terrible fuss with my phone. I couldn't remember the code, I normally use my thumb. Anyway, William got there in the end. He's been a dear friend."

I smile and nod, patting her hand again when I can't think what else to say. I'm like a snowdome of emotions that's been tipped upside down, so my feelings are scattered all over the place. I barely know which way is up anymore.

When the porter arrives, I'm forced to move aside as they disconnect Mummy from her various machines. I scoop up her handbag and a plastic bag stuffed full of her jacket and the nightie she was wearing when the paramedics came for her. "Okey dokey, I think we're good to go," the porter announces.

He maintains a constant stream of chirpy chatter that avoids the need for any of the rest of us to speak, which is good because my thoughts are chaotic and discordant. I attempt some deep breathing but have to stop when I start to feel dizzy.

We process through the hospital corridors, like ducklings behind our mother duck, following the trolley down this one and then that. Passers-by look down at Mummy, then send me sad smiles. I recognise their expressions as pity. Mummy must look really poorly.

She's going to get well, I tell myself, because she has to. I simply can't begin to imagine any other option. What do I need now? I need her to be better again. That's literally the only thing I need. Nothing else matters.

They settle her into a ward containing three other women of a similar age, drawing the curtain around us to offer a little privacy. Unfortunately, it can't block the sounds of snoring coming from the lady opposite. I half expect the floor to be covered in sawdust. She sounds exactly like a chainsaw.

"Jesus, that's an awful racket," I whisper to a young nurse who's rearranging Mummy's pillows and making sure everything's plugged in to the monitors again. "I don't know how she's meant to get any rest with that going on."

She smiles down at Mummy. "You'll hardly notice after a while, and if it's too bad we can offer you some earplugs." The nurse sends me a practised smile before disappearing through the curtain.

I seriously doubt there will be any chance of ignoring it and say as much to Mummy. "Oh, darling, it's fine," she says with a weary wave of her hand. "It's no worse than I put up with from Daddy for years. Really, don't bother yourself."

"But wouldn't you rather have a bit of peace and quiet? I know I would. I'm sure, if I ask, they'll do something about it."

"Thank you, sweetheart, but no. I'm fine where I am. Really. I don't have the energy to move again, if you don't mind. It's been a bit of a day, all in all."

She does look very tired. "Well, if you're sure? Can I get you anything? Something to eat or drink?"

She leans back against the pillows. "No. darling, thank you. I'm fine. I'll just get a bit of sleep for a minute or two."

I flutter around beside her, finally settling into the chair next to her bed. The snoring's louder if anything, but true to her word, Mummy's already asleep again. I attempt to concentrate on mirroring my own breaths with those coming from the bed opposite. In and out, slow and calm. Centred.

"Have you got a moment, Mrs Everett?" A young doctor accosts me as I step back onto the ward, heading back from the café having fetched myself a cup of coffee.

"Of course," I say, following him back out into the corridor.

He adopts a grave expression. "I just wanted to take a moment to update you on our plans. I won't lie, your mother is very poorly," he says. "The blood flow to her heart through her coronary artery is severely restricted. Fortunately, it doesn't seem to be entirely blocked."

Well, that sounds promising. It could be worse, surely?

"Our intention is to operate in the morning. First thing. We'll perform a coronary artery bypass graft. You need to be aware, though, as with any operation in a woman of your mother's age, this is not a simple procedure. It comes with some risks attached."

Icy fear prickles my scalp. "I understand." No, I don't understand. Why is this happening?

"It's important we monitor her closely until she's taken down. She needs to remain calm..." He looks at me questioningly, seeming to say *can you manage that?*

I nod. "Yes, of course, I quite understand." Is that all I can say?

He appears satisfied. "Afterwards, she'll be in intensive care for a day or so, until we're happy she's recovering as we'd hope. I just wanted to inform you, so you know what to expect over the next day or so."

"Of course, thank you. Is there anything else I should do?"

Now he smiles. "Just being here will be as much as she needs. Help us to keep her calm. We don't need her to be under any more stress than her body already is." He pauses. "If you have any other family, you may wish to call them."

I shake my head, his words reawakening that gripping fear in my chest. "No, there's only me." It's dark outside; visitors are beginning to drift out of the ward. "Is it okay if I stay?"

He frowns. "For a little while longer. Visiting hours finish at eight. After that we like to maintain a quiet ward, for all the patients' benefit. There are some poorly people here. If there's any change in the night, we'll contact you immediately."

Mummy's awake when I return to her beside. She insisted on changing into the nightie she'd been brought in wearing. The pink, frilly collar frames her face like the petals around a flower, the sight making me smile. "Everything okay?" I ask, plumping up the pillow a little behind her. Do you want me to brush your hair?" It's come loose from its pins. She hates it when it does that.

"Would you, darling? That would be wonderful, thank you."

I release her long hair from its chignon, feeling carefully for the pins hidden amongst the long silvery strands. It falls almost to the middle of her back when I'm finished, still thick and shiny despite her years. I'd kill for hair like hers compared to my own ragged mop. I took after Daddy. I suppose I can be grateful it hasn't all fallen out.

I reach into the bag Sarah brought in and retrieve the natural bristle hairbrush she has always insisted on using. I cursed the bloody thing when she used on me as a child. "I've always loved your hair," I say, sweeping the bristles down the silvery length of it.

"So did Daddy. He insisted I wasn't to cut it, even when it turned grey. So I didn't."

That sounds like him. He was forever telling Mummy how much he loved her. Every day. "He adored you. You were very lucky."

She sighs. "I was, I know that. It's the reason why I want so much better for you, darling. I know what real love is all about.

It's completely different from any other feeling. That's why I know you haven't found it yet."

I continue to concentrate on her hair, now gleaming like mercury under the brush. "But I do love Ben."

"I know you think you do. And he's very lucky to have that love. He just doesn't love you the same way. Maybe he never will. Maybe it's beyond him. I don't know, really."

I pause to look at her. "How can you say that? He's always been lovely to you."

"It's not about him being lovely, or otherwise. It's about who he is. And that's a little bit selfish. He can't help being made that way. He will always want you because you make his life easier. You enable him to be lazy. That other missy he went off with will make him work his little behind off. He won't like it in the long run. You mark my words, he'll be back with his tail tucked between his legs before you know it."

"He already is," I admit, rolling the hair into a fresh chignon.

Mummy purses her lips. "I thought as much." She looks over her shoulder at me. I have one pin in my hand, a second clamped between my lips. "And what does he want?"

I remove the pin from my lips and spear it into her hair. "I shouldn't be bothering you with all my nonsense. Not when you're poorly."

She makes a *pfft* noise. "It's exactly because I'm poorly we need to talk about this. I can't be going anywhere until I know you're going to be alright. Until I know you've heard me. We made such good progress at Briar Hill. You were like a different woman. I can feel you slipping back again."

"You're not going anywhere," I say, ignoring her comment about me slipping. She's right though, I have. I've lost some of that confidence and joy I came away with. I'm silent as I press the last pins into her hair. "There," I say. "That should hold until tomorrow. I'll bring some hairspray in with me then."

She settles back against the pillows. "Darling," she says, reaching out to touch my arm. *Crack*.

"Why do you always do that?"

"What?"

"The static. You give me shocks. Always have."

"Oh, I don't know. It's a funny thing. Daddy used to get them too. He always told me it was because I was brimming with positivity. It couldn't wait to get out of me and pass on to other people."

I smile. "I like that."

"Me too. I miss him terribly, you know."

"Who, Daddy?"

She sighs deeply. "Yes. It's been lonely without him these last few years." I draw breath to respond, but she continues, "It's not any reflection of what you have or haven't done, Claire. Just a fact that one half of me is missing. You can't spend fifty years with someone and not miss them when they're gone. For all his annoying little ways, we were good for one another. He made me better as a person than I was on my own, and I like to think I did the same for him."

"You did. You know you did. He'd have been a disaster without you. We both would have been. I still am."

She shakes her head. "No, darling. You've got all the tools you need now to make yourself a wonderful life. You don't need anyone because you're enough just as you are. So, when you choose to be with someone, it should be because you want to. What people don't realise is that you don't just feel love – you act upon it. It's about doing, not purely emoting. It's a moment by moment decision and re-commitment, deliberate and conscious, even when times are tough."

"But how will I know it's the real thing? How will I know the difference between loving Ben and being in-love with Ben?"

She presses a hand to my cheek. "You'll know because you'll decide to be. It's love when you can do that. Every time."

"You make it sound so easy," I say. "I still think it sounds a lot like what I feel for Ben most of the time."

She picks up my hand. "Maybe so, but if you're constantly sacrificing yourself, expecting nothing in return because you love unconditionally, then in the long term it won't work. You'll become resentful. 'Most of the time' is not enough. You're settling for second best again."

Is that what I'm doing now? Do I love Ben unconditionally? Does he love me the same way? I'm just not sure. Maybe he does love me because I make his life easier. Is that enough? I fear not.

The nurses are bustling around the other beds on the ward, turfing out visitors. I'm going to have to leave in a minute.

"Will you be okay, Mummy?" I ask. I'm reluctant to go.

"I'll be just fine, darling. Daddy will watch over me." Her expression turns serious as she looks at me and holds my gaze. "Will you be alright?"

I nod a little uncertainly and press a last kiss to her cheek. *Crack.*

We both smile.

"I love you, Mummy."

"I love you too, my darling. Always."

Chapter 27

My phone rings at four a.m. Icy fingers drive straight into the marrow of my bones. They have nothing to do with the sub-zero temperatures outside. It's dread. Because I know calls in those last hours before dawn bring life-changing news.

I lunge for my phone, rousing from sleep to wakefulness in the moments it takes for me to connect the call. "Hello?"

"Mrs Everett?"

"Speaking." I swallow, mouth dry from the same fear that's now electrifying every cell in my body.

"I'm the Sister on Keller Ward. I'm afraid your mother's taken a turn for the worse. We think you should come down here, now if you can."

I remember nothing more of our conversation, whether I said goodbye or just disconnected the call. I become a scramble of arms and legs, pulling on whatever items of clothing come first to hand, no thought of what or why, so that in mere minutes I am out of the door.

My breath is snatched away by the cold. A quick look up tells me the sky is clear, the air crisp and showing the stars off to best effect. The car is also frosted with ice.

Cursing, I grab my scraper and start the engine, turning the air vents on to full. Then, with shaking hands, I attack the windscreen. Another five minutes are wasted until it's clear enough I can see to drive. Shivering, I slip behind the wheel. It's as cold inside as it is outside. I should have thought to wear a coat.

The usually thirty-minute journey to the hospital takes me fifteen. I don't waste time buying a parking ticket. Instead, I run straight inside. I hurry past a group of drink-addled casualties who call out, "Where's the fire?" and try to step into my path. I don't stop. I use the stairs rather than wait for the lift and arrive panting at the door to the ward, where I ring the bell. Twice.

A young doctor slips out from behind the reception desk. The ward is calm and quiet. I'd expected to find it filled with doctors, all shouting to one another over my mother, a tornado of medical activity. "I'm Mrs Lane's daughter, Claire Everett."

"We've been expecting you," she says.

She leads me along the corridor, away from the room where I last saw Mummy. "How is she?" I ask. We're in a sitting room now. I look around, confused. "Where's my mother?"

"Please, sit down, Mrs Everett."

There is a sense of unreality as I slide heavily onto one of the chairs, staring at the stranger in front of me. News that requires sitting down is not going to be good. The young woman holds my gaze and my stomach does a somersault.

She reaches out to me and I look down, at my hand now encased within hers, with a sense of detachment. It's as if my hand doesn't belong to me. As if I'm a spirit floating somewhere near the ceiling watching this scene unfold. A voice in my head is shouting *no, no, no, no, no.* As if it can stop what's about to come.

The young woman breathes in and says, "I'm very sorry to have to tell you that your mother passed away a short while ago."

"Oh." My single word is more of an expulsion of breath.

"She suffered a second heart attack – a more serious one this time. There was nothing the doctors were able to do. They worked on her for some time, but I'm afraid there was no response -"

She continues speaking. I have no idea what she says or how long we sit there. Five minutes or fifty. I don't register very much of anything really. My head is full of white noise. It's only when the doctor stands and leads me from the little room into a side room that it stops.

Silence.

Mummy is laid out on the bed, perfectly still, a sheet pulled up to her chin. Her hair still looks perfect, I note. She'd be pleased about that. "Please, take as long as you need," the doctor says, hesitating in the doorway. "Is there anyone you want me to call? Anyone who can be with you?"

I stare at her. "No. No one, thank you. I'm alone." And I am. No parents, no siblings, no cousins, no husband, no children. No one. Just me.

I walk to Mummy's side and take hold of her hand. There's no static this time, only the press of rapidly cooling flesh.

I don't know how to explain the difference, but I know it's not her. Not anymore. She's gone. Hopefully to wherever Daddy is. They'll be happy to be together again. But I wish she didn't have to leave me.

Tears come then and all I can do is cry. First, great heaving sobs, then afterwards hot, silent tears that roll down my cheeks relentlessly. I can't seem to stop. Is it possible to cry so much you empty your body entirely of tears?

I cry for what I have lost, and how much I will miss her. Both my parents gone already – the only people who unfailingly had my back, who always loved me, even when I behaved like... me. I'm scared of being alone to face whatever may come. Will anyone care what happens to me now?

The sun rises. Winter-weak, its pale light slowly pushing away the shadows in the room, enhancing the absence of life beneath Mummy's skin.

"I'm sorry to disturb you. Can I get you a cup of tea?" It's the same young doctor I saw before.

I shake my head. The thought of eating or drinking anything makes me feel sick. "What happens next?" I ask. I'm not sure if I mean to Mummy, or life generally. Perhaps both.

"Well, when you're ready we'll move your mum downstairs. We'll keep her here with us until you select an undertaker, then they'll come and collect her. You don't need to do all that today. There's no rush."

I nod and look down at Mummy again, but now my only urge is to get as far away from here as I can. "I think I want to go home," I say.

The doctor smiles. "I quite understand. Do you need me to order you a taxi?"

It's nice of her. Or maybe she just wants me away from here so they can move Mummy and make space for another patient. "No, thank you. I drove here."

Concern clouds her kind eyes. "Will you be okay to drive home?"

Will I? I suppose so. I must make enough of the right responses to reassure her because she lets me leave. I'm handed an envelope on my way out. "What's this?"

"It's the medical certificate. You need to present it at the Register Office to get her death certificate." This is rapidly getting to be a bit much for me. A bit too real. Mummy dealt with all of this when Daddy died.

I back away from her. "Thank you," I manage. Then I turn and run from the ward. Tears threatening again, I sprint back down the stairs, back along the corridors, through the reception and out the front doors where I stop to gasp a deep lungful of air.

It's a beautiful day. Icy cold, the winter sunshine sparkling off every frosty surface. Brittle blades of grass crunching under my feet as I tread slowly back along the path to my car. It's where

I left it, a parking enforcement notice slapped onto the front windscreen. I ignore it, sliding straight in behind the wheel. I sit there for a moment and try to breathe. I can hardly manage it. There is no relief for me in this moment. Everything's wrong.

It takes me nearly an hour to get home through the morning rush hour traffic. With the engine idling, I wonder at all the people rushing around without a care. As if nothing important has happened at all. As if no one just died. As if their lives are completely unaffected by the funny, kind generous soul who left us last night. As if I'm the only person in the world who cares.

By the time I pull up in front of the apartment, I'm crying again. I sit there for another half an hour, trying to summon the strength to walk inside.

Tapping on the glass of my window drags me from my thoughts.

It's Jack.

"Where did you get that?" He points at the enforcement notice, still resolutely plastered to my windscreen. "Not round here, surely?" He looks down at the kerb, as if to check whether they've come along and painted yellow lines in the night.

I stare at him. I want to shout, *my mother's dead.* Instead, I open the door and get out, and what I actually say is, "Oh, your boot's gone." He's walking without any support.

He grins at me. "They're delighted with my progress, said I didn't need it anymore." He takes a step away from me and scans me from head to toe. "That's an interesting outfit. Whoever said *purple and green should never be seen* had clearly met you. Remind me never to employ you as an interior designer." I attempt a smile. It's obviously not terribly convincing because he says, "Hey, are you okay?"

I nod, aware my eyes are filling with tears again. "I'm sorry, I have a terribly important -" I push past him. I never actually say what it is that's important. By that time, I'm at the top of the steps, fumbling with my key to let myself in. I rush inside and up the stairs. Another fumble at the keyhole and I'm inside the flat. I let the door slam shut behind me. Sukie's startled by the noise and darts out through the cat flap. She's up the tree in moments.

I ignore her, I ignore everyone – especially when the calls start later that afternoon. Instead, I go to bed and stay there.

"Claire! I need your help." I've turned all my phones off. I've even disconnected the landline. My voicemail box is full, but I haven't bothered to listen to any of the messages. "Claire!" It's Jack.

I remember the last time he tempted me out of my flat under the pretence he needed my help, only for me to find Mummy and Nicole waiting to pounce on me. Mummy won't be there this time. I burrow my head back under the duvet. Jack can wait.

"Claire! Seriously, this can't go on." He does sound a little desperate.

What does he mean, it can't go on? I can stay wallowing in my flat for as long as I need to. I just lost my mother, for Christ's sake. If that doesn't warrant a bit of wallowing in self-pity, I don't know what does.

"Claire! Are you really going to make me climb up on to that shed roof again and risk breaking my leg for a second time to retrieve that bloody cat of yours? Mr Wilson says he'll call the RSPCA this afternoon if you don't do something about her."

Dear God! Sukie. I've been holed up for two days and in all that time I haven't seen her once. She must still be up the tree. I throw back my duvet and run to the back window in the lounge. Sure enough, there she is peering down from the nest of branches she perches upon. It's been bloody freezing the last few days. I'm a disgrace of a human being.

I jam my feet into an old pair of trainers I haven't worn for months, probably since I went to Briar Hill, pulling a gilet over the top of the flannel pyjamas I'm still wearing, and then open the door. Jack looks harassed. "Thank God!" he says.

We bundle down the stairs and out into the back garden. "I would have done it myself," he says, "but I've developed a fear of falling."

"I'm sorry?" My voice comes out a little croaky from lack of use.

"Since my fall. I can't go downstairs now without holding a banister, or climb onto anything without becoming terrified I'm going to lose my balance." He shrugs. "It's a bit inconvenient, but I'm sure it'll get better." I stare at him. "So, can I help with the ladder at all?"

"I've got it," I say, dragging it up against the side of the shed. I bound up the steps onto the roof, then drag the ladder up behind me. I prop it against a branch near to where she's sitting, blinking down at me with reproachful owl eyes. I look up at her. Instead of my usual saccharine torrent of abuse, I stick with the facts. "I'm so sorry," I call. "I'm so sorry, I've been a little distracted since Mummy died, I should have noticed you weren't in the flat with me. If you want to move out then I quite understand."

"Your mother died?" Jack sounds a little shocked. I assumed someone would have told him before now. But then again, who would there have been to tell him? Who actually knows but me? And I've been bunkered away for days. Now that I think about it, I've not only left Sukie freezing up in the tree, I've left Mummy in the hospital mortuary on her own too. I haven't organised a damn thing for her funeral or let anyone know what has happened. And while we haven't got lots of relatives, she had an army of friends who deserve to know what happened to her. I'm a terrible person. Horrible and selfish, wallowing in a pool of my own self-pity like a hippo in mud. I should be ashamed of myself. Correction, I should be even more ashamed of myself.

I turn and look down at Jack, who's staring up at me with such compassion in his face that all the grief I thought I'd already cried away comes bubbling back up. I burst into tears, still holding onto the ladder, standing on top of the shed roof. Sukie, who'd placed one tentative paw onto the first rung, retracts it again at the sight of the blubbering wreck I've become.

"Oh, bloody hell," Jack says. He grabs onto one of the fence posts and uses it to heave himself up against the side of the shed. Through a series of undignified scrabbling and heaving motions he worms his way up onto the roof. He slithers on his belly towards me, casting fearful looks down to the ground around him.

The sight of him slithering up to my ankles distracts me enough to stop my crying. "You shouldn't be up here," I say.

With a deep breath, he pulls himself to his knees. A further swallow to, I presume, gather his courage, and then he's standing in front of me on very shaky legs. "You should have told me about your mother," he says, pulling me into a hug.

I still have the ladder on my hip. I let him hold me, feeling the quiver of his terrified muscles. "You shouldn't be up here," I say again.

"Your mum died and you were crying," he says simply.

I press my face into the crook of his neck and cry while he holds me.

"Are you two going to stop canoodling and get that poor benighted creature down or do I have to call the RSPCA?" Mr Wilson's voice booms over the garden fence. He huffs. "Really, Claire, you should be ashamed of yourself. Two days that poor cat has been stuck up there. Two days I've had to listen to her yowling all day and all night. They should take her away from you."

I cry a little harder.

"Her mother just died. Give the woman a break," Jack snarls.

And he does. Mr Wilson emits a little grunt of surprise, then says, "I'm very sorry to hear that, Claire. Daphne was a wonderful woman. I'm very sorry indeed." And then he walks off.

Chapter 28

It takes Jack and me another half an hour to coax Sukie down. Her reduced girth makes me burst into tears again. Sukie's a little less concerned. She runs along the fence and up into the flat. It takes us a little longer to get back up there. Mainly because, with the immediate emergency resolved, Jack's new fear of falling comes back in full force. There's a lot of him worming on his belly again, keeping as flat against the shed roof as he can manage whilst I manoeuvre the ladder into position beside him.

I coax him down in much the same way I coax Sukie, minus any abuse, until in the end we're both back on terra firma. For a moment it looks like he might kiss the ground like the Pope.

He doesn't. He wraps an arm around my shoulder and leads me back inside, past his own front door, up the stairs and into my apartment. "Don't you need to go to Bertie?" I heard him yipping when we walked past the door to Jack's apartment.

"He had a long walk this morning. He'll be fine for a bit. Anyway, I suspect it's his fault Sukie wouldn't come back down the tree. He'd taken to sitting beside the shed barking up at her."

"Oh, no," I assure him. "Once she's up there she never comes down. I should have realised she wasn't in the flat. I haven't been quite myself these last couple of days."

He squeezes my shoulder. "I think that's very understandable, all things considered." He pauses. "Why don't you settle yourself on the settee and I'll put the kettle on? What do you fancy?"

For the first time in days, my stomach doesn't roil at the prospect of putting something inside it. "Perhaps one of my apple teas?"

He smiles. "Coming right up."

As he clatters about in the kitchen, I pick up my phone and begin to work my way through the twenty odd messages that have filled up the mailbox. Most of them are from Sarah. She must have gone up to the hospital and been told the news. I'm terrible. I haven't called her. She's still living in Mummy's house, I presume.

When I dial her number, she answers straightaway. "I'm so sorry I didn't call to tell you," I say, when she breathes my name into the phone.

"Oh, thank goodness you're okay. I was so worried about you. I nearly came round when I couldn't get you on the phone, but I didn't want you to have to deal with Gavin on top of everything else. I was hours away from calling the police."

My heart warms at her concern. "I'm okay... well, as okay as I'm likely to be. I'm sorry I went to ground. I just kind of shut down. I didn't expect it, you see. She's always been the strong one, I've always leant on her. I needed a day or two to come to terms with it."

"You don't have to justify yourself to me or anyone. You take as much time to feel what you're feeling as you need. Grief is not a race. Can I help at all? With any of the arrangements?"

My stomach lurches at the thought of everything I've been ignoring. I track Jack as he walks back in with a steaming mug of tea for me and a coffee for himself. He sits down next to me. "I've done nothing," I admit to Sarah. "I need to choose an undertaker and register the death and choose a day for the funeral and let everyone know. . ." That last task alone fills me with dread.

"One thing at a time," she says. "Why don't you let me tell some of her friends? Her address book is here, I'm happy to work through it. I'm a bit useless for everything else."

Relief wraps itself around me. "Would you? I can't face long conversations with all her friends rehashing what's happened. It'll be bad enough at the funeral."

"Do you know what she wanted?"

Do I? Did we ever talk about it? After my father died, we'd had enough of death for a while. Then I realise I do know exactly what she would have wanted. "To be with Daddy."

I choose the same undertaker we used for my father, explaining that Mummy would want to have her ashes interred with his. She'd watched one episode of The Walking Dead and then declared that there was no way either she or Daddy were going to be buried, for fear of a zombie apocalypse. Daddy had had little say in the matter. Although, that's how he'd quite liked it. His ashes are kept in a little cemetery about ten miles away, because they have the best cut lawn and Mummy knew Daddy would have been pleased about that. The undertakers assure me they'll have Mummy collected from the hospital by this evening. I'm beyond relieved about that. I've even set a provisional date in two weeks' time – it's all contingent on me picking up the death certificate.

"How's it all going?" Jack asks later. He disappeared to take Bertie for another walk, but now he's back again.

I tell him what I've accomplished.

"Gosh, well done. That's a lot. What's left?"

I sigh and describe all the legal shenanigans to come. And then the funeral arrangements: choosing flowers, a coffin, a venue for the wake, caterer. The list goes on and on, my courage falling with each additional task. It's a mountain.

He must sense some of what I'm feeling. "You don't have to do this all alone," he says.

"In case you haven't noticed, I'm not inundated with family."

"Maybe not, but you've got lots of friends – Sarah, Nicole, me. Even Ben, dare I say it?"

I snort. "Mummy wasn't terribly keen on Ben, or him on her. Plus, he can't organise finding his way out of a cardboard box. I used to do everything for him. No, I think we'll leave Ben be for now. I do need to let Nicole know, though. She loved Mummy nearly as much as I do."

"I can come with you tomorrow, if you like?"

"Where?"

"To register the death. You shouldn't do that alone. I can come. I've got some work to do in the afternoon, but I'm free in the morning. That's if you want me to? Bertie and I will both come."

Yet more tears are my response. "I'd like that," I manage some time and several tissues later. "If you're sure you don't mind?"

The three of us – Jack, Bertie and me – take the half-hour walk to the Register Office. I'd had to pop over to Mummy's house first thing to collect the documents and papers we needed, so I didn't want to be in the car again. I need to clear my head. Being at the house without Mummy being there had been harder than I'd expected. And Sarah's sympathetic hug only made me cry again.

It's another cold but bright day. Were it not for the purpose of our trip, I'd have enjoyed the walk immensely. When Jack proffers me the bag containing Bertie's business, I even manage a giggle as I shake my head. "No, thank you very much, I've seen what your discount store bags can do. I'll leave that deposit in your capable hands. I hope not literally this time."

"Oh, very funny. Planning any more bin-surfing?" he asks, as we pass the rubbish bin he last saw me rummaging in.

I have to admit, I'm enjoying his company. The thought brings some guilt. I should be more sombre, I'm sure.

I shouldn't have worried. By the time we reach the Register Office my good humour has fled, and I'm dragging my feet. Jack hooks my arm in his. "It'll be okay," he says.

I'm less certain. I give my name, the purpose of our visit, and take our ticket for the registrar. We're surrounded by two couples with new babies whose dark shadows under their eyes suggest they've been awake all night, and a couple who must be getting married judging by all the petting going on.

"Mrs Everett?" A woman in a sober, dark suit calls from the doorway to the waiting room. She frowns down at Bertie. Perhaps dogs aren't allowed. "Will you follow me, please?"

Jack and I trail behind her, Bertie scampering along beside Jack. He's definitely getting bigger.

"Wedding, is it?" the woman asks, looking between us.

"Erm, no," Jack says quickly. "We're registering a death."

The woman's face flushes. "Oh, I'm so sorry. I just assumed… You look like such a lovely couple. Forgive me, I'm letting my mouth run away with me again. I'm so sorry. Here we are." She opens the door in front of us. "The registrar is waiting for you."

We're ushered into a small office. This woman is clearly aware of the purpose of our visit – a box of tissues is strategically placed on the corner of her desk beside two empty chairs. Jack pulls one out for me, then sits himself down in the other. Bertie sits obediently on the floor beside him. I hand over the death certificate.

"I'm very sorry for your loss," the woman says. She might as well have said *she sells sea shells on the sea shore*. I mean, how can she be sorry for my loss? She didn't know my mother. Mummy might have been a terrible woman, for all this lady knows. We might all be over the moon she's dead. We're not, of course, but the registrar doesn't know that.

"Claire," Jack says. He nods meaningfully towards the woman.

Oh, she's been asking me something.

"I was asking what your relationship was to the deceased?" she says with practised patience.

"Oh, I'm so sorry. She's my mother. Was my mother." I sniff. It's still a little unreal to be talking about her in the past tense.

The woman pushes the box of tissues closer to me. "And where and when did she pass away?"

Pass away. Such an odd turn of phrase. "On Sunday. A little after four in the morning. She was in the hospital at the time because she'd already had a heart attack. They told me she suffered a second one – heart attack, I mean."

The woman taps the details into her computer, refers to the death certificate beside her, then looks up. "And her full name?"

"Daphne Marigold Lane. Her maiden name was Pitt."

Jack smiles at me, reaches over and squeezes my arm. *Crack*. I receive a static shock from him.

I stare at my arm. No one other than Mummy has ever given me a static shock.

The registrar is already tap, tap, tapping away again. Pecking at her keyboard like a bird picking ants out of the lawn. Meanwhile, Bertie is starting to get bored. He begins with sniffing about under the registrar's desk, soon fixating upon her foot. His long, pink tongue unravels, then he starts licking it. She surreptitiously tries to shove him away with a sweep of her leg, but there must be something he likes about either her foot odour or something she's trodden in – doesn't bear thinking about – because he's straight back in there, pink tongue lolling out again for another big lick.

Jack finally notices what's going on and calls him back to his side.

The woman's expression never changes. She carries on peering at her screen and typing. She only looks up after a full minute has passed. "And where was she born?"

"Bromley, on the sixth of August, nineteen forty-four."

Bertie will not leave her feet alone. He runs straight back under the desk the moment Jack stops paying him attention. He's retrieved a second time, this time courtesy of a sharp yank to his lead. Jack threatens him in a low, soft voice with the removal of his favourite toy when they get home. Bertie looks up at him and wags his tail.

"I assume she was retired then?" The woman says, as if she's noticed nothing at all of Bertie's goings on.

I nod.

"And where did she live?" I reel off the address as the woman squints at her computer screen. "Any husband or civil partner?"

"No. Daddy died three years ago."

She looks up at me. "I'm very sorry to hear that." *Peter Piper picks a peck of pickled peppers.* Then she's back to staring at her screen again. "Was she receiving a state pension?"

"Yes, I believe so."

"And what about any adult social care? Did she need any help at home?"

"Oh, no, she was very independent, right up until the end."

The registrar smiles benignly. "Well, she was a very lucky lady then. Would that we were all so fortunate." She taps a little more into her computer. "The good news is, I should be able to let all the agencies know at once, rather than you having to contact them all separately."

Bertie has now spotted the potted plant the woman keeps in the corner of her office. A robust yucca. Jack seems to think this is less likely to be a problem than the woman's feet and is letting him sniff around it to his heart's content.

She glances across at Bertie and then back towards me. "Have you got any supporting documentation with you?" I sense we must be on the homeward stretch and she's very glad about that. I have a feeling she'll make this as quick as possible.

"Oh, yes." I reach into my bag and retrieve Mummy's passport, birth certificate and her most recent council tax bill. All the things I'd collected this morning. There had also been a letter instructing where her will was held, but I couldn't think about any of that yet.

"Oh, very good," the woman says with approval. "Everything I need." She stands to make a copy of the various documents. "How many copies of the death certificate will you need?"

I blink back at her. I have no idea. How many do people usually need?

She takes pity on me. "People normally take three or four. You'll need to send them to the authorities – the bank and any insurance companies and similar she may have had policies with – you know the sort of thing. All the different people you need to inform of your mother's passing. You'll need more than one, anyway. Otherwise it can be a slow process if you're always waiting for the single copy to come back."

Your mother's passing. The phrase irritates me. It makes her sound like the Coca Cola lorry. "I'll take four then," I say.

"Very well." She prints four and then signs them in what she explains is special ink that won't fade over time. I'm just pondering why it is that we all don't use that sort of ink when Bertie chooses to cock his leg and pee up the trunk of the yucca.

"Bertie!" Jack sounds mortified. As well he might.

The woman raises her eyebrow. "Well, that's a first."

Despite everything, I giggle.

Chapter 29

I'm still giggling when we get back to the apartment. It wasn't only the leg cock, it was Jack's efforts to blot it up with some of the tissues from the box on the desk, which he then attempted to hand back over to the registrar to place in her bin. Her expression... I giggle again at the memory.

"Claire."

My good mood evaporates like air from an untied balloon. I groan. Gavin. I haven't seen sight nor sound of him for a few days, and I can't say I've missed him. I turn reluctantly in his direction.

He looks terrible; several days' worth of stubble on his chin, crumpled clothes that look slept in with traces of what may have been his last meal – or even a meal from a few days ago – drizzled down the front, though I'm hardly one to judge. "Hello, Gavin."

He steps closer and I get a strong waft of the alcohol on his breath even from this distance. "Where is she? I know you know where she is. You need to tell me. You need to tell me now."

Jack steps smoothly between us. "Back away, mate."

"Says who?"

"Me." Jack says it simply enough, but there is no hesitation in his voice. He means it.

Gavin bristles in response. Tension thickens between the two of them. Bertie growls, the sound deep and low in his throat and surprisingly threatening for something that looks like a cuddly toy and pees on yucca plants.

"Go home, Gavin, there's no point in you even being here." Nothing, no flicker of response from him. I try again. "Jack, stand down."

Neither of them listens to me. Their eyes are fixed on one another. "Did you know the ex was here the other day, sniffing about her again? Into sloppy seconds, are you?" Gavin offers Jack a twisted smile, enjoying sticking the knife in.

Jack clenches his fist and takes a small step towards him. I'll be damned if I'm going to let him start this fight. "Jack!" My voice is sharper this time. He freezes.

Only once I'm satisfied Jack has his temper back under control do I turn to look at Gavin. "Go home," I tell him. "I've had enough of this shit. If you don't leave right now, I'm going to call the police. I'm not messing about anymore." I reach inside my bag and retrieve my phone.

Gavin stares at me, perhaps assessing whether or not I mean what I say.

Jack still hasn't relaxed a muscle. Bertie's eyes are also fixed on Gavin.

"Go home," I say again, my finger poised over the call button.

Gavin must see enough to convince him I mean business because he staggers a half step backwards. The threat is over. Without another word he turns and walks off up the street.

Jack doesn't fully relax until he's out of sight.

He turns to look at me. "That guy is out of control. You need to watch yourself around him. I wouldn't trust him further than I could throw him."

"Believe me, I don't trust him either. But there's not much I can do about it for now. Except be grateful Sarah got herself out of there."

Jack frowns, still looking in the direction Gavin disappeared in. "I sense it's going to come to a head sometime soon. He's going to blow. Please try to make sure you're not around when he does."

I throw my arm around his shoulder. "Aw, I didn't know you cared."

Jack tenses.

Shit, I just majorly overstepped the friendship boundary. I snap my arm back to my side, trying to ignore the inappropriate heat touching him sent through me. "Anyway, thanks again for coming with me today. I owe you one." I cringe at how awkward I sound. I owe you one? Seriously? I run up the steps before I can embarrass myself further.

"Claire," Jack calls after me.

I turn.

He's still on the pavement, watching me, a quirky smile on his face. "Look after yourself. You know where I am. Anytime."

And now I don't know whether to laugh or cry. I give a sharp nod, then run inside before he sees.

Nicole pours Sarah and me another large glass of wine. "I can't believe Daphne's gone," she says, slumping back into her chair. We're already on to a second bottle. At the rate we're raising glasses in toasts to Mummy, I'm going to be badly hung over by the morning. And given we've been doing this most evenings, I'll probably be an alcoholic by the time we reach the date of the funeral.

I'm drinking faster than normal tonight. It's something to do with being here – in Mummy's house. It's funny, the funny strange, not the funny ha-ha type. Without her being here the house lacks … something. I can't put my finger on what the difference is – I've been in this house plenty of times when she wasn't, like the time she and Daddy went on a month-long Alaskan cruise, and I never noticed any difference – but tonight I'm finding it hard to relax. Thankfully, the wine is helping. "It never crossed my mind that one day I might be without her," I say. "Barring the time I went away to university, she's always been such a major presence in my life."

"And look what a mess you got yourself in to there," Nicole says, rolling her eyes towards Sarah and mouthing "*Ben*".

Sarah laughs.

"Daphne was a major presence in all of our lives," Nicole continues. "She knew me far better than my own mother ever did. She had this knack of always knowing exactly what we were up to."

I smile. "I always had a feeling that was because she'd done whatever it was before we'd even thought of doing it."

Nicole snorts. "Do you remember that time when she caught us smoking up on the roof? I thought she'd go ballistic, but she just warned us about the risks to our skin if we carried on – that it would make us wrinkly – and how hard it was to quit. Oh, and how bad we'd smell. That did it for me. I never really smoked after that."

"Changing the subject, how did you get on today?" Sarah asks.

Now that we have the death certificate, I've been able to book the funeral. That meant I needed to choose a coffin too. Thankfully, Nicole volunteered to come with me for that experience. "I never imagined there were so many different types of coffins to choose from."

Nicole laughs. "I still think it would have been fun to go for the wool. Your mother loved a lovely yarn. Imagine all the static she'd be able to build up in there."

Sarah's eyes widen. "A wool coffin?"

"And then there were cardboard ones," Nicole says. "Just imagine if it was a very rainy day and she'd wanted a burial. It would be a disaster."

"I think they have that covered. It's tougher than a cardboard box, I imagine. I quite liked the idea of the cardboard. It's biodegradable and all that. Good for the planet. Plant a tree over me too and I think I'd be happy." I look at Nicole. "Make a note of that if I snuff it before you."

Nicole's eyes narrow. "You've changed."

"What do you mean?"

"Well, there was a time you'd have been all about the satin interior coffins. Brass handles and excessive floral displays. Now you're talking biodegradable and planting a tree on top. That Mindfulness course really did a number on you. It's turned you into a sandal-wearing hippy."

"Not at all," I say, a little put out by the sandal slur. "Sarah will vouch for the fact I've not been near a single pair of sandals since I started the course."

"That's only because it's winter. I bet in the summer you'll be bringing out the Birkenstocks."

I know for a fact I already have a pair in the back of the wardrobe. I also know I'll be wearing them next summer. "Is that so bad?"

She sighs. "No, it really isn't. I'm happy for you. Even after everything you've had to cope with this week you still seem much more in control. Peaceful even. If you'd had to cope with all this before you went on the course, you'd have had a full-on nervous breakdown." She looks across at Sarah. "You should have seen her when she was having her panic attacks. You wouldn't have recognised her."

"I think we were all in rough shape when we started that course. We were all there for our own reasons."

"I only went because Mummy suggested it. And when I nearly lost it again halfway through, she was the one who picked me up, dusted me off and told me I needed to love myself. She was right too."

Nicole peers at me as if I might be some new exotic animal she's never seen before. "So, are you alright now?"

I wish. "No, not nearly. But I'm trying. I think Mindfulness taught me not to spend my time worrying about what will happen in the future. Just to focus on what is within my control right now. Sometimes that's easier said than done, like now, with Mummy and everything. But I do think I spent a lot of time before worrying about everything that might go wrong – and finding ways to blame myself for it."

"See. You're different. You never would have known that about yourself before."

I sigh. "I'm not that different. She's still in me – the woman who wants to tear me down every time I do something good.

Those voices still shout at me daily. Maybe I just recognise them for what they are when they do it now."

Sarah grunts in agreement. "The way I try to explain it is that I made friends with myself. I know my situation was a bit different from yours; your voice was in your head, mine was my courtesy of my husband telling me I was worthless all the time. Ultimately the result was the same. I believed every bad thing he said about me."

I nod. "Exactly. I believed everything I told myself."

"The course helped to mute the voices a little, but they're not gone. I hear the echoes of everything Gavin ever said to me and I'm still working on the fact that just because he said it, it doesn't mean it's true. I'll get there in the end. It's a journey. I'm working on it."

This seems like the right moment to tell her about today's visit. "He came round again today," I say.

Her face drops.

"I'm sorry to be such a downer."

Nicole looks first at me and then at Sarah. "Your husband, is this? The one who hit you?"

Sarah nods without taking her gaze off me.

I meet her eyes. "It was okay, Jack was with me for backup. But I had to threaten to call the police again. Next time, and I know for a fact there will be a next time, I'm not going to hesitate to call the police. He's a mess. Angry beyond reason. Jack reckons he's on the edge. Could step off at any point. I'm scared what might happen if he does. What he might do to you. . . or me, or anyone really. I know you don't want to involve the police, but I think for your own safety you should really think about it. You can't live in hiding for the rest of your life. You shouldn't have to."

Sarah wraps her arms around her middle. "I know you're right. I know he's dangerous. I even know what he did to me was criminal and that he deserves to be punished for it."

I nod encouragingly.

"The problem is, he's also the man I loved. Perhaps even still love, despite everything. He's the man I married. You know," she nods at me, "you don't do that lightly."

Do I know that? When I married Ben, I believed I was in love with him. But on reflection I may just have been desperate for someone to love me. He spoke to my affection-starved soul. Was I just happy enough – whatever enough was at that time? Was it a case that it was better Ben than no one?

"However dark the time we were together was, there were always some good moments, moments when he was the man I first met and married again."

I stare at her. "What does that mean?" I'm terrified she might be tempted go back to him when the memory of what he's really like fades along with her bruises.

She hugs her knees. “Only that it’s not quite so cut and dried as we like to think. He hit me, therefore he’s bad. He wasn’t always a bad man -”

The deep chime of Mummy’s doorbell silences us. We look at one another, eyes wide. Who the hell can be at the door? All three of us are sat here. Who else knows about this place, but doesn’t know about Mummy?

Chapter 30

"It'll be one of her friends," I say, pushing to my feet, even as I know that's unlikely. It's after nine p.m. Most of Mummy's friends will be tucked up in front of Call the Midwife by now. And quite right too. The thought it might be Gavin, that somehow he's found us, is uppermost in my mind. Perhaps we summoned him by speaking his name in some Harry Potter-esque style. My hand hesitates on the door latch. It's a man, judging from the blurry outline. He's tall-ish, maybe not as tall as Gavin, and wearing a dark overcoat. But that's about all I can tell from what little the porch light is showing me through the dappled glass.

I take a deep breath and pull the door open. "Ben!"

"You sound surprised to see me. You must have known I'd come as soon as I heard."

"Oh." I'd actually thought no such thing. I hadn't really thought about him much at all. He's staring at me. Waiting for me to say something. "Well, you'd better come in." I regret the words as soon as I utter them. What the hell will Nicole say when she sees him here?

"I didn't know if you'd be here or back at your flat. I went over there first. That loser was there."

"Who? Gavin?" Oh, God, what if Gavin's followed him here?

Ben strides towards the front room. He's been here enough times; he knows exactly where he's going. "No, that idiot Jack Wilton." He pushes into the lounge and then stops dead. "Nicole." No nice to see you, how are you, long time no see. Just *Nicole* in a voice that says it isn't nice to see her. They exchanged some pretty heated words after the Bella incident, by all accounts. I wasn't there, but I heard it got nasty. They've not really spoken since.

"Ben." Her voice is Arctic.

I wring my hands, staying in the hallway, out of Nicole's line of sight and the disapproving looks I have no doubt my friend is sending whether she can see me or not.

"What are you doing here, Ben?" Oh, Nicole is fierce. She never backs off from a fight.

He straightens. "I came to check on Claire."

She tuts. "Claire's doing fine. She has lots of friends all looking out for her. In fact, she's been doing fine for the last nine months." Umm, I don't think that's exactly true. "How's Bella? And the baby? You must be getting excited." Ben winces at the reminder of his soon to be baby mama.

"Can I get anyone a drink?" I say with false cheeriness. Inside, I'm dying a little. I just want this car crash over and done with. For Ben to leave. Or do I? There is a piece of me that doesn't want that. A little bit of me that's kind of happy he bothered to come round and check on me in the first place.

Another, slightly larger part, that doesn't want him to leave because then I'll be forced to face Nicole's wrath. This is the first she's heard that he's been sniffing around me again.

Ben looks towards Nicole then back at me. "No, I won't stay. I can see you're busy." He raises an eyebrow at the empty bottles on the table. "I just wanted to check when the service is and to see if there was anything I could do to help? Who did she make her executor?"

"None of this has anything to do with you," Nicole says, getting to her feet.

"Don't be ridiculous, of course it's to do with me. She was my mother-in-law for fifteen years. I think I have a right to come and check how Claire is doing."

Nicole steps around the coffee table. "You gave up that right when you fucked her daughter's friend. Daphne was glad you were out of Claire's life. She'd be horrified if she knew you were using her death as an opportunity to creep back in again."

"Nicole!"

"I think it's probably better that you leave," Sarah says to Ben. Her voice is calm and reassuring as she adds, "We'll make sure she's okay."

Ben looks at me, then across at Sarah. "Thank you." He heads back out into the hallway. I follow, a couple of steps behind. He halts on the doorstep, turning towards me. "You know you can call me," he says in a low whisper. "Anytime. I don't give a shit what that bitch says -"

Okay, now he's going too far. "Ben! Nicole's not a bitch. She's my best friend, and she's concerned about me with good reason."

He splutters with frustration. "I'm not going to do anything to hurt you."

"You already have. You broke my heart into tiny pieces and then trampled all over them. I've only just begun to piece myself back together again, and now here you are. They have every right to be concerned about me."

"But I know better now. Have you been thinking about what we talked about? This could be just what we wanted."

It's too much. I can't do this right now; in whispers, in the hallway, with my mother only recently dead and still unburied, Nicole with steam coming out of her ears listening behind the door to the lounge. "Let me bury my mother, Ben. I've thought about nothing but her over the past few days. Let me see her off as she deserves to go – in peace. Please, don't ask more of me right now. I need my focus to be on that, not my own shit. She had enough of that to deal with when she was alive."

He bends to kiss me, but I turn my face at the last moment and his mouth hits my cheek instead of my lips. He winces as he straightens.

"Haven't you seen the GP yet? Why are you still in pain?"

"I had to cancel. Bella needed a lift to the midwife. I've rearranged the appointment for Friday."

The same day as the funeral. It upsets me a little to think he might not bother to come.

"I know what you're thinking," he says. "The appointment is at nine. I'll be there Claire, I promise." He squeezes my hand in his and then slips out the door, hunching his shoulders against the chill wind as he runs back to his car.

The second the door clicks shut she shouts; "Claire Everett! Get your arse back in here this second!"

I cringe. "Do I have to?"

"No, I'm quite happy to come into the hall and shout at you," Nicole says, filling the doorway, hands on her hips.

At least in the lounge I can drink my wine. I pretend nonchalance and saunter back into the front room. Sarah sends me a grimace in sympathy. "Anyone need a top up?" I ask, reaching for the bottle.

"What the hell are you thinking? For a whole second, I actually thought you were getting your life sorted again. That you knew what you needed to be happy. That this course," she gestures towards Sarah, "had done you some good."

"All of that's true. Nothing's changed."

"Then why is it I'm only learning now that Ben's been skulking around to see you again? This isn't the first time, is it?"

I frown at Sarah, who blushes. "He's been round once or twice." I lift my chin in defiance.

Nicole's complexion morphs from mottled pink to red then on to something that might be called purple. I'm worried she's going to have an aneurysm. "What the bloody hell are you thinking?"

"I've done nothing wrong."

"I'm not sure Bella would see it quite like that."

Just the mere mention of her name sends my own temper flaring white hot. "Oh, so we're worried about hurting her feelings, are we? No matter it was my husband she fucked in the first place? Oh, no. Just because she's pregnant we all have to tiptoe around her? Well, I'm sorry, if Ben's not entirely happy with her and if he chooses to spend time with me instead, that's not actually my problem. He's still my husband."

Nicole gapes at me. "This is worse than I thought. You're terminally stupid. There's no hope for you. Even after everything he's done, you still can't see it. You actually think I give a shit about that bitch? I couldn't care less about her or her kid. What I care about is that you seem willing to let a man who's perfectly happy running straight from one woman to another, trample all over you for the second time. It's not enough that he's left you once and got another woman pregnant, you want a repeat performance. And then, what do you imagine will happen when the baby arrives? Oh, yes. He'll be running back to Bella again, ready to be Daddy, sneaking back to you for sex."

"What if I want to have sex with him? It's my right, my body, my husband."

She raises her arms in a gesture of despair. "How can you let him walk all over you? Again?"

"He wants us to be together again. To raise the baby together, like we always wanted."

"Oh, because Bella's bound to be happy about that, isn't she? The woman's positively rabid at the mere mention of your name. You don't know the half of it. I heard that after you met the pair of them in the café to give back the folder, Ben and she had a big row and she made him sleep in the car for two nights before she'd let him back into the house. I thought she was turning into a bunny boiler, but now that I know he's been sneaking round for visits with the ex, I think she might have more sense than I gave her credit for. There is no way in hell she's going to let him waltz off to play happy families with you and her baby."

"I think you've made your point, Nicole," Sarah says in a quiet voice. She leans over and pulls me into a hug. I'm crying. When did I start crying?

Nicole throws her hands into the air again. "What the hell would your mother say?"

I take a deep breath. "She knew," I say in a quiet voice.

"She knew? She *knew* Ben was sniffing around again and she didn't say anything? I don't believe you."

"She posted the divorce papers without my knowledge."

Nicole scratches her head. "What? Back up a bit. What have the divorce papers got to do with anything?"

Jesus, in for a penny, in for a pound now. I might as well tell her everything. "Ben started coming round after he saw me at the café." I hold a hand up as Nicole splutters again, about to launch into another tirade. "Marjorie saw him on my doorstep and told her. Before you get your knickers in a twist, nothing happened. I haven't slept with him. Well..."

"I knew it!"

"You know nothing. He stayed over one night, the night after I had a row with Mummy. That was the only time. I was very upset. He slept in my bed BUT NOTHING HAPPENED!" I shout the last words over her spluttering. It shuts her up.

"Why did you have a row with your mum?"

"Because I found out from Ben the solicitor had received my divorce papers. I knew I hadn't posted them and I realised she had. I was upset with her. She had no right to do that without my permission."

"When did all this happen?" Nicole's circling like a shark, getting ready to move in for the kill. She can scent blood.

"The day before her first heart attack." And there it is: one plus one equals two. I shouted at my mother and then she had a heart attack. And now she's dead. I might as well have killed her. I collapse back onto my chair, I'm not sure when I got to my feet. Nicole's on her feet too. She stares down at me, a look of shock and horror on her face. She looks like she might say something, the killing blow, but Sarah steps in first.

She takes hold of my hands in hers. "Look at me, Claire. Your mother had acute atherosclerosis furring up her valves and arteries, including the ones in her heart. You didn't cause that. She smoked all through her youth. You said that yourself," she says with a look towards Nicole, "and she told me the same in the hospital. A piece of plaque broke free and caused a blockage in her heart. It could have happened at any time. I'm not saying this for any other reason than that it's the truth. She knew you would do this. That you would look to blame yourself. I'm telling you what the doctors told me: You cannot blame yourself for your mother's heart attack. I won't let you blame yourself. She would never have wanted that."

I'm crying so hard my head aches.

"I think I'd better leave," Nicole says quietly.

Chapter 31

The morning of the funeral dawns cold and grey. I dress in silence. Even Sukie barely bothers to lift her head, choosing instead to stay asleep on top of the wardrobe. I wish I had that choice.

Mummy hated black. She asked that any mourners come in bright colours, so that's what I choose. I have on a pink skirt with a purple flower print on it, and a matching purple jumper. My mother always said I looked bonny in this outfit. I don't feel bonny. I feel ugly. Inside. I can't get rid of the memory of Nicole's expression of horror when she realised I had caused Mummy's death. Sarah can dress it up as nicely as she wants, and she's done her best over the last few days, but the facts don't lie.

I'm a horrible person. That's no random thought. That's a fact. I know it because I took my childish anger out on a seventy-five-year-old woman and the very next day she had a heart attack. Fact.

Mummy may have forgiven me, but that doesn't mean I deserve forgiving.

I deserve to be alone.

And I am.

Fact.

I have a car arriving in ten minutes to take me to the funeral and I'm going to be all on my own inside it. Because that's what I deserve. Fact.

When we first planned the funeral, Nicole was going to be here with me. We'd agreed to travel to the funeral together. She's always been like a sister to me, and Mummy treated her like a second daughter, so it seemed only right that she share Mummy's last journey too. Not now. Now she probably can't face being in the same church with me, let alone car.

What if she doesn't come at all? She wouldn't do that, would she? Whatever she thinks of me, I hope she'll be there for Mummy's sake. Mummy deserves a good send off.

I'm crying again. I dab at the corners of my eyes carefully with a piece of tissue, trying not to remove my pathetic attempt at eye make-up. I don't know why I bothered to wear any at all. It'll be running down my face before I've even made it out of the apartment.

I'm jolted out of my self-pity when the intercom buzzes. "It's Arthur here from Bennetts'. Your mother's arrived," he says in a rich, professionally sombre voice. "We're ready when you are."

I tell them I'll be down shortly, then promptly sit down in the middle of the floor and burst into tears. I don't think I can do it. I don't deserve to have people feeling sorry for me. I should be locked up. They'll all be better off without me. My breaths quicken, coming in short, fast pants now, my vision narrowing as darkness descends.

I wake when the intercom buzzes again. Sitting up slowly, I press my fingers to my forehead. It's throbbing and tender to the touch, a large lump protruding from just above my temple. I stand and inspect myself in the hall mirror. I have the makings of a fine bruise. I must have passed out and bashed my head on the floor. Now, I have no idea what time it is, or how long was I out.

The intercom buzzes yet again. I ignore it. Perhaps if I don't go down, they'll travel on without me. I'm not sure anyone would notice. It might be for the best. Best for Mummy. Best for everyone.

The doorbell rings followed by hammering on my apartment door. Shit, someone got past the street door. "Claire?" It's Jack's voice. That's okay, I can ignore him. "Claire?" *Bang, bang.* He keeps this up; the banging, the doorbell ringing and name calling, for another five minutes.

He's not going away. He's a bloody nuisance. "What?" I shout, annoyed now. My head throbs in protest.

"Open this bloody door. Stop wallowing in self-pity."

Oh, he has a bloody cheek. What does he know about anything? If anyone has a right to a bit of wallowing right now, I have.

"Claire! I'm not going away."

I yank the front door open. "What do you want?" My voice dries up.

She's there. Nicole.

Standing next to Jack. Dressed in a buttercup yellow dress that Mummy would have loved.

I try and fail to produce any words. "About time too," she says. "Come on, we have a mother to pay our last respects to. Have you got everything you need? Keys? Purse?"

I pick up my handbag from off the side and nod, still dumbstruck to see her here.

"Well, come on then." She grabs my hand and pulls me out the door. "Thanks, Jack," she says as we pass him on the stairs.

"I'll see you at the wake," he calls after us.

I stumble down the steps behind her, out the front door and then stop, my body frozen to the spot. My mother's there, her coffin right in front of me. It's all so real. So final. "I don't know if I can do this," I say.

"You bloody well can. You have to. She deserves a good send-off, so that's what we're going to give her. It won't be easy." Nicole looks at me sideways, perhaps assessing how close I might be to another full panic attack. "But we're not going to let her down. Are we?"

"No," I agree. I take a deep breath, exhaling slowly. Then a second. I keep my steady breathing up until we're both seated in the back of the second big black car. "Thank you for coming," I say when the door closes behind us.

She leans back against the creaking, leather upholstery. "You can't really imagine I would miss this?"

"I wouldn't blame you if you'd decided you wanted nothing more to do with me."

My best friend sighs. "Look, I know you think I blame you for Daphne's death, but I really don't. That'd be stupid. Just cruel." She takes hold of my hand. "I'll admit I was angry with you, okay? But that was because of you seeing Ben again, not this. This was just an unhappy coincidence."

I dab at my eyes with a bit of tissue that's already disintegrating from overuse.

"That's disgusting," says Nicole, brushing bits of tissue off my lap and handing me a fresh tissue from a pristine packet she whips out of her handbag. "Just because I get cross with you doesn't mean I don't still love you." She dabs at her own eyes this time. "Same as your mum still loved you, no matter what."

I stare at the hearse in front. A photo of Mummy has been propped up at the back. In it she's throwing her head back in laughter. It perfectly captures her. "She and Daddy will be living it up in heaven."

"Can you imagine?"

"I'm going to miss her terribly." I swallow. "I mean, it was bad enough when we lost Daddy. But now..."

Nicole squeezes my hand again. "You're not alone. Not today or any other day. You always have me, no matter what stupid things you do." She pauses. "Which is probably just as well, because you do a lot of really stupid things."

I slap her arm.

"Speaking of, would you like to explain to me why you've got a lump the size of a small duck egg on your head?" She fishes in her bag and whips out a small compact mirror.

I angle it in front of me until I can see. She's right. It's quite a lump. "I had a panic attack."

She frowns at me. "I thought you'd got over those."

"It appears not. With enough stress they're still my body's go-to coping mechanism."

"Here." She passes me some pressed powder.

I dab enough on that it's only the lump that's still visible, not the purpling bruise around it.

"Brace yourself," she says. "We're here."

Mummy would have been thrilled with the turnout. We're a rainbow array of colours in a hall filled with flowers. Marjorie and William did beautiful readings, and then when Nicole read the eulogy, there wasn't a dry eye in the house. We'd written it together, before our big bust-up. It managed the right blend of funny reminiscences and observations. I've been touched by how many friends have come up to me to tell me how Mummy touched their lives in some way. By the time we finished with one of her favourite hymns – Morning Has Broken – my throat had closed up altogether, clogged with emotion.

"Here, take this," Jack says, handing me a glass of whisky. We're standing by the bar in the Old Ship Hotel, and the wake is still in full swing. Mummy's crowd don't get out much. I remember her saying they love a good funeral. Judging by the state of their hairpieces, they really do. "You look like you need it," he says, nodding towards my glass before bending to look at me a little more closely. "What happened to your head?"

"A close encounter with my lounge floor, I'm afraid. Thank you," I say, raising the glass to him. "It was good of you to come." He's wearing a salmon pink shirt with a lilac tie.

"I liked her. I'll never forget her calling Bertie the Durex puppy. Still makes me smile whenever I think about it."

I laugh. "I'm scarred by a lifetime of such things."

"Doesn't sound all that bad. She adored you, you know?"

I nod. "I know. She made that very clear."

He smiles. "Did you know she told me to ask you out?" He stares at me intently.

It sounds exactly like my mother. "I'm so sorry. That's the sort of thing she did all the time. I hope she didn't make you feel too awkward. She had all the subtlety of a pneumatic drill."

He puts up a hand to stop me. "No, I don't think you understand. I -"

"Claire." I turn towards the familiar voice. It's Ben. He's wearing a dark suit and a black tie. He clearly didn't get the message. He looks at Jack and frowns. "Wilton." They exchange a curt nod.

"Hello, Ben," I say, feeling a little irritated by the interruption. I really want to know what Jack was about to say. Today there's none of the spark of excitement I used to get at seeing my husband. Just a sense of weariness. And sadness. Maybe it's the day – that's what funerals do to people. Suck away some of the joy of being alive. Jack's moved to stand by my shoulder. "Thank you for coming," I say.

"Don't be ridiculous. Of course I came. Are you okay?" Am I? "What am I saying? I know you're not, how could you be?" Typical Ben. He asks a question and answers it for me. "Come here."

Before I really know what's happening, he's pulled me into his arms. He's hugging me close, stroking his hand through my hair. I'm assaulted at once by both the familiarity and unfamiliarity of his touch and smell. Most surprisingly, I want to pull away. When I try, Ben just holds on to me a little tighter. "I'm here," he whispers. "You'll be okay now."

Irritation prickles. Does he really think his presence is going to make all the difference? I do pull away this time. Jack's stepped back but I sense Nicole's laser glare beaming into me from the other side of the bar. "I'd be happy to help with any of the probate stuff," Ben is saying.

I look at him. "No, that's okay. It's all under control. The solicitor is on to it. Should be relatively straightforward, he thinks."

Ben steps back a little, surprise showing on his face. "Goodness. Get you, being all independent. There was a time you barely knew how to read a bank statement."

That same feeling of irritation is back. "Well, it's amazing what you can learn to do when you have to," I say, the bite in my voice surprising both of us.

"Sure, yes, I didn't mean to offend you."

I sigh. "You didn't. Not really. I'm tired. It's been a long day is all."

"Of course," he says again, all compassion and understanding once more. He hugs me a second time. I let him, standing there rigid as a totem pole as he wraps his arms around me, just wishing he'd let me go so I can drink some more of my whiskey.

"Ben!" The second voice has the same effect on me as nails down a chalk board.

Bella.

We both turn. She's blossomed since I last saw her. She must be approaching the final trimester because the baby bump looks huge compared to her skinny frame. She has a face on her like thunder. "You could have waited for me," she says to Ben.

He huffs. "You couldn't wait to try and chat up that ex-client of yours. I assumed you'd be hours." I presume he means William. I'd forgotten Mummy had torpedoed that working relationship.

Bella turns to me with a scowl. "I didn't know William was friends with your mother, Claire," she says.

I meet her gaze. "Neither did I until recently. They played bridge together, apparently. Were you at the service? He gave a lovely reading."

Bella doesn't respond immediately. She's wound tight as a cotton reel. The muscle in her jaw's ticking faster and faster. "Did you make sure he pulled out of the contract with me? That's low, even for you."

Hold on a cockadoodie minute! What the hell is she talking about?

"You must have loved it when you realised you could get your own back on me without even lifting a finger. You effectively destroyed my business. You knew I couldn't survive and meet our overheads if we didn't have that contract..."

Actually, I knew no such thing. I barely paid any notice to what the overheads were or how much money we made. I just went and created lovely rooms for my even lovelier clients. That's why I was so blindsided when my friend and business partner ran off with my husband.

Ben steps towards her, looking annoyed. "Bella! This isn't the time or the place, for goodness' sake. You're at a funeral."

She whirls towards him and I swear her eyes flash red. We both take a step backwards. If I'm not mistaken, this woman is about to blow.

"Are you sticking up for her? After everything she's done? After she's ruined me?" We're drawing a little crowd now, people finding the raised voices irresistible. Mummy's friends love a bit of drama. Personally, I want nothing more than to slide into the background and leave them to it, but as I try to slip away Bella turns on me again. It seems she hasn't finished with me yet. "It may be a funeral, but it hasn't stopped *her* from playing the *poor little me* card. Yet again." She draws a breath and I brace myself for whatever's to come. "There's nothing poor about Claire, especially not once she hoovers up Daphne's money. She's determined to kill my business and take the food from the mouth of our child with that greedy divorce settlement. She's a scheming, manipulative bitch!" Bella finishes her tirade with a stinging slap across my cheek. It leaves my ears ringing.

Up until that point, my mouth was hanging open. Now it snaps shut.

"Bella, control yourself, for God's sake, woman!" Ben is shouting now. "You're a fine one to talk. You're the dictionary definition of a scheming, manipulative bitch. In fact, I think you'll find if you look it up, all they have is a picture of you, so don't go accusing Claire."

I really wish they'd keep me out of this. I'm beginning to wish the floor-swallowing thing was real. I look around for any sort of help. Nicole and Jack are both leaning against the bar with their arms crossed over their chests. They look like they're enjoying themselves. I glare at them.

"You started all of this in the first place, Bella. Claire and I never stood a chance once you decided what you wanted and stuck your talons in," Ben says.

Bella huffs with derision. "Oh, give me a break. You weren't complaining when you were getting your dick wet."

Okay, this has descended into bad daytime television land.

Bella's on a roll. "So, don't give me the *I didn't stand a chance* line. You knew perfectly well what you were doing. And you were happy to do it."

I have my hands clapped around my face, in part because my cheek is still stinging but mainly because this whole situation is mortifying. For everyone concerned. Is there any way I can extricate myself from this diabolical domestic without drawing any more attention to myself? Unfortunately, the crowd is now six-deep around us. At any moment I'm expecting someone to start chanting *fight, fight, fight.*

"Oh, but I didn't know everything, did I?" Ben's skin has turned puce, spittle flying from his mouth as he leans in towards her, his finger jabbing against her chest.

Bella rolls her eyes in dramatic fashion. "What are you talking about, you stupid little man?"

"I'm talking about the fact I didn't know you were fucking someone else at the same time as you were fucking me."

Okay, this is totally Jeremy Kyle territory, but I'm as riveted as everyone else now. Bella's skin turns a full shade paler. She splutters a little. "I don't know what you're talking about." Her defensive posture suggests she might be telling a porky-pie. She definitely looks uncomfortable now.

She glances over her shoulder as if looking for a way out. I suspect if she thought she could get past the crowd she'd be out of here in a shot. But we're not budging anywhere. We're all on tenterhooks waiting for the punch line we sense is coming.

"Oh, don't you? You see, when Claire and I were trying for a baby we started having tests to find out what was wrong. I always thought it was her. Turns out it wasn't. When I went to the doctor for my back this morning, the GP gave me the results from the sperm test I did ages ago but never picked up. It turns out I'm completely infertile. Not even a couple of lame ducks. A complete Jaffa. So, you see, there's no way that baby can be mine."

And there it is.

The truth at last.

Boom.

Chapter 32

"Will you please stop tiptoeing around me. I'm fine," I say to Nicole, as she slides another whisky in front of me. I knock it back in one large gulp.

"Oh, yes, completely fine," she says. She's watching me, one elbow propped on the bar, hand supporting her head. "You're the very definition of fine."

She has a point. I caught sight of myself in the bathroom toilet mirror earlier. There was a manic look in my eyes. "Well, I'm considerably better than Ben and Bella, I imagine." They were last seen in the hotel car park, still shrieking at one another, before Ben tore away in the car and Bella was observed rolling herself into the back of a cab.

"It's been a wonderful funeral," Marjorie says, clapping me on the shoulder. "One of the best I've ever been to. Your mother would have been delighted." She chuckles, years of cigarette smoking making the sound bubble around inside her chest. I give her a minute as she coughs up half a lung. "Yes, I've got to say, this will be a hard one to beat. You've set the bar high for the rest of us."

I press a kiss against her powdered cheek, trying to ignore the small grey man bobbing about at Marjorie's shoulder. Her latest squeeze, no doubt. "I'm so glad you enjoyed it. Thank you for coming."

"No. Thank *you.*"

I've had this all afternoon. No one seemed to want to leave. Eventually, several concerned offspring turned up to collect their parents because they were worried after they'd been gone so long, assuming something awful must have happened. Nothing had in fact happened beyond repeated retellings of the showdown over copious amounts of booze – leading to several inebriated parents being led away, wigs even more awry, by their shamefaced children.

Nicole spins herself around on the stool next to me. "Is that the last of them?"

I visually sweep the now-emptier bar. I can't see anyone else I recognise, but I haven't checked under the tables and chairs yet. "Dear God, I really hope so. I'm not sure I can take much more."

"This one's on the house," the barman says, topping up our glasses with another shot of whiskey. "We've done a roaring trade this afternoon, thanks to you."

I drop my head into my hands. "Do you think I'll ever live it down?"

Nicole looks at me, her head cocked on one side. "It probably won't be forgotten in a hurry, but I'm not sure you came out of the whole scenario too badly. Now, Ben and Bella are another matter..."

"Is it wrong that I feel sorry for them. What a freaking mess."

"Yes, it's wrong. I'm sorry, I think that's just karma. She got her comeuppance."

I can see her point, but still. "Maybe she was right. Maybe I *was* glad that William took away that business from her. Maybe I could have done something to stop it from happening."

She holds my gaze. "Look, think about it. How rich is he?"

"Very rich." He bloody well is. I'd seen the new Maserati he pulled up in.

"He didn't get that way by giving in to whims, now did he?"

"No, I don't suppose so."

"No. He's a hard-nosed businessman. Trust me, if he'd really liked what Bella was designing for him, he'd have kept the contract on. He must have already had concerns if he could be so easily swayed. Stop making the shit-storm they created for themselves all about you. This had nothing to do with you. You didn't tell William to dump Bella. You didn't tell Bella to cheat on Ben. You didn't make Ben infertile. You didn't choose to air all your dirty laundry in the middle of someone's wake. All of that is on them."

When she puts it like that my guilt does ease a little. I really need to meditate. Maybe I'll go round to Mummy's tomorrow and see if Sarah fancies it. "Marjorie was right though," Nicole continues. "Your mother would have had a ball today. I think we gave her a terrific send-off. Your dad and she must be rolling about on their cloud up there as we speak." We gaze up at the ceiling.

I imagine the cracked, yellowing, artexed plasterboard is gone and I can see straight up to the heavens. Mummy's holding Daddy's hand, perched on the edge of a cloud, kicking her feet up and chuckling at the funeral shenanigans. "She would have loved it," I agree. "To Mummy," I say, raising my glass.

"To Daphne," Nicole echoes as we clink glasses. "Another one for the road?"

"Bertie, you bastard, leave her alone. No! Stop it! Oh, fuck! Not again." The shouts are loud enough to be heard all the way from the back garden into my lounge.

I blink, heave my reluctant body into a sitting position and look around. I'm in the lounge. Why am I in the lounge? The last thing I remember was Nicole tipping me out of a taxi. We'd had several more for the road. I must've fallen asleep on the settee.

I stand and sway, nausea rolling through me as I gather my sea legs. My head's thumping – boom, boom, boom – with every move I make. Ugh, a whiskey hangover. I attempt to tiptoe. Maybe I can fool my head into not noticing the movement. It doesn't work. Ouch! I crack my shin against the coffee table. Someone must've shifted the bloody thing whilst I was asleep. Bending to rub the tender spot, nausea swills inside my belly again.

It's still dark. Too bloody dark to be up and staggering about in my flat. Somehow, I make it out to the kitchen. The digital display on the cooker says five thirty-five. What the hell am I doing? I grapple my way towards the window, gripping on to the sill for balance.

In the silvery moonlight I can just about see Jack. He's dragging the ladder over towards the shed as Bertie bounces about by his ankles. He's only wearing a pair of pyjama bottoms. He must be bloody mad. Who in their right mind goes out half dressed in the middle of the night when the temperatures are sub-zero? Light glitters off the slight sheen of ice on the top of the shed.

What the hell is the stupid man thinking? He's not going to try and climb it again, is he? Surely not with his fear of falling. Not when the top of the shed will be slippery.

I follow the dark line of the tree trunk upwards and catch sight of Sukie's bright eyes peering down at Jack from between the branches. Bloody Bertie must have chased her up there again.

Jack's got the ladder propped up against the shed now. Both his hands gripping the metal uprights. He pauses, as if he's taking deep breaths and trying to give himself a good talking to. He places his first foot on a rung and I swing into action. I'm wide awake now. I can't have this on my conscience. Not again. I almost call out to him, then remember how that ended last time. Instead, I grab my keys and sprint down the stairs, swinging round the bottom of the bannister and running out the wide-open back door.

Jack is halfway up the ladder by the time I reach the garden. His panicked breaths are loud in the night-time stillness. I approach slowly, not wanting to startle him, only picking up my pace when Bertie decides to try to follow him up. The bloody creature jumps, his front paws catching on the first rung. In slow motion, the ladder begins to slide sideways. Jack takes a second to realise what is happening. He should grip on to the roof. He doesn't. He leans back, his arms doing the comedy wind-milling I saw just before he fell the last time.

I find a burst of speed from somewhere, arriving at the base of the ladder at the very moment he's falling off it, and stick my arms out, imagining somehow that I am going to catch him. He hits my arms but his weight's too much. He drags me down with him. There's a sickening crunch in my wrist as we both hit the ground. Jack landing on top of me. The breath whooshes out of my lungs.

"Fuck! Claire, are you alright?"

I make a sound, to let him know I'm still alivc. I mcan to say, 'Oh yes, I'm perfectly fine, thank you.' It sounds more like ummph.

He scrambles off, the removal of his weight allowing pain signals from my wrist to scamper along the nerve synapses all the way to my brain. "Ow!" It bloody hurts.

"Oh God, look at your wrist!"

I don't want to. From the tone of his voice I know that, if I do, I'm going to see something horrible. It's the kind of voice people use to say, 'Oh dear god, look at the size of that hairy spider.' The dull throb tells me it's not going to be good. I now have stereo throbbing in my wrist and my head. It's all making me feel a little nauseous again. Correction, very nauseous.

I deposit three generous heaves all over the bottom of Jack's pyjama bottoms.

"Oh, fucking hell!"

The vomit smells strongly of whiskey. The thought of whiskey makes me heave again. But it's when Bertie starts licking it up that I really get into my stride. I heave until there's nothing left. Then I catch sight of my wrist; it's bent at a sickening angle. At that point, I hit the patio tiles a second time.

"Well, this is a turnaround of events," Jack says, sipping on a cappuccino. The rich smell of coffee is excruciating. I'm gasping for something to drink, but they won't let me have anything until they decide if I need to have an operation or not. In the meantime, my tongue feels like it's swollen to twice its normal size. And while they've given me some IV paracetamol, I still have a cracking headache and a throbbing pain in my wrist.

He turns in his seat. "Tell me again, how did you know that fireman?"

Of course, when Jack reported a cat stuck up the tree along with my broken wrist, they sent a fire engine as well as an ambulance. And because God is laughing at me, it had to be Chris who wandered into the back garden to find Jack and I covered in my vomit. I've already relayed the lasagne-in-the-eyebrow story – he doesn't deserve it again.

I'm in a foul mood.

"Who'd have thought -"

"Please stop," I say, cutting him off mid flow. It must be the fourth or fifth time he's remarked on the fact it's funny we're back in the hospital, only with me as the patient this time. Maybe the first time he said it I agreed with him, even managing an attempt at a smile. Not so much now. Now it's frankly just plain annoying.

A doctor brushes in through the curtain, stopping us from a full-scale bicker. "Good news, Mrs Everett, Mr Everett."

"I'm not Mr Everett," Jack says, holding his hands up as if in horror at the thought.

The doctor looks at him. Then turns back to me. "Yes, well, Mrs Everett, at least?"

I nod.

"The good news is your wrist doesn't need an operation. We're satisfied now that we've straightened it that a cast should do the trick. You'll need to wear it for six weeks, but then you should be right as rain." He grins at me.

Jack joins in the grinning. "Well, isn't that good news."

I'm feeling a lot less cheery than the pair of them. "Yes, in a 'my wrist is still broken kind of way, and I now can't drive for six weeks'."

Jack shuffles a little in his chair. "Yes well, believe me it's better than an operation, and cast and pins, for twelve weeks."

I huff. "This isn't a broken bone competition."

The doctor stares at us both, then slowly backs out of the room.

We take the taxi home in stony silence. I use the time to list all the things that are now going to be a complete arse to do because of the cast. Thankfully, it's my left hand, not my right. Jack's given up trying to make perky comments.

"Who the hell is that?" he says, as the taxi driver looks for somewhere to pull in.

I look up. There's a figure, huddled on the steps outside our building. Whoever it is, is bundled up against the cold, wearing a long black coat, hat and gloves.

Jack scowls, readying himself for a fight. "Is it that guy again? If it is, I insist you call the police this time."

Is it? I can't tell from here. The person looks too small to be Gavin. Could it be Ben? I could really do without another scene. All I want is my bed. My wrist throbs in agreement.

The person looks up as our car brushes against the kerb. "It's Sarah!" I say, surprised. What's she doing here? I scan the street, fearing Gavin might be around too. Did he find her at Mum's? Is that why she's here?

She stands up as we get out, Jack taking a moment to pay the driver. "Sarah! Are you okay?" She looks awful, big red splodges marking the skin under her eyes. I run towards her, ignoring the ache now. It doesn't matter anymore. "What's the matter? What's happened."

She collapses into my arms, and I wince a little as my broken wrist protests the pressure. Then she promptly bursts into tears.

Chapter 33

It takes me half an hour to get her inside, sitting on my sofa clutching a cup of sweet tea, and calmed down enough that she can talk to me. "Tell me what's happened," I say softly, holding her hand with my one good one.

She sniffs, rubbing her eyes with a tissue. "Gavin's been arrested."

I can't imagine I've heard her correctly. "Did you say he's been arrested?"

She nods.

"How? What happened?"

She sighs. "I'm not sure of all the details. The police turned up at your mum's late last night."

That makes no sense whatsoever. "But how did they know where to find you?"

Guilt twists her face. She takes a minute or two to gather herself. "I went to see them yesterday. To report him."

I sit back in my chair, surprised. I never thought she'd go to the police. "You did?"

She nods again. "It was when you were at the funeral. I was angry because I wanted to come with you, but I didn't dare. I really liked your mum. She was so kind to me – offering me a place to stay when I needed one – I wanted to be able to pay my respects. But I couldn't because I knew Gavin had been watching you. And I didn't want to go to the church and worry about him turning up and making a scene."

"You needn't have worried about that," I mutter. "You'd have fitted right in."

"Sorry?" she says, looking confused.

I shake my head. There'll be time enough for telling her about all of that after she's told me about whatever happened to her. And Gavin. I encourage her to continue.

"So, I was mad with him because once again he was keeping me away from living the life I wanted to live. I'd had enough." Her fingers worry the edge of her jumper now. "I was so cross with him, I decided to go to the police. I'd had enough of hiding away; I wanted to report him for what he'd done to me. I wanted to be free to live the life I want to live. So, I called a taxi, and walked into the police station."

I'm on the edge of my seat now, desperate to know what happened next.

She takes a sip of her tea, then puts the mug back down on the coffee table, drawing a deep breath. "The officer was very kind. An Officer Brown? When I told him where I'd been staying, he mentioned he knew you?"

I wince. "We've met once or twice," I say. Is it a good thing to be so known by the local constabulary? I don't think so.

"Anyway, he was very kind. I showed him all the pictures I took after the last attack – of my bruises and whatnot."

"I didn't know you'd taken pictures."

"Yes, well, I might not have been ready to report Gavin, but I knew what I'd need if I did want to. I took photos the day after it happened. I also told them about all the previous attacks and the times I've been taken to hospital. There was enough for him to be arrested. But it turned out they didn't need to. . . Not for that anyway."

"What? Why?"

"Well, they said they'd issue a warrant. Asked if I wanted to be taken to a local refuge. I told them I didn't need to because I was still staying at your mum's, and he didn't know where that was. I left feeling pleased with myself – not brave enough to come and join you at the wake because they still hadn't found him by then – but like I'd done something positive. Officer Brown promised me they'd let me know once my husband was in custody. When I didn't hear anything, I assumed he'd got wind of the arrest warrant and gone to ground, so I went to bed. They turned up at a little past four."

I look at my watch, it's only just past ten now. "What happened?"

"You remember you said that Gavin had been in a bit of a state that day you last saw him?"

"Yeah." I remember only too well.

"Well, you were right. Last night he went to a bar and got himself very drunk again. He picked a fight and ended up stabbing the guy in the neck with a broken bottle. The police said it was a bit of an unlucky hit, by all accounts; Gavin didn't mean to kill him, but he caught the man's jugular and that was it. The man bled out too quickly for them to do much about it. He died before the ambulance even reached them. So Gavin was arrested for manslaughter."

I turn cold and lean forward to hug my friend. "Oh, Sarah, I'm so sorry. That's awful. I don't even know what to say... I won't lie – I didn't like the guy – but I'd never have wished this to happen... to any of them. It's terrible. I know how much you love him, despite everything."

She nods, dabbing at her eyes with the new tissue I pass her. "He wasn't always like this – so angry all the time. He didn't start out like it. Even when it was really bad, he didn't hit me every day. He just got mad with me sometimes and couldn't control himself. And if he drank too much it made him much, much worse. I'm not trying to excuse him – I know I did the right thing at the time when I left him – but..." She looks down at her feet, her voice when she does speak again little more than a whisper. "Now, I just keep thinking that it's all my fault that he's in prison." She starts to cry again, her shoulders shaking.

I pull her back into my arms. She comes willingly, collapsing against me as her tears flow in a seemingly unending stream. "How on earth can you possibly think that it's your fault?" I ask her gently.

She looks up at me with bloodshot eyes. Her face twisted with anguish. "If I'd been there – been at home with him – he wouldn't have taken himself out to a bar or gotten himself drunk. He would have been home with me. He wouldn't have started a fight and he wouldn't have stabbed anyone. He'd be here now."

I want to shout at her, to tell her how stupid she's being, but I know that's not what she needs right now. "I hear what you're saying – what your thoughts are telling you. None of those are facts, though, are they?"

She shakes her head, slowly, her gaze fixed upon me.

I rub the still very obvious bump on my forehead from where I smacked it during my earlier panic attack. I'm knackered. It's been the longest day followed by an equally long night. I feel like I haven't slept in days. Barring the short nap on the settee, I haven't. But my friend still needs me. I make sure to look her straight in the eyes. "Do you believe you made the right decision when you left?"

She stills, thinking hard, weighing up the pros and cons. Eventually, she nods. "Yes, I do."

"Then that's all that really matters. Gavin made his own choices. Bad ones. You can't control that."

"But what if I could have saved that other man's life?"

I hold her gaze. "You made the choice that was the best for you. If you hadn't, there's a chance you would be the one who wasn't here today."

Sarah goes home – or at least back to Mummy's, because she can't face going back to her own house just yet. I used the time before she left to fill her in on everything she missed at the funeral. The fact I managed to make her laugh, albeit faintly, was one small highlight in an otherwise dismal day. To make matters worse, I agreed to accompany her to visit him this afternoon. She insists she needs to see him. She's going to drive us there in my car, because she doesn't have one and I can't drive with my broken wrist.

I have a deep desire to take a shower and wash my hair, but I spend ten minutes more trying to work out how I can manage both and not get my cast wet. I've got as far as taping a huge black bin liner onto my arm – not an easy task with only one arm – but am still scratching my head as to how to rub shampoo into my hair when the doorbell rings.

Cursing, I drag on my dressing gown. "What?" I say when I open the door to and meet an anxious-looking Jack.

He thrusts a bunch of flowers at me. "These are for you."

I grab them, forgetting I have a bin liner on my arm. "Thank you, they're lovely." They are. He shouldn't have. What with the funeral, I've had quite enough of flowers – especially lilies – for a while

"Good look," he says, nodding down at my arm. "Very Doctor Who."

I'm too tired for jolly banter. "Look, I'm sorry but was there anything else?"

He shifts his weight a little, his colour rising. "Well, I was just a bit worried about you managing on your own." He nods down at my arm. "With that. I wondered if I could help at all? I feel sort of responsible. I did land on you."

"If anyone's responsible it's my cat. Shit! Where is she?" We both hear the barking from the back garden now. "Is she back up the tree again?" I stare at him. "How the hell am I going to get her down?"

Jack swallows, his Adam's apple bobbing in his throat, before he straightens, and says, "I'll do it."

"Really? You don't have to. I could call the fire brigade again. I'm sure Chris won't mind."

He pouts. "You don't need a bloody fireman. I insist. My dog chased her up there, it's my job to get her down." He stands, his fist clenched, looking like a soldier off to fight in a war. Also, he looks terrified.

I can't deny I'm relieved not to have to do it myself, but a little concerned he might break something else – perhaps his neck. "May I suggest you might want to put Bertie inside your flat when you do it?"

He looks at me seriously. "Yes, I was thinking the same thing."

"Do you need me to hold the ladder for you?"

He considers me for a minute. "No, you go and do whatever it was you were planning to do with that." He glances down at my arm, waiting for some sort of an explanation.

"Shower. I wanted to wash my hair."

He looks a little doubtful as he assesses what I've done so far. "I'll go and sort the cat out. Perhaps you ought to leave your door on the latch, so I can let myself back in, in case you need any help."

Although I'm sure I'll be fine, he insists. So, as he heads off to do battle with a ladder, the shed, a tree and my cat, I face myself in the bathroom.

The bump on my head has turned a vivid shade of purple with some yellowing now around the margins. I'm still wearing my makeup from yesterday – although what's left of it, which isn't much, is giving me a slightly lopsided appearance – and my hair looks like I've stuck my fingers into an electrical socket.

I step under the spray of water. The water pressure struggles to cope in this flat, and the supply is patchy probably due to limescale clogging up the head. Today, I really miss the rain shower Ben and I had back at the house. Regardless, it feels good to wash away some of yesterday. I turn my face to the water, letting it drum into me, massaging my head, my thoughts of nothing but this moment. Too soon it passes. The first niggling concerns that Jack might be lying on the ground with a broken neck press in and spoil the moment. Do I know it as a fact? No. Do I believe it might be so? Abso-fucking-lutely.

I press a handful of shampoo into my one good hand and smash it into my hair. My plastic bag wrapped hand is useless, but I manage to get a lather up with the one good hand I have. My bad arm is aching, a dull throb reminding me I'm meant to be resting it, but that's easier said than done when you're used to using two hands to do everything. It takes me another ten minutes or so to rinse, condition and wash myself. In all that time I'm listening for anything that will reassure me Jack is okay. Nothing.

I bundle out of the bathroom intending to look out the lounge window, a towel hastily wrapped around me and my hair still dripping, to find Jack sitting on my sofa with Sukie perched on his lap. He beams up at me, "She came down on her own! I didn't even need to -" His voice dries up as he stares at me, his Adam's apple bobbing up and down in his throat.

"The door was on the latch, I've let myself in," a second voice calls from the hallway. Ben walks in a moment later.

Chapter 34

"So, what happened then?" Sarah asks, her eyes wide and fixed on me rather than the traffic.

I keep my eyes on the road ahead. "Ben made lots of spluttering noises, Jack laughed until there were tears coming out of his eyes, which annoyed Ben immensely so he started shouting. And then Sukie ran out of the window and straight back up the tree."

Sarah turns back to look at the oncoming cars, before risking a second glance at me. "Lordy. And then what? I mean, how did you leave it with them?"

I sigh, remembering Ben's very hurt expression and Jack's complete hysteria. "I told them both to leave. That I had to get ready for this."

Sarah's expression darkens at the reminder of what's to come. She's wearing all black. "And you didn't bother to try and explain anything? To Ben, I mean?"

I look at her. "No, why would I? We're divorced – or very nearly. I don't need to explain myself to him anymore."

She makes a small noise of surprise. "So, if he wanted to get back together you wouldn't be tempted? I thought that's all you wanted."

Was it? Maybe once upon a time. Now I just fancy a few quiet days without any drama. "What Ben wanted was someone to help him raise that kid with him. He knew he and Bella were heading for the rocks, weeks ago. Now he knows it isn't his, he doesn't need to worry."

"I'm not so sure. Anyway, why was the street door open? How did Ben get in?"

"Jack opened it so the window cleaner could get through to the back garden."

"Huh! Timing really is everything. So, how's your wrist this morning?"

I glance down at my cast. "It aches. I guess it's bound to really. At least it's only for six weeks." I stare out the window. It's a dank day, a grey mist hanging in the air from where slightly warmer air has collided with a cold front. It's hard to know where the mist stops and the clouds start.

Sarah pulls up in front of a brick building, walls towering above us, into one of the many rows of empty parking spaces. I peer out at it through the windscreen. The place looks deserted. "Is this it?"

She looks down at the piece of paper she was given and checks the address. "This is where they said."

I place my hand on the door handle but stop when Sarah doesn't move. Her face is pinched with fear and her wide eyes seem even wider than normal. "Shall we get this over with then?" I suggest gently.

She still doesn't move. Only grips the steering wheel until the skin across her knuckles turns white. "I don't know if I can do it."

This is why I'm here. For exactly this moment, and all the ones to come. Her breaths are coming in short fast pants now and getting faster. I know where this is headed if we don't calm her down. "Take a deep breath," I say.

She gasps a quick breath.

"No, deeper this time. And close your eyes."

Her eyes blink closed. She inhales, pulling air into her lungs so that her ribs expand beneath her polo neck.

"Good. Now push it out again."

Her lips part and she exhales a long, soft breath, her hands still gripping the steering wheel.

I need to get her to relax somehow. I think back to what Alex might have said in one of his sessions. "Rest your hands where they're comfortable," I suggest, watching as they flutter down towards her lap. "Now, notice your body. Inside." I pause. "Feel the sensations and touch of the car seat." Pause. "Relax. Feel any areas of tension or tightness in your body and let them go. Let everything soften."

Her shoulders drop, her muscular tension relaxing just a little.

"Good. Now focus on your breath. Let it be natural, a gentle in and out. Notice where you feel it in your body. In your abdomen, your chest or throat. Feel the sensations, one breath at a time. When one breath ends the next begins."

She's breathing more deeply now, her body more relaxed with every inhalation. I let her sit there in silence for another five minutes, just breathing, until eventually her eyes open and fix on me. "Thank you," she says. "I think I'm ready now."

Sarah looks terrible when she comes out. "Are you okay?" I can't help myself asking, even though she very clearly isn't.

"I told him I want a divorce. He didn't take it very well."

I can only imagine. What can I say? I help her into the car, hating the fact I can't drive her home.

She weeps silent tears. They roll down her cheeks and drip onto her coat, glistening there for a second before the wool sucks them away. I'm not sure if she's crying for the man she loved and lost, or from the anger at what she's been forced to overcome. Or maybe from fear of what may yet come. Because one day he'll be let out again, and then what?

We weave our way through traffic reduced to a crawl in the fog. It's thickened, rolling about us in swirls as we cut through it, disorienting, the buildings around us swallowed by it. Visibility is now down to less than ten metres. The radio reports of a terrible pile up on the M25. Too many people driving too fast to stop in time. Seven people dead. Here today and then gone, just like that. Alive and then... not.

When Sarah pulls up outside my apartment Ben is waiting for me on the front steps. His hair is plastered to his head and his clothes look wet through. He raises his head as the car pulls to a stop. Our eyes meet.

"Will you be okay?" Sarah asks.

I turn to look at her. "Will you?"

"Eventually."

"Exactly." I reach across to open the door with my good hand.

She stops me with a hand to my shoulder. "The meditation helped, you know. A lot. It didn't stop me from feeling all my stuff, but it helped me separate those natural feelings from the thoughts I was layering on top. It helped me feel strong enough to say what I needed to."

I nod. "I'm glad." I am.

"If you need the same," she glances towards Ben. He's on his feet now, waiting for me, "You only have to ask."

I nod again. "Will you be back at yours? You're welcome to stay at Mummy's if you'd rather?"

She smiles. "No, thank you though. I think it's time I went home again. Call me this evening?"

"Sure," I promise. I don't feel sure. She hands me back my keys and I open the car door, the fog swirling towards me.

Ben hurries in my direction. "Are you okay? When did you do that?" He nods towards my broken arm. He doesn't wait for me to answer, taking hold of my other one and leading me up the steps. The curtain at Jack's lounge window twitches. He's watching us, I'm sure of it. "Let's get you inside. You must be exhausted. Where have you been?"

I tell him. He frowns. "That was a bit much to expect you to go with her today, not just after breaking your wrist. And only a day after burying your mother."

He talks on and I let him, trudging up the stairs beside him. At the door he takes my keys from me and moves me aside gently before unlocking it. Sukie blinks up at us from the middle of the kitchen table. She got herself down again.

"I think you need to sleep," Ben says.

I agree.

He leads me into the bedroom and unpeels my clothes. I'm like a rag doll, letting him lift this arm here and then that leg there. His touch is familiar. He tucks me into my bed. The last thing I remember is him sitting beside me before I fall asleep.

I wake to an eerie grey light. It's early, I guess, but still foggy judging by the halo visible around the streetlight. It flickers, preparing to switch off and welcome the start of a new day. But what day? How long have I slept? I think Mummy's funeral was the day before yesterday, and that was a Tuesday, so assuming I haven't slept for more than twenty-four hours, today must be Thursday.

Ben stirs beside me on the bed. He's still here then.

I slip from beneath the covers, grabbing my robe as I plunge my feet into my monster slippers and shuffle out into the kitchen. The kettle is already half full of water, so I flick the switch and use the time while it boils to empty the dishwasher and give Sukie some chicken.

The tea bag bubbles a little as I pour over the boiling water. I leave it to steep, watching the hypnotic the way the fog eddies around obstacles outside. The tree at the end of the garden's barely visible now.

Sukie surprises me, once I'm settled onto the sofa with my book, by jumping onto my lap. I place the book on the seat beside me and run my hand along her fur. She emits a low rumbling sound I've never heard from her before. My god, she's purring.

We stay like that for more than half an hour, me stroking and her purring. I'm just wondering how we might ever call a halt to something so lovely when Ben makes us both jump. "You're awake."

Sukie shoots from my lap and disappears under the kitchen table. I watch her go, wondering if there might be room for me under there too. I look at him. "So are you." But only just. He's got a crumpled look about him, pillow creases still marking the side of his face.

"Can I make you a cup of tea?"

I hold up my empty mug, "Just had one, thanks."

He disappears into the kitchen and comes out again five minutes later with two steaming cups in his hands. He holds one up. "Just in case you change your mind, I know how much you love a cup of tea."

I don't. Not anymore. I prefer my fruit teas most of the time. I force a smile. "Why are you here, Ben?"

He scrubs a hand through his hair, leaving it pointing in every direction but the one it ought. "Straight into it, eh?" He offers me one of his smiles. I used to think they were cute. When I don't respond he straightens a little. "I wanted to apologise for the scene the other day. It was unforgivable."

"Oh that." I'd almost forgotten about it. I wave my good hand. "Really, don't worry yourself. Mummy's friends loved it. You made their day."

He winces. "That's what I was afraid of." He rubs the back of his neck, looking a little uncomfortable. "When Bella started having a go at you, I'm afraid I lost it. I didn't mean to reveal everything in public like that. I'd been planning to tell you, but then with the funeral and everything I didn't get a chance."

"How is Bella?"

His eyebrows lift. "What?"

"How's Bella? It must have been a bit of a shock for her too. Is she okay? She's only got a few weeks or so left, hasn't she?"

He looks at me like I must be speaking in a foreign language. "Why do you care about Bella? She's fine. She's always fine, you know her. She's probably already shacked up with someone else."

Now I'm surprised. "She left you?"

"I kicked her out!"

I can't think what to say to that. I only stare at him.

I suspect something of my shock must show on my face because Ben hurries to explain himself. "She lied to me, Claire, the whole way through. I only agreed to our divorce because of the baby. I didn't think it was fair to keep you tied to me when I'd made another woman pregnant. She told me it was mine. All the way through. She never said she was sleeping with someone else at the same time as me."

An ember of the anger I knew all those months ago flares a little at his words. "Not very nice when someone does that, is it?"

He puts his cup down on the table and then comes and kneels on the floor in front of me. "If I could go back and live that time again, I'd never touch her."

"What, knowing what you do now? That you'd end up with nothing? You still chose to sleep with her before she ever announced she was pregnant. You made that choice when we were still married."

"I know. I know. I made a mistake. A stupid, stupid mistake. I should never have strayed. We were happy together. I want to be happy together again. I want to show you that you can trust me. I want us to give it another go."

I stand up, walking to the window, trying to clear my head. Not so many weeks ago this was everything I wanted to hear from him. Now my mind feels as foggy as outside. Can it really be that simple? Ben is no longer with Bella, so we fall back into what we once were. What even was that? Who was I back then? I can't remember myself, only Ben and Claire – the couple. And Ben, the man I looked after. The man I did everything for to make sure he was happy, and still it wasn't enough. Still he went off to find something else from someone else. What is there to stop that happening again? What did Mummy say? That sort of unrequited love grows into resentment. Is that what I'm feeling?

My gaze is drawn back down to the garden by barking. It's Bertie. He's grown even since the last time I saw him. He's going to be a giant of a dog by the time he's full sized. Jack walks into my view, waving a stick and Bertie bounces on all four paws at once, like Tigger. Jack waves the stick again. Bertie lunges for it, gripping it in his slathering maw. They wrestle together for several minutes until Jack wins it back. Bertie, obviously unimpressed, jumps up with his big furry paws planted firmly into the centre of Jack's chest, making Jack lose his balance. He topples over backwards, doing that funny wind-milling thing again with his arms. Thinking this is part of the game, Bertie bounces straight onto the middle of Jack's chest. *Oof*, I lipread.

It makes me laugh.

"Something funny?" Ben says, coming up behind me and slipping his arms around my middle. He rests his chin on my shoulder. I resist the urge to shake him off. He stiffens when he realises what I've been watching. Or rather, whom. "What's going on between you and Wilton?"

I turn my head to look at him over my shoulder, making sure I'm staring him straight in the eye when I say, "Nothing."

Ben releases me and walks back to the sofa, his expression stony.

I turn back to the garden to find Jack staring up at me. Our eyes lock for a minute before he looks away. His nose wrinkles as he pulls his jumper around and inspects it. He turns to look at something on the ground where he fell and that's when I see it. It could be mud. If I were being kind, I'd say it were mud, but by his expression I know it's not. And whatever it is is now smeared all over the back of his jumper. He turns back to look up at me and I grin down at him. He grins too before walking back towards the house, pulling at his jumper as he goes.

I turn back to Ben, now that Jack and Bertie are no longer there to look at. I must still have a smile on my face because Ben's face lights up in response. He stands, and hurries towards me. "God, I love you," he says. Then he kisses me.

Chapter 35

Five days later, the fog is still hanging about. Flights have been cancelled, there have been numerous accidents and generally the fog news coverage has been wall-to wall. It's all due to a weather front that seems determined to hover over us for the foreseeable future, thanks to the fact there's little in the way of any wind to get things moving again. It's all rather like living inside a white glove.

Ben's still hanging about too. I haven't slept with him – yet. He's slept over once or twice, sleeping in my bed and taking up rather more of it than I might have wished, but sexually there is nothing doing. Much to his frustration, I suspect. We've come close once or twice, but something always stops me. I think it might be Mummy's ghost.

I've been surprised by how quickly my life seems to have reverted into something akin to normal. Or normal for me, anyway, barring the very obvious gaping hole left in all the parts of my life my mother filled. It's been a revelation how many times I've found myself reaching for my phone thinking *I must tell Mummy about that*, only to come up short when I remember that I can't. Those are the moments I have a little cry.

"Have you got time to drop some dry-cleaning in for me this morning?" Ben calls through from the bathroom. "I'm up in the office all day, and then I want to speak to the solicitor about the company. We need to get Bella to dissolve it completely or buy me out. It would be a massive help if you could drop that stuff off. I'm running out of shirts. Bella did none of that sort of thing. She's a complete waste of space. Would you mind, darling?"

Can I? Maybe. I've got two clients this afternoon but not much on this morning. Should I? That's a more difficult question to answer. I'm still chewing over what he said about dissolving the company. Poor Bella can hardly be in a good state to deal with all that when she's about to give birth. Then he lobs in, "I was thinking we should start packing your stuff up this weekend."

"Sorry?" A sharp pain in my chest makes me wince. I have to sit down on the sofa for a second to catch my breath.

He pokes his head around the bathroom door. "Your stuff. It's going to take a while to get it all moved back. I mean, we could book a packing company, I suppose, but it's hardly worth it. You don't have much we'll want to keep."

I look around my apartment, at the 'seen better days' furniture, and feel another bubble of irritation pop inside my gut. It's been happening more and more often lately. Sure, my furniture might be crappy, but it's mine, and he doesn't get to decide what stays or goes. Same as he doesn't get to decide if I stay or go. And I haven't yet – decided, that is.

I stand, grabbing the cushion off the sofa, and heading for my bedroom. "Where are you going?" Ben calls after me.

"To my room. To meditate."

"Not again. More bloody mindlessness. I wanted to talk about things. I haven't got long, and we need to plan and get things moving."

That's exactly why I need to meditate. I slam the door closed behind me, throw my cushion onto the ground and settle myself upon it. It takes far longer than normal for me to clear my mind, not helped by the fact Ben's pacing around the apartment outside my bedroom door.

"I was thinking we could book a few gites again in France for the summer, what do you think? Shall I do it?" he says as soon as I walk out again.

Ben loves France, but mainly he loves the Tours de France. We'd spent most of our married summers travelling miles to what he considered a good vantage point, then sitting beside a road until the cyclists all trundled past. Then repeating the whole exercise on another day on a new patch of road. Personally, I fancied something a little different. A beach or maybe even an island, perhaps Greece. Or what about a meditation retreat somewhere? Sarah and I had been looking at a couple only the other day. Ben looks as if I've stolen his favourite toy when I suggest it. "But I've already made a few provisional bookings. I wanted to surprise you."

It's hardly a surprise. It's the same thing we always did. When exactly was this booking made? And was it done with me or Bella in mind? How delighted would Bella have been, traipsing around after the Tours with a new-born baby in tow? Ben really has no idea sometimes. "Maybe next year," he's saying. He stands and picks up his briefcase, as if that's all decided.

"So, do you want packers, or shall we do it? It's stupid to keep camping in this shithole when we've got a rather lovely house five miles away."

Okay, now several hundred bubbles of irritation spill their bilious juices into my gut. "I'll be late back tonight," I say, taking a deep breath to try and calm my racing pulse. "I'm going for a pizza with friends. You might as well stay at your own place."

He looks at me. "Oh, that's a shame, I was looking forward to spending the evening with you. Diet's over then is it?" He squeezes me, grabbing my bottom and pinching it for good measure like a character from a 1970s sitcom. "Never mind, I think you're perfect exactly as you are."

He thinks I'm fat, he thinks I'm fat, begins to loop around my brain. Then it morphs into *I am fat. I'm disgusting.*

I put down the banana I'd picked up off the side for my breakfast. I'd stopped watching my food so closely since I'd been to Briar Hill, just trying to make better choices whenever I could, and things seem to have stabilised a little since then. Now I'm filled with a deep urge to stuff my face with a fried egg sandwich.

A sharp pain pierces my chest, making me gasp.

"I'll see you later then, love," Ben says, oblivious to the slicing agony lancing through me. I force something of a smile. He swings out of the door and runs down the steps.

As soon as he's gone, I collapse onto the floor.

Is this another panic attack?

Or is it my heart?

Am I dying?

I've never had a pain like this in my chest before. What if I am dying? My breaths are coming shorter and faster. I'm dizzy. Do I want to die alone?

I decide not.

Somehow, I crawl to the front door and open it, hoping to catch Ben before he leaves. I'm too late; a car engine roars outside then accelerates away down the street. "Help," I croak. "Help." My breaths are nothing more than shallow pants now, my body screaming for more oxygen. The last thing I remember is my head hitting the doorframe.

I wake to Bertie lying beside me. He's licking my face, stretched out along the length of my body. "Eugh, stop it," I say, pushing him away.

"There you are," Jack says, "what the hell are you doing up - " He pauses, catching sight of me on the floor next to Bertie, shielded by his girth. "Claire? What are you doing down there?"

I push another of Bertie's big licks away from my face, trying to heave myself up to sitting. My body is aching as if I've tried to run a marathon. "I had a bit of a funny turn," I admit. After all, he's seen worse from me. Where Jack's concerned, I have no dignity left to lose.

"A panic attack? I thought you'd cracked those," he says, bending and offering a hand to help me back onto my feet.

I wobble a little, but he keeps a tight hold until we're both confident I'm not going straight back down again. "So did I. I don't know what came over me."

Jack grimaces. "Don't you?" He schools his expression, helping me back into my apartment. Bertie follows us in, appearing delighted to be back.

Sukie watches him from the table in the kitchen, licking her paw, but doesn't appear overly concerned. Bertie, having learned just how sharp her claws can be the last time they met, keeps a respectful distance. Instead, he curls up on the lounge rug and promptly goes to sleep. "Well, he's made himself at home," Jack says. "Can I get you something to drink? Or eat? You really ought to eat something if your blood sugar is low. You've got another nasty bruise coming up on the other side of your head. Maybe I should call an ambulance?"

"No! With the amount you and I have made use of emergency services lately, they'll be sending Social Services round to check up on us. A cup of tea would be lovely. And maybe a banana," I say, telling the thoughts shouting, *'I'm fat, I'm disgusting'* at me inside my head to do one. "And an icepack. There's one in the freezer," I call after him.

I listen to him pottering about in my kitchen, re-emerging five minutes later with a mug of tea, the icepack and a banana. "Take it slowly," he says, passing me the mug. "I added a couple of spoons of sugar to replace some of the energy burnt by adrenaline." He sits down next to me. "So, do you want to talk about it? What was the trigger?"

"Oh, just some stuff Ben said." I slap Jack's arm, "Don't roll your eyes!"

"Well maybe that ought to tell you something. Maybe it's time to listen to what your own body's trying to tell you. I'm not your mum, Claire, but I know what she'd be saying right now if she were here. She'd say, love yourself. Are you loving yourself?"

Am I?

Chapter 36

"Is that another bruise on your head?" Nicole asks, immediately noticing this morning's misdemeanour as I walk up to the table.

"She didn't have that when I saw her yesterday," Sarah adds, unhelpfully. Her face drops. "He's not hitting you, is he?"

"No, of course not!"

Nicole sits back in her chair and crosses her arms. "Then what?"

I huff in annoyance. "I had a bit of a funny turn this morning. I went down and banged my head on the way. There, now you know everything." I pick up the menu. "Can we order our pizza please?"

Nicole plucks the menu out of my hand. "Not so fast, lady. One minute." She calls the waiter over and orders a bottle of wine. When he's disappeared to fetch it, she places her elbows on the table. "Now talk."

I could lie to them, but I don't. I tell them exactly what went down, literally as far as I'm concerned, and finish with Jack picking me up again. In the middle, the waiter returns with the wine. Nicole pours us each a large glass. I need it. "So now you really do know everything," I say, when I finish with what Jack said about Mummy.

"To Daphne," Nicole says, raising her glass. "Mummy," I say, lifting my own as Sarah echoes, "Daphne."

"To loving yourself," Sarah adds. We raise our glasses a second time. For some reason it brings tears to my eyes.

"Right, what pizza are you having?" Nicole asks, passing me back the menu.

I can't believe it. "What, that's it? You're not going to have a go at me? Tell me about all the crappy decisions I'm making in my life and how I'm a terrible person?"

She looks at me. "Claire, first of all you're about as far from being a terrible person as it is possible to be. I don't need to have a go at you, because you're doing that all by yourself. You're beating yourself up so badly you had a panic attack bad enough that you thought it was something to do with your heart. Your own body is screaming at you to do something different than what you're currently doing. That should tell you something. I believe in you. I believe you'll make the best decisions *for* you. I believe you'll learn to love yourself as much as we all love you. And in the meantime, we'll eat pizza and drink wine."

And now I am crying. And I don't know why.

Sarah takes hold of my good hand. "I'm here, Claire. Whenever you need me. No judgement. I'm here for you. You just have to tell me what you need." They're the exact same words I said to her.

"Good," I blow my nose on my serviette. "I know for sure I'll need one of you to slice up my pizza."

I enjoy every mouthful of it when it arrives, quieting the little voice that wants to tell me I'll be less loveable if I eat it. And, when I've had enough, I put the knife and fork down. "When's the trial likely to be?" I ask Sarah.

"I'm not really sure. He went in front of a magistrate today. The police contacted me to let me not know they're not letting him out on bail. They tell me it should all be fairly straightforward. They have the fight on CCTV. There's no doubt about what happened. Gavin's planning to plead guilty to the manslaughter charges."

"And what about you? Do you need any help? When you do, you only need to ask."

She smiles at me. "I think you've got enough of your own stuff to sort out with your mum's estate and Ben. Anyway, David's offered too. And Willow and Alex contacted me when they saw the report in the paper. I'll be fine. Over time. Emotionally, our relationship was damaged a long time ago, but I still have some stuff to work through. Willow's given me the number for her counsellor. Hopefully, with some help, I'm going to get myself through this." She pauses. "What about you?"

What about me? That's the question really. "I'm thinking that I still have some stuff to work through too. Some decisions to make." I make sure to meet her eyes and hold them. "I'm going to get there though."

Ben is waiting on my doorstep when I get home. And whilst I'm annoyed, because I asked him to go home tonight, I'm also glad because there are things I want to say to him. Things I have been working though all night. All week. Maybe for the last year or more.

He stands, bending to kiss me when I approach. I turn my head, so he hits my cheek. "Did you have a nice evening? How was Nicole?"

I press my key into the lock. "I did, thank you. She's well."

He paces up the stairs behind me. "I booked a packer," he says as we let ourselves into the flat. "I got the sense you were a little reluctant to do the packing yourself. This way we can get you moved across without any stress. You can keep any stuff you don't want in the garage until we decide what to do with it."

I take a deep breath, centring myself on the way the air feels as it rushes in through my nose, down my throat and into my lungs. Then I push it back out again, every drop. "I'm not going to move back in with you, Ben. I'm sorry." A deep blanket of peace settles over me as I say the words aloud.

Ben frowns. "What do you mean, you're not going to move in with me? This weekend? When are you going to move?"

I sigh. I don't want to make this more difficult than it needs to be. "No. I mean at all. I'm not going to move in with you at all. I don't think this – this relationship – is good for either of us."

He stands now, taking a step towards me. "Don't say that. You don't mean that. I love you. And you've always loved me."

"I have always loved you," I agree. "But it's not enough. And you don't love me. Not enough. Not really." He begins to protest again, but I plough on. "Maybe in your own way you do a little – as much as you can – but I need more. And before that, before I can love someone else, I need to learn to love myself first."

He looks like he doesn't understand, head tilted with confusion. I so want him to understand.

"When I learn to love myself, only then will I be able to find someone who loves me in the same way. Completely, utterly, devotedly, every day."

"But I do! I do love you like that."

I believe he wishes he did. But he doesn't. We both know it. "No, Ben. You don't. Because if you did, you'd never have looked twice at Bella." I take a deep breath, knowing that once these words would have broken me, but not now. "I'm not enough for you, Ben, and that's okay, because I don't think you're enough for me either. It's just taken me a long time to realise it."

He scrubs his hand over his face. "What can I do to prove it to you? You're wrong."

I reach a hand out and press my palm against his heart. It's racing rhythm thunders underneath my fingertips. "I'm not wrong. And you know it in here," I tap his chest. "We were always good friends, and hopefully we can be that again one day, but the romantic love died a long time ago. We started hurting one another because we became lazy about our love. We were a habit neither of us knew how to break. Until Bella came along and gave you what you thought you were looking for. I couldn't see it at first; I really believed all I wanted was for us to get back together. That doing so would make everything better. But I realise now that we'll never work." I brush tears off my cheeks with the back of my hand. "What caused you to go with Bella would still be there." He's staring at me with wide, wounded eyes. I hate hurting him. I take another deep breath, to give me the strength to continue, pulling on the deep sense of certainty inside my chest telling me this is the right thing to do, however much it might hurt right now. "I want a divorce, Ben. I want you to find someone you want to love more than you love yourself, and I want to find someone who feels that way about me." I think of Mummy then and send her thanks for the words she offered that helped me to understand the difference between what I have and what I really want. To not accept second best for fear of being alone. To be happy with who I am right now.

We stand and he pulls me into a hug. Despite everything, both of us are crying. But even then, even when it would be so easy to take the path we know, to say, "Stop! No! I'm sorry. Please take me back. I don't want to be alone." I don't. I keep quiet, just holding him closer, trembling a little. Because, as much as I want to comfort him, to sooth away anything that might trouble him as I always have in the past, I know the right thing for me to do is to let him feel this pain. And find his own path through it.

The same as I must find mine.

I wake to flickering light in the corner of my room. Sunshine, dancing through the cracks in my curtains, making patterns against the creeping damp in the corner of my room. I really must do something about the damp one of these days.

I stretch, long and languorous, then reach for my phone and start a body scan meditation. Mid-way through Sukie jumps onto the bed and curls up against my leg. I carry on regardless. I push away the thoughts chattering inside my head; I'm alone now, I should be afraid. I'm unlovable and unloved. Instead, I recognise I'm okay. Right this minute, I need nothing more than this. Except maybe breakfast. My stomach growls in agreement.

I have no meetings today. It's the perfect day to speak to the solicitor and find out what I need to do to settle Mummy's estate. I've not even read her will yet. And maybe I'll raise the issue of my divorce again – with everything that's happened I'm not quite sure where I stand. With that thought in mind I strap up my hand in a bin bag and shower.

So far, so good.

My luck seems to be holding when I glance out the window and find it's still sunny. There may be a few white clouds, but the day looks alive with the prospect of the best kind of December day. Maybe I'll walk to the solicitors.

I meet Bertie and Jack returning from their own walk as I step out onto the street. I smile as Bertie pulls away from Jack, yanking his lead out of Jack's hand. He's getting so strong now. I laugh as he bounds towards me.

"Don't let him -"

I don't hear any more as Bertie reaches me and rises up to place his front paws onto my chest. I keel over backwards with the momentum his extraordinary weight provides, hitting the pavement with a thump. All of my breath whooshes straight out of my lungs. A long, pink, very wet tongue runs up the length of my face.

"-lick you," Jack says, arriving a little late and slightly breathless to retrieve his wayward dog.

He puts out a hand and helps me to my feet. "Are you okay?"

"Nothing broken this time," I say. "Nice to see you too, Bertie." I sit up and pat him on the head, giving him a quick scratch behind the ear." His tongue lolls out again, looping around my hand.

"You might not want to let him do that," Jack says, looking a little green.

Bertie's still licking me. "What? Why?" I pull my hand away. I'm not sure I really want to know.

"He's taken to eating other dog's shit. Loves it in fact. Gobbles it down in seconds if I don't get there first. He's just eaten an enormous -"

"Stop! Please don't tell me any more." I turn back towards the apartment. I need to wash my face. Right now. And hands. In fact, I may have another shower. Bertie trots along beside me looking like butter wouldn't melt in his mouth. "How can something that looks as gorgeous as him be such a monster?"

"T'was ever thus," Jack says, walking quickly to catch me up again. "Never trust the pretty ones. Where were you going anyway?"

"The solicitors."

He quirks an eyebrow.

He's wearing the same jumper he had on the other day. "I see you managed to get the shit out of your jumper."

He grins. "I see you managed to get the shit out of your life."

I turn and stare at him. "How can you possibly know that?"

He reaches out and cups my face. Static cracks against my skin. I barely notice. "You're glowing. You look alive with possibility. Bright eyed and bushy tailed. It's a good look on you. Your mother would be proud." He grins.

I find myself smiling back, the voices quiet in my head for once.

"Yes, I think she would be."

THE END

Acknowledgements

This story has been a labour of love. Some of you may know I also sometimes write contemporary romance (have a little look for my other Isobel Hart books, if that's your bag too). I wanted this to be different. It really mattered to me that this book was about Claire learning to love *herself*, rather than finding her sense of self worth through the love of a man. Even if he is the perfect man for her, like ahem, Jack. Go on, you know it's true!

Like a lot of women, I've spent too many years filling my head with a tsunami of negative thoughts about myself. I'd get arrested if I spoke them aloud to anyone else. I think a lot of us do it. It took a Mindfulness course to help me recognise what I was doing. The NHS wrote a policy document called 'No Health Without Mental Health'. It's true. If this book does nothing else, I hope it makes you smile and maybe be a little kinder to yourself. Or even take a Mindfulness course.

It was whilst I was meditating that the idea of Claire first came to me. I should have let the thought float past, but she just held on. She's an amazing blend of bits of me plus some of the other amazing women I've met in my life. With a big dollop all of her own. Perfectly imperfect.

I have to thank a few people who made me believe this book should be out there when I doubted myself. Lucy Unwin – my amazing critic partner – who never runs away screaming no matter how awful the drafts are I make her read. She nags me to edit more than I want to, but I don't think I'd enjoy this writing business half as much without sharing the journey with her. Then #Pitchwars – the amazing online writing community and competition set up by Brenda Drake. I never quite made it to selection but came close enough to make a connection with the mentor Gwynne Jackson – whose gentle guidance helped me shape this manuscript into something I'm proud of.

Finally, my husband. I can write about what love should be because he demonstrates it to me every day. Even after thirty years. I'm lucky, I know.

I really hope you laughed, and even cried a little. If you did, and you enjoyed it enough, please leave me a review on Amazon and Goodreads. Or maybe tell a friend. It all helps.

Printed in Great Britain
by Amazon

62071291R00225